6

07

17

# KLEBER'S CONVOY

# Kleber's Convoy

*Antony Trew*

ROBERT HALE · LONDON

ISBN 0 7090 7021 7


Robert Hale Limited
Clerkenwell House
Clerkenwell Green
London EC1R 0HT




2 4 6 8 10 9 7 5 3 1

Printed in Great Britain by
St Edmundsbury Press Limited, Bury St Edmunds, Suffolk.
Bound by Woolnough Bookbinding Limited.

## AUTHOR'S NOTE

1. The characters in this story, the ships, U-boats, aircraft and events are entirely fictitious. Where authorities, such as Captain (D) Greenock, are referred to their incumbents are fictitious though the appointments did exist.

There were not, as far as I know, a Nineteenth Cruiser Squadron, a Fifty-Seventh or an Eighty-Third Escort Group, nor any ships in service in World War II of the names I have used. If there were it is an inadvertence on my part for they had nothing to do with this story. It is possible that those who served with me in HMS *Walker* – what a fine ship's company they were – may look for characters they knew in that ship but they will do so in vain, for *Vengeful* and her company are figments of the imagination and any resemblance can only be coincidental.

2. *Page* 147 – Recent British research suggests that U-47, commanded by Guenther Prien, was sunk by the corvettes *Arbutus* and *Camelia*, and that *Wolverine*'s kill after a long stern chase was in fact U-70.

'The Russian convoys are a northern saga of heroism, bravery and endurance. This saga will live for ever, not only in the hearts of your people, but also in the hearts of the Soviet people, who rightly see in it one of the most striking expressions of collaboration between Allied governments without which our common Victory would have been impossible.'

Ivan Maisky
Soviet Ambassador in London
during World War II

# CHAPTER ONE

It was wet and cold and the wind from the south-west came gusting and eddying across the loch, bringing the rain and the smell of peat and rotting heather.

In the sternsheets the big man hunched his shoulders, seeking protection under the canvas hood of the motor boat. He was dark and angular with shadows under eyes which regarded stonily the ships at anchor, so many that they faded in the distance until the farthest were lost in the mist. Thirty-seven, he recalled, with twenty-six escorts by the time they'd passed the Faeroes. Pity it hadn't always been like that. He thumped his chest hoping to stop the wheeziness and thought of the specialist at the RN hospital at Bridge-of-Weir.

'Any previous history of respiratory trouble?'

'What sort of trouble?'

'Difficulty in breathing. Frequent attacks of bronchitis. Asthma?'

He'd shaken his head.

'Nothing like that?' persisted the specialist, a wartime surgeon-commander.

'When I was about six I had some sort of breathing trouble. It lasted for about two years.'

'Do you remember what sort?'

'Just that I found it difficult to breathe and then I'd panic and it'd get worse.'

'Were there any pressures on you at the time? Can you remember? You know. Being pushed hard at school. Trouble at home?'

He wondered what the specialist was driving at.

'I wasn't at school. My mother died when I was five. My father remarried a year later.'

'I see. Now let's get those things off. We'll have a look at your chest.' He'd seen the surgeon looking at his fingers. 'No,' he said, 'I don't smoke and haven't for years.'

'Good.'

And so the examination had proceeded.

The big man's thoughts were interrupted by the leading-seaman's order, 'Stop engines.' The boat lost way and drifted in towards the landing stage at Aultbea, waiting for a berth. Other boats moved off and it went alongside. The big man stepped on to the wooden jetty. 'Lay off, Harvey,' he said. 'Make room for the others. We'll be about an hour.'

The leading-seaman saluted. 'Aye, aye, sir.'

The gaunt figure of the captain joined others on the path and strode up through the rain towards the Nissen hut. 'Fine bloody day to be starting one of these,' said Harvey to the stoker tending the motor boat's engine.

'Don't worry,' said the stoker. 'There'll be worse to come.'

The boat went astern from the landing stage. The badges on her bows showed, beneath a naval crown and the name *Vengeful*, a mailed fist holding the hilt of a sword.

The big man reached the door of the old hall. The sentry saluted. The big man returned the salute. 'Captain of *Vengeful*,' he said.

The chief petty officer next to the sentry looked at his list and ticked off a name. 'Lieutenant-Commander Redman, sir?'

He said, 'Yes,' and went into the hall. It was old and dingy and smelt of long ago. A low platform confronted rows of wooden seats reminiscent of church gatherings and school concerts. Redman looked round. He was in good time. Half of them were there already. He nodded to those he knew, mostly captains of *Vengeful*'s escort group, the Fifty-Seventh, spoke briefly to one of them, and sat down.

He wondered if those near him could hear his wheeziness and was mildly ashamed. He felt through the raincoat into the pocket of his reefer, found a lozenge and slipped it into his mouth. It's will-power, he told himself. Goes if you try hard enough. But it didn't and he swore under his breath.

The convoy commodore came in, a time-wrinkled white-haired man with blue eyes in a pink face. Redman looked at him curiously. Wonder why they do it, he thought. Must have retired as a rear-admiral ten, fifteen years ago. Volunteers for this. Ought to have his feet in front of a fire reading the war news. Redman turned to the officer next to him. 'Know him?'

The lieutenant-commander shook his head. 'Incredible old

boys, aren't they?' he said. 'Can't imagine a more bloody job.'

The commodore sat at the centre of the table on the platform flanked by several officers. One, a commander, Rory McLeod, was staff-officer operations to CS19, the Vice-Admiral commanding Nineteenth Cruiser Squadron; another commander, a lanky red-haired man with humorous eyes, Ginger Mountsey, was senior officer of escorts. Next to him sat the naval control service officer, beside him a second officer Wren with notebook and pencil. She was looking at the faces in front of her, the captains of escort vessels and merchant ships, with the polite but impersonal interest of a visitor at a school prize-giving.

When it was decided that everyone had turned up the commodore opened the proceedings. Rory McLeod explained that the Vice-Admiral would be flying his flag in the escort carrier *Fidelix*. He would join the convoy off the Faeroes, bringing with him from Scapa Flow the carrier, a heavy cruiser and a flotilla of Home Fleet Destroyers. The SOO explained briskly that the Vice-Admiral would be responsible for passing convoy JW137 through to Murmansk and, as CS19's orders emphasised, a prime purpose of the operation would be *to seek out and destroy the enemy*.

Waste of time this, thought Redman, like reading the book after you've seen the picture. Damn this bronchitis or whatever it is. He leant forward trying to ease the congestion.

Ginger Mountsey was now saying his piece but Redman wasn't really listening. In a vague detached way he was looking at the convoy diagrams on the blackboards. They showed the station numbers of ships, distance apart of columns, disposition of escorts and covering forces. These things interested him but he was oblivious to the posters on the wall behind. Old now, torn and damp-stained: 'Don't join the stragglers' club,' a lone merchant ship sinking, the balloon from the periscope in the foreground inscribed, *'Wunderbar! Ein verdammter Straggler'*; another, 'Careless Talk Costs Countless Lives', a sinister, emphatically Teutonic character listening in to a telephone conversation. And there were others, too familiar to make any impact. Vaguely, as if it were part of a long-distance telephone conversation on a bad line, he heard snatches of what Mountsey was saying: formation of the convoy, disposition of escorts on close and outer screens, the carrier's procedure when flying off and recovering aircraft, communication arrangements, role of the rescue vessel, and the weather.

The weather, thought Redman, you can say that again. We can look after the rest but not the weather. Mountsey switched to enemy forces likely to be encountered. *The enemy,* the words tumbled discordantly through Redman's mind – the *enemy.* That meant Germans. Every time he thought of Germans he saw not U-boats and swastikas but Marianne and Hans. Then he would apply a discipline practised over the years and get rid of the images. But it wasn't easy.

'No stopping for survivors,' Mountsey was saying. 'We can't afford to present sitting targets to U-boats. Throw floats and rafts to the chaps in the water. Leave the rest to the rescue vessel.'

Five to ten minutes, thought Redman, exceptionally fifteen. That was about the longest a man could survive in Arctic water. A picture formed in his mind of wet blackness, the winking of survivors' lights, the slap and wash of seas unseen but ice cold, the sound of Patterson's hoarse croaking in the darkness – 'Are you all right, sir?' With a shiver of head and shoulders, Redman shook away the recollection.

The lieutenant-commander beside him looked up. 'You all right?' he muttered.

'Quite,' said Redman.

Ginger Mountsey was on to something else. U-boat shadowing? 'Weather permitting we should keep them down with air patrols and the ships on the outer screen,' he was saying. 'But don't underestimate the difficulties which will confront the carrier's pilots. Almost continual darkness for the greater part of the journey, frequent gales and blizzards – and icing problems. They'll do everything possible. You can be sure of that.'

Redman remembered a row with some Fleet Air Arm sub-lieutenants a few days before. It was in the billiard-room of the officers' club at Greenock. They'd drunk too much and made a lot of noise, skylarking and upsetting a tankard of beer over the green baize cloth. He'd choked them off and they'd become suddenly silent and apologetic. Afterwards he remembered how dubious their chances of survival were and

10

felt ashamed. They flew mostly in darkness, in appalling weather, and even if they found the carrier on return a safe landing was often no more than an even chance.

Time went on. The second officer Wren was making notes with one hand, arranging her hair with the other. Now it was the naval control service officer giving advice to the merchant captains. Action to take if contact with the convoy was lost, the dangers of straggling, of showing lights . . . Redman sighed with tired boredom. Merchant captains who'd survived to the end of 1944 knew just about all there was to know about convoys. He wondered if the naval control service officer had spent much time at sea. Or was he one of those people at Greenock with a flat and a car, going steady with a Wren. He decided it was an unkind thought and disliked himself for it. After all, some people had to do the shore jobs, ships couldn't operate without them and many of them had done sea time. His laboured breathing irritated him. He cleared his throat, stifling the noise with a handkerchief. A few days in dry clothes, hot meals and plenty of undisturbed sleep. That'd put him right, he assured himself, knowing these were things he wasn't going to get.

Ginger Mountsey, still sounding far away, was addressing a final word to the escort captains. 'Radio silence except for TBS.[1] Unless we know the convoy's sighted. If you find yourself carrying out a pounce attack on a submarine close to the convoy, switch on fighting lights if there's any danger of collision – not otherwise.'

For God's sake, thought Redman, let's get back to the ships. We know this stuff. He took his mind off what was going on by concentrating on the Wren. She looked a nice girl. Peaches and cream complexion. Beneath the table she showed good legs. He wondered about her. Was she a virgin? Highly improbable. He hoped not. Such a waste. Who did she belong to? Was she always as demure as that? Difficult to be demure in bed. The commodore was saying something. Telling the merchant captains what he expected of them and wishing them good luck. They need it, thought Redman, they're the targets. The commodore asked if there were any questions. There were several. When the old man had dealt

[1] TBS – Talk Between Ships. A very high-frequency two-way radio telephone with limited range.

with them he said with genial finality, 'Well, gentlemen, I think it's time we returned to our ships.'

Redman sighed with relief. Once the thing started the tension went. It was like waiting in your corner for the bell for the first round. Come to think of it, he decided, convoy conferences were rather like those preliminaries. Of course only one of the contestants was present, but the other was there by implication, and the injunctions to escort and merchant captains all sounded rather like, *No holding, break clean. No punching on the break. You know the rules. Now go to your corners and come out fighting . . .'*

Outside it was blowing harder and the wind drove the rain cold and prickling into his face as he went down the slope towards the landing stage. He was joined by two captains in his group and they chatted desultorily, their thoughts on other things. Up in the belly of Loch Ewe the wind snatched plumes of white steam from the funnels of the ships at anchor, and sea birds swooped and screeched for offal.

'Hope we get this lot set up before darkness,' said a bearded lieutenant-commander, the captain of *Vectis.*

'My dear boy, you *are* an optimist,' said the other.

'We won't,' said Redman. 'But they'll be settled down by morning. They usually are.'

'You sound hoarse.'

'Bit wheezy,' said Redman. 'It's nothing.'

'What about the weather?' asked the bearded man.

'Poor outlook. Haven't you see the forecast?'

'It's wrong sometimes.'

'Thank God for that.'

They reached the jetty and Redman beckoned his boat alongside. Down at the landing stage motor boats were coming and going. A busy scene: the noise of engines, shouted orders from coxswains and bowmen. It cheered Redman. Busy like . . . like what? He couldn't think of a simile. But it was good to see movement and things happening. It was when nothing happened, when you had time to think, that you felt depressed. *Vengeful's* boat came alongside, he climbed down into the sternsheets and they headed out into the anchorage. He was aware of the noise of the boat's engines, the slap of small waves and douches of spray, but though he was looking at the merchant ships, the destroyers, the sloops, frigates and corvettes, he was thinking about his breathing. He hadn't told the surgeon-commander that the childhood attacks had recurred twice. Once after the ski accident, then after Paris. He always thought of that time as 'after Paris'. He didn't like to put it into appropriate words. They were too stark, hurt too much. This time the attacks had started after the second Reykjavik trip. He wondered why. Then his mind emptied. It was part of his tiredness that his mind often switched off. The boat approached *Vengeful*'s starboard quarter and he saw a little group at the head of the side-ladder. The first-lieutenant, the officer-of-the-day, the coxswain, the chief boatswain's mate, a quartermaster and a sentry. They stood to attention and the thin treble of the boatswain's call cut through the curtain of rain. Redman climbed the ladder to more piping. On deck he exchanged salutes with the first-lieutenant. 'We're sailing at fourteen hundred, Number One.'

'Aye, aye, sir.'

Redman went through the door into the after deckhouse, down the steep ladder to the officers' flat, and along it to his day cabin. It was well furnished and comfortable, the chairs and settee covered with chintzes, a blue-and-white pattern like Dresden china which reminded him of his aunt's house in East Horsley where he'd spent so much of his time. Off the day cabin, on the port side, was the sleeping cabin he used in harbour. He took off the wet cap and raincoat and, as if waiting for this moment, Topcutt, the able-seaman who was his servant, came in. 'Take those and dry them for you, sir?'

'Thank you, Topcutt. I should have taken an oilskin. More rain than I thought.' Topcutt had been with him for two years. They'd survived a sinking together and the able-seaman did much to make Redman's life more comfortable.

Too old, though, thought Redman as Topcutt left the cabin. Must be every bit of forty. Too old to be on a job like this. Redman felt old too. He was thirty-four. The first-lieutenant was twenty-four. There were only two officers in the ship older than its captain. Emlyn Lloyd, the engineer-officer, and Baggot the torpedo gunner.

Redman looked round the cabin, yawned, stretched himself into an easy chair and stared at the coloured photograph on his desk. A flaxen-haired girl sitting on a farm gate, a field of corn behind her. In spite of the smile there was a wistfulness, a certain tragic beauty about her. The photo reminded him of two things: a gendarme's shrill whistle, the shriek of brakes, an urgent throng through which he'd broken, a crumpled figure at their feet, a man leaning over her; an Alpine crevasse, the glacier beneath a slope, broken skis and blood, a tall fair man smiling as he took his hand.

To have the photo there at all was a contradiction. It recalled two of the worst moments of his life. A time when he'd been overwhelmed by tragedy and guilt. A time before that of fear, pain and desperation. But there were things one could do and things one couldn't, and to do away with the photo was unthinkable. An act of betrayal. The least he could do was keep her memory alive. He drew his hand across his eyes. I'm tired, he thought, bloody tired. There was a knock on the door. Gavin Strong, the first-lieutenant, came in with a signal sheet in his hand.

'What is it, Number One?'

'Signal from Greenock, sir. From Captain (D).[1] About Leading-seaman Tregarth.'

'What's the trouble?'

'His wife died in labour yesterday. Captain (D) wants us to land him if we can.'

'Can we spare him?'

'I think so, sir. I think we must.'

'Right, do that Number One.'

There was an attractive ugliness about the first-lieutenant; smiling grey eyes and a nose on one side, like the face of a much-punished boxer. His manner was direct and his lop-sided smile warm and friendly. He had an assurance, an air of confidence, an enthusiasm which infected the ship's company. This strongly recommended him to his captain.

Apart from Redman, the only Royal Naval officers in the ship were the first-lieutenant and Pownall, the navigating officer. The rest, but for Baggot the torpedo gunner, a warrant officer, were Royal Naval Volunteer Reservists. On the whole a good bunch of officers who made for a cheerful wardroom. He had reservations about Pownall. The navigating officer was competent but often supercilious at the

[1] Captain (D) was the title given to the officer commanding a destroyer flotilla or destroyer escort group. In the latter case he was usually based ashore.

14

expense of others. Then there was Sutton the new doctor. A queer fish. Pale, apprehensive eyes. A serious, joyless, detached sort of man. He'd joined the ship a few weeks back. Redman had his doubts about him. But he was sure of *Vengeful*. She was a good ship. Her chiefs and petty officers were all RN – some of them Fleet reservists – sound men, the hard core around which the ship's company functioned. She was a Chatham-based ship, the majority of her crew 'hostilities only'; mostly young Londoners in their late teens and early twenties. Life on the messdecks of a V and W destroyer in northern seas was hard and appallingly uncomfortable. But these youngsters, pitch-forked into the Royal Navy by the fortunes of war, endured it all with a stoicism which Redman admired. Of course some of them annoyed and worried him at times. Did stupid things like going absent without leave, usually because of some girl, and getting into other unnecessary trouble. And there was Cupido, the captain's steward. Small, dark, taciturn. He worried Redman. Somehow he couldn't get through to the man. They had a bad effect on each other. Cupido seemed unable to bring a hot meal to the sea-cabin. And he smelt of garlic.

Redman lunched early and alone in his day cabin. He had just finished when the first-lieutenant reported that the ship's company was assembled in the seamen's messdeck. When Redman got there he outlined to the ship's company in straightforward, simple language the operation on which they were about to embark: the escorting of convoy JW 137 to Murmansk. He drew on a blackboard a diagram of the convoy. For the first twenty-four hours *Vengeful*, with the rest of the Fifty-Seventh Escort Group, would be on the close screen. Off the Faeroes the carrier, the cruiser and the Home Fleet destroyers would join and the Fifty-Seventh Group would then move to the outer screen, eight miles ahead of the convoy. Distance apart of ships on that screen would be three thousand yards and it would cover a front of twelve miles. *Vengeful* would be the port wing ship.

There were a few quiet good-o's. Norway lay to starboard.

Redman turned from the blackboard. 'Don't forget where we'll be on the return journey.' The dark shadowed eyes smiled. 'Norway'll lie to port then.'

15

That produced some coo-ers.

On the last convoy, on the journey north, *Vengeful* had been starboard wing ship, one of two destroyers detached to sweep the Norwegian coast between the Ofoten and Alten Fiords during a long Arctic night. Their task had been to find and sink ships hugging the coast with supplies for German air and naval bases in Norway. Navigating the Norwegian coast with its straggle of offshore rocks and islets, without shore lights and in frequent blizzards, was not an experience anyone was keen to repeat. And they hadn't found any enemy shipping.

With firm strokes Redman rubbed the chalk from the blackboard.

'JW 137 is a big convoy. Thirty-six ships. But we've a large escort force – twenty-six of us including the carrier and a cruiser. Worst problem will be the weather. There'll be U-boats and enemy aircraft, of course. We'll have to be on the top line. But we're a good ship in a good group – and we know how to fight her. We can't ask for more. So,' he hesitated, 'the best of good luck to you all.' He turned to the first-lieutenant. 'Right, Number One. Carry on.'

Down in the wardroom not long afterwards they were discussing the captain's talk. O'Brien, a burly Irishman with tousled red hair and beard, said, 'I suppose the Old Man's fireside chats do some good?' O'Brien was next in seniority to the first-lieutenant.

'They add a touch of drama to the mundane,' said Pownall.

The first-lieutenant swallowed the last of his sherry. 'I think they're good. The Old Man takes the ship's company into his confidence. They understand the object of the exercise. Know what's expected of them. Much better than the remote sort of skipper. Tight lips, sealed orders, a grim look, and tell the ship's company nothing.'

'Hear, hear,' said Rogers, one of *Vengeful*'s two midshipmen. A thin youth with mousy hair.

'The young should be seen and not heard,' said Pownall. 'And say *sir*.'

'Yes, *sir*.'

A dark man in overalls, wearing a greasy cap and gauntlets, came into the wardroom. It was Emlyn Lloyd, the

16

engineer-lieutenant. He had crowsfeet at the corner of his eyes and seemed always about to smile.

The first-lieutenant suggested a drink.

Lloyd nodded to the steward. 'Sherry, please, Guilio.'

'You're not sitting down to lunch with us in that rig, are you, Chiefy?' Pownall raised a disapproving eyebrow.

Lofty Groves, the sub-lieutenant, went to the dartboard, took the darts and handed three to the engineer-lieutenant. 'Give you a start of ten,' he said.

'No respect,' said Emlyn Lloyd, shaking his head. 'No respect. That's the trouble nowadays.' He flicked a dart into the board. Wilson, junior of *Vengeful*'s three lieutenants, picked up his cap. 'Better show myself on the upper deck.'

'About time,' said the first-lieutenant. 'The officer-of-the-day should be available on deck at all times,' he quoted.

'Article one-one-five-two,' said Pownall. 'King's Regulations and Admiralty Instructions.'

'Holy Saint Patrick,' growled O'Brien.

'What's the trouble?'

'Nothing, Number One. Just the punishment returns. Forgotten to send them in.'

'Dereliction of duty, is it?' said Emlyn Lloyd. 'Forget them, lad. Never do today what you can put off until tomorrow. Indeed, we may be sunk and they won't be necessary at all.'

'Now that's a fact,' said O'Brien. 'That's a really practical attitude.'

There was a burst of laughter from the two midshipmen in the corner, Rogers and Bowrie. Lofty Groves turned on them. 'Pipe down. Can't hear myself throw a dart.'

'He's losing,' said the engineer-officer.

O'Brien went over to them. 'And what's amusing the children?'

'N-nothing, sir,' Bowrie had a slow stammer. 'Rogers was telling me what he d-did on leave.'

O'Brien shook his head. 'What midshipmen do on leave. Bless my soul.'

'Rather sad, really,' said Pownall. 'Caught between childhood and adultery.'

'Anyone seen Huff-Duff?' asked the first-lieutenant.

'In his c-cabinet calibrating h-his . . .'

'Steady lad,' said O'Brien. 'Speak no evil.'

'H-his set, sir,' finished Bowrie.

Huff-Duff was the wardroom's name for Sunley, a specialist branch RNVR lieutenant who maintained and operated *Vengeful*'s high-frequency direction-finding apparatus – HF/ DF, known in the Navy as *huff-duff* – a key weapon in tracking U-boats.

A man with a horse-like face, pale eyes and straw-coloured hair came into the wardroom. He went to the notice-board and took from it an OHMS letter addressed, 'Surgeon-Lieutenant E. B. Sutton, RNVR.'

He sat down on the padded seat round the Charlie Noble, the wardroom's coke fire, its circular iron body topped by a shining brass chimney.

The first-lieutenant said, 'Ship's company fit, Doc? Clean bill of health?'

The doctor frowned, looking up from the letter he was opening. 'Beer, please, Guilio. Yes, Number One. I think so. Common cold, VD. A few old friends. Nothing operable.'

'L-lucky for someone,' murmured Bowrie. The doctor's pale eyes regarded him with distant contempt.

The wardroom steward brought the beer. The doctor finished the letter, looked thoughtful and put it in his pocket. While the others laughed and chatted he worried. Redman had at the doctor's request visited the RN hospital at Bridge-of-Weir for examination. The captain had stalled, postponing the visit to the day before the ship sailed from the Clyde. The OHMS letter was from the consulting physician. 'Lieutenant-Commander Redman,' it reported, 'is suffering from bronchial asthma brought on by nervous exhaustion; too long at sea, too much stress, too little sleep. There is a childhood history of the complaint. With a suitable period of rest and freedom from anxiety it will probably disappear. The patient makes light of it and is not amenable to any suggestion of leaving the ship. He has particularly requested that no medical report be submitted to Captain (D) until *Vengeful* returns to the Clyde in three weeks' time, and then only if the complaint persists. Since the X-ray plates only became available the day after the examination, Lieutenant-Commander Redman was not informed of the diagnosis.'

The consulting physician's diagnosis did not surprise Sutton – at least not the part about stress and nervous exhaustion.

It accorded with his own. But Redman hadn't told him of any previous history of bronchial asthma. That had been unhelpful of him.

Stress and anxiety symptoms were not uncommon among escort captains in the Western Approaches, but the doctor's problem was what to do about the letter. When Captain (D) Greenock, the group's administrative authority, received the medical report he would no doubt act. Put the captain ashore for a rest whether he liked it or not. The doctor decided it wouldn't help to tell Redman the result of the examination now. He'd probably blame him for having organised the visit to Bridge-of-Weir. The doctor was unsure of Redman. Sensed that the captain had not yet accepted him.

The Maltese messman reported that lunch was ready. The first-lieutenant said, 'Come on. Let's get cracking. We haven't much time.'

The wardroom officers of HMS *Vengeful* sat down to what promised to be their last normal meal for many days.

## CHAPTER TWO

In his cabin Redman was preparing for what lay ahead. At least the next eight days would be spent on the bridge and in the tiny sea-cabin adjoining the wheelhouse. There would be little sleep, frequent alarms, appalling weather, almost continual darkness – the exception being a couple of hours of feeble twilight during the forenoon – no change of clothing, cold or at best lukewarm food, no comforting gins or whiskies – captains did not drink at sea in wartime – and few opportunities to ease his bowels. There would be explosions in the night and sudden disaster. And having got one convoy to Russia they would have to bring back another. The gauntlet had to be run twice. He'd done six: three outward, three homeward. Others in *Vengeful* had done more. He wondered how long the ship's luck would last. With these thoughts he changed into the clothing he would wear until they reached the Kola Inlet. Thick, loosely-knitted grey wool underclothing provided by the Admiralty; then a flannel shirt, over it a heavy wool jersey; uniform trousers, well-worn; an old uniform reefer; woollen socks, seaboot stockings and felt liners to the leather seaboots which he pulled on last of all. Slowly and methodically he tied the Mae West – the inflatable life-belt – round his waist, secured the tapes, tested the survival light, slipped a rope picking-up harness over his shoulders and adjusted it. He hated the harness but wore it in accordance with Admiralty Fleet Orders to set an example to the ship's company. There was another reason. He knew that if he'd paid more attention to these things in his last ship fewer lives would have been lost. He thought of that night – the agonising reality of icy water, the knowledge that one was weak from injury. Worst of all, Patterson's cries for help. Cries to which he'd made such a feeble response. He tried to shut the picture from his mind.

The clock on the bulkhead showed 1350. Ten minutes to go.

He put away those things on the desk which would roll off. The last of these was the photo of the flaxen-haired girl. Before putting it in the drawer he looked at her face, trying to recall the sound of her voice, but failing. He picked up his duffel coal, uniform cap; mittens and night glasses and stood uncertainly, looking round the cabin wondering what would have happened by the time he next saw it – during those eight or nine days that must pass before they reached the Kola Inlet.

Topcutt came from the sleeping-cabin with an anorak suit, fur cap, fur-lined gauntlets, spare jersey, steel helmet, handkerchiefs and a bag of shaving and washing gear. He said, 'I'll be taking these up to the sea-cabin, sir.'

'Thank you, Topcutt.'

The able-seaman popped his head back through the door. 'Be back shortly for the bedding, sir.'

'Yes,' said Redman absent-mindedly.

Topcutt hesitated. 'The – the bronchitis. Better, sir?'

Redman said an irritable 'Yes.' Topcutt took the hint and left.

When he'd gone Redman looked through a navigating notebook, checking data he'd recorded before they left the Clyde. He was interrupted by a knock on the door. 'Ready for sea, sir.' It was the first-lieutenant.

After the first-lieutenant came the engineer-officer, Emlyn

Lloyd. 'Engines ready for sea, sir,' he reported. Next it was the gunner (T). When he'd made his report Redman said, 'That starboard depth-charge chute all right, Mr Baggot?'

'Yes, sir. We've got it fixed.'

'Good. We shall need it.'

Then came Pownall, the navigating officer, to make his reports: radar tested and in order; master gyro running, repeaters checked and found correct. He was followed by Lofty Groves, the asdic control officer.

'A/S equipment tried, tested and in order, sir.'[1]

'Thank you, Groves. Dome housed?'

'Yes, sir.'

Redman was referring to the asdic dome from which sound waves were transmitted and received when searching for a submerged submarine. It protruded from the bottom of the hull in the forepart of the ship and could be raised and lowered. In harbour it was normally raised – 'housed' – but lowered at sea.

When steaming into head seas at speed the dome was housed to avoid weather damage. The asdic search equipment could not function with it in this position.

Finally Sunley, a thin grey-faced young man, reported that the HF/DF equipment had been tested and found correct.

'Good,' Redman looked up from the desk. 'We couldn't do without your Huff-Duff, Sunley.'

'Thank you, sir.' Sunley blinked, then withdrew, closing the door in slow motion as if apologising for the intrusion.

[1] I  *Radar* – used by warships to obtain the range and bearing of ships, including surfaced submarines, aircraft and other objects on or above the surface. Also used for navigational purposes, e.g.: to obtain the bearing, distance and configuration of the land.

II  The principal use of *Asdic* (now called Sonar) was to obtain the range, bearing and depth of submerged submarines.

III  During World War II, *HF/DF* (High frequency direction finding) – known affectionately in the Royal Navy as *huff-duff* – gave the bearings of ultra high-frequency radio transmissions made by U-boats. The existence of equipment with this capacity was unknown to the Germans until after the war.

Five minutes to 1400. Redman went to the door of the cabin and took a last look round. At the back of his mind was the thought that he might not see it again. He shut the door and made for the bridge.

At 1400 the shroud of silence over Loch Ewe was broken by the sound of windlasses turning and the squeak and groan of anchor cables coming home. The ships in the loch had begun to weigh. The Fifty-Seventh Escort Group was first to leave, led out by the senior officer, Ginger Mountsey, in the sloop *Bluebird*. The sloop *Chaffinch* followed, then *Vengeful,* after her *Violent* and the remainder of the group. The south-westerly wind continued to gust and eddy, driving the rain before it under a lowering sky. *Vengeful* steamed out into the North Minch between Rubha nan Sasan and Ploc an Slagain, the two headlands looming through the rain, the monotony of their greyness relieved here and there by the russet of dried heather. As she left the shelter of the land the destroyer began to move about in the seaway.

A group of men in oilskins were clustered together on the small bridge: Redman, Pownall, Burrows, the yeoman of signals, the first-lieutenant and the lookouts. On the fore-castle other oilskins glistened wetly in the fading light as the cable party put the final touches to securing anchors and cables under the watchful eyes of O'Brien.

Redman stood in the forefront of the bridge searching the sea with binoculars. Away to port he could see the lighthouse at Rubha Reidh, a thin grey pencil poking into the wet sky. Moving to starboard he looked astern to where *Vectis,* the last ship of the group, was clearing the headlands.

The movement of the ship, the slap of water at the bows and along the sides, the whirr of the turbines, the *ping* of asdic transmissions relayed on the bridge-speaker, the steady sweep of the radar scanner on the tower – these things reassured him. The ship was alive, her equipment was at work in capable hands, for him the party had started and the worst of the tension had gone. And so, oddly enough, had the wheeziness which had troubled him.

Behind *Vectis* the frigates and corvettes of the Eighty-Third Escort Group were emerging from the mist. Astern of them the freighters would be lining up to leave the loch. He turned to Pownall. 'Time of sunset?'

'Fifteen sixteen, sir. Nautical twilight ends at sixteen fifty-seven.'

'It'll be dark long before that in this weather.'

'I imagine so, sir.'

Redman thought, why does he say 'I imagine so' when he knows bloody well it will be. He said, 'That gives us about two hours of daylight in which to get the convoy formed. I think . . .'

The crackle of the TBS speaker on the bridge interrupted him. It was *Bluebird* ordering the Fifty-Seventh Group to carry out an anti-submarine sweep to seaward. Redman called to Pownall who was on the compass platform. 'Port fifteen, one-six-oh revolutions. We'll take station on *Bluebird*'s port beam.'

The navigator repeated the orders, passing them by voice-pipe to the quartermaster in the wheelhouse below.

Redman spoke into the asdic voice-pipe. 'Carry out an all-round sweep. Resume normal sweep when we're in station.'

The asdic operator repeated the order.

*Vengeful* trembled as her speed increased and she swung over to port to pass astern of *Bluebird*.

Before long the group had formed line abreast, the eight ships pitching and rolling, whipping up douches of spray as they swept up the North Minch under a pall of rain. Pownall had a sense of poetry and to him the ships looked like grey-hounds casting for a scent. No such thought crossed the captain's mind. Though a U-boat in the Minches was most unlikely, he was thinking that the A/S sweep was important. A convoy was particularly vulnerable to attack when leaving harbour, before the ships had formed into columns with their protective screens of close and outer escorts.

The yeoman answered the buzzer from the W/T office. 'Captain, sir. Signal from NOIC to *Bluebird*. Liberty ship *USS Jonathan Nash* has furnace trouble and will not repeat not be joining convoy.'

'One less to worry about,' said Redman. He went back to his thoughts. It was late 1944, the Battle of the Atlantic had been won. The anti-submarine forces – sea and air – had gained a decisive upper hand. But U-boats fitted with *Schnorchels* – and so able to charge their batteries by running on diesels while submerged – were venturing closer inshore in their search for targets. He felt that the chances of making contact with one that afternoon were remote with such powerful escort forces about, but it was like fishing for salmon on a bad day. Just as the monotonous *ping* of the asdic kept sounding on the bridge-speaker without anyone seriously expecting to hear the answering *pong* of a submarine contact, so you could go on casting a fly into pool after pool without expecting a fish to rise. Then suddenly – usually when you least expected it – there was the sudden swirl of water and the tug of a salmon taking.

Once they got going – particularly rounding Norway between Bear Island and the North Cape, up in the Barents Sea – there would be U-boats. And long before that enemy aircraft from German bases along the Norwegian coast might find the convoy. Much would depend on the weather. Bad weather and almost continuous darkness, for all the discomfort they brought, were useful aids to concealment. But even if the convoy was found the sinkings were unlikely to be heavy. Prevented by strong escort forces from getting to close quarters with convoys, U-boats now concentrated on attacking the escorts with *gnats,* acoustic torpedoes which homed on the target's propeller noises.

The escorts had counter-measures, mainly noise-makers called *foxers* which were towed astern and into which acoustic torpedoes homed and exploded. But escort captains disliked using them. Long wires trailing astern hampered manœuvring, and the noise of the *foxers* reduced the asdic operator's chances of making contact with a submerged submarine.

These were Redman's thoughts as he listened to the *ping* of the asdic and watched the PPI, the instrument which relayed the images from the screen in the radar office at the back of the bridge. Redman was not consciously doing these things. He'd done them for so many years now that it was a conditioned reflex – as was his reaction when the call-up bell from the asdic cabinet sounded three *Ps* in rapid succession.

'Hard-a-port. Full ahead together,' he shouted down the voice-pipe to the wheelhouse. 'Start the plot.'

*Vengeful* swung round, laying over to starboard, her hull vibrating with sudden urgency as the turbines responded to a full head of steam.

24

Three *Ps* was the asdic operator's emergency warning to the bridge that he had heard on his hydrophones the sound of a torpedo approaching from the port side.

Within seconds the first-lieutenant had rung a series of shorts on the alarm bells for *anti-submarine action stations*, and the yeoman had broadcast a general alarm by TBS.

## CHAPTER THREE

Redman assumed the torpedo to be acoustic and acted instantly. The running time would be under a minute. When *Vengeful* completed her turn he steadied the ship on the HE bearing and ordered, 'Fire one – set shallow.' Seconds later the depth-charge exploded astern of the ship. He at once called, 'Starboard twenty. Stop engines. Anything on radar along that HE bearing?'

'No, sir,' said Wilson, the officer-of-the-watch.

The buzzer from the quarterdeck sounded, followed by the voice of the gunner (T), 'Torpedo passing astern.'

From the wing of the bridge Redman saw in the fading light the tell-tale track crossing the ship's wake. It was less than fifty yards astern, turning away, making for the turbulence created by the depth-charge. The torpedo's acoustic device had locked on to the noise of the explosion just in time. Redman sighed with relief and informed *Bluebird* by TBS. Mountsey immediately ordered the group to stop engines. They've already done it, thought Redman, as the escort commander's cheerful voice added, 'Thanks for passing us your hot potato.' Not long afterwards they heard the torpedo explode at the end of its run.

In *Bluebird* Mountsey was looking at the chart of the Minches, doing some quick thinking. The U-boat somewhere south of *Vengeful* was probably a loner. Several had been reported in the Irish Sea close to the Minches. But it might be a trap. An attempt to draw escorts to the south of Loch Ewe. U-boats waiting to the north would then be freer to deal with the merchant ships as they came out. This was the first time Mountsey had experienced an attack on leaving Loch Ewe. It was by no means unusual at the other end, outside the Kola Inlet. But not here. It might be a new tactic. To play safe he assumed it was. Over the TBS he ordered *Vengeful* and *Violent* to hunt the U-boat while the remainder of the group continued the A/S sweep over the ground to be covered by the convoy.

'Can't spare you for long,' he said. 'Try for a quick flush. Rejoin in thirty minutes if no joy.' He then reported the contact to C-in-C Western Approaches. The operations room there would decide whether to call on coastal command for aircraft. With a ten-tenths sky, cloud ceiling almost zero and heavy rain, Mountsey didn't think aircraft could do much.

*Vengeful* was the senior ship. As Redman ordered *Violent* to take station a mile on his port beam, the buzzer from the asdic cabinet sounded. 'Plot gives one-nine-five as probable bearing of U-boat's firing position.' It was Groves reporting.

'Steer one-nine-five,' ordered Redman. 'One-five-oh, revolutions.' Then to the asdic cabinet, 'Carry out normal sweep.' He went to the chart-table in the wing of the bridge. Pownall was plotting the ship's position. Redman waited impatiently. Every minute counted. 'Shake it up, Pilot,' he urged. He knew he was being unfair but couldn't contain his irritation.

'We're here, sir.' Pownall made room for him under the screen, pointing with his pencil. 'Three-two-one, Rubha Reidh, five-point-two miles.'

Globules of rain fell on to the chart from the sleeves of their oilskins. Pownall dabbed at the damp patches with a towel.

'Good. He'll have dived immediately after firing. Sliding away south now on electric motors. Making for deep water.' Redman screwed up his eyes, concentrating on the chart. 'Down in that long reach towards Rona. Outside the fifty-fathom line.'

Pownall was silent, weighing what the captain had said. It was not in his nature to agree out of politeness. Nor did he like being told to 'shake it up' when he was plotting a position. But he knew the captain was tired and that allowance had to be made for occasional outbursts.

'Yes, sir,' he said eventually. 'I think that's possible.'

'Probable,' snapped Redman. 'He won't go north into a pack of escorts. He wants to stay alive.' Redman stared at the chart, deep in thought. 'Tell the plot to assume a course of one-eight-oh, speed six knots. Where does that put him now?'

While Pownall spoke to the plot Redman looked at his watch: 1437. Three minutes since the firing of the torpedo. The destroyers were doing fifteen knots. The U-boat was somewhere within half a mile if his assumptions were correct. He went to the forepart of the bridge. 'Steer one-eight-five. One hundred revolutions.' The yeoman passed the new course and speed to *Violent* by TBS, adding, 'Captain thinks U-boat's making for the deep water towards Rona.'

Jackie Dixon, *Violent*'s Royal Naval Reserve captain, said, 'Probably. Cheeky bastard joining the party uninvited like that.'

Redman heard him on the bridge-speaker and sighed. He wished he had Jackie Dixon's temperament. The light-hearted approach to war was the only one that made sense. Yet Redman knew it was impossible for him. Was it a façade or did it really all seem rather fun to Jackie?

Minutes went by. For the men on the bridge the *ping* of the asdic dominated all other sounds. The wind freshened, bringing squalls of rain from the south-west, wet grey curtains drenching the bridge and upper deck. Visibility was down to half a mile at times and *Violent* would be lost in the mist. But the PPI showed her in station as the destroyers moved south, their ships' companies closed up at anti-submarine action stations; ASCO's and their operators hunched over asdic sets, concentrated and alert; depth-charge parties standing by the throwers and chutes, charges primed, itching to fire them; gun's crews at their guns hoping desperately to see a submarine surface.

There was tension and a high degree of alertness in both ships but an underlying cynicism. The attack had come too soon, too unexpectedly. Only a handful of men in *Vengeful* had seen the torpedo track though in both ships the terminal explosion had been heard, but even that many believed to be just another depth-charge.

At least on *Vengeful*'s and *Violent*'s bridges it was known there *was* a U-boat. It was known, too, that it might at any moment fire another acoustic torpedo from its stern tube. In the asdic cabinets the operators were listening for HE – the hydrophone effect which would give warning of this.

Redman looked at his watch. It was 1452. Mountsey had given them thirty minutes. Eighteen had gone.

'Position, Pilot?'

Pownall's head and shoulders jerked nervously behind the chart-table's canvas screen. He was plotting a snap bearing of the lighthouse at Rubha Reidh, taken in a brief clearing of rain.

'Position, Pilot?' Redman's voice was insistent.

Pownall's head came out of the screen. 'Two-eight-two, Rubha Reidh, four miles, sir.' Redman looked at the chart and checked the depths ahead of the ship . . . 64, 66, 68 fathoms . . . about 400 feet. He *must* be round about here, he thought. U-boats dived deep after firing a 'gnat', otherwise it might circle and home on the submarine's own diesels. If the U-boat had surfaced in the rain, mist and failing light, in an attempt to get away at high speed, the destroyer's radar would have picked it up.

Redman said, 'We'll hold this course for . . .' He stopped as the asdic's *ping* was echoed by an unmistakable *pong*. The buzzer from the asdic cabinet sounded. 'Contact, sir. Green oh-two-seven . . . drawing right . . . range eight hundred . . . closing . . . submarine.'

Redman contemplated a pounce attack, but they weren't often successful. He wanted to get this U-boat. Not just scare it. With *Violent* in company he could carry out a 'creeping' attack. He reduced speed, ordered, 'Starboard ten, steady on two-one-two.' He put on the TBS headset. From now on he'd speak direct to *Violent* instead of relaying messages through the yeoman. He found time to glance through the small window into the asdic cabinet where Lofty Groves and his operators sat at their instruments. He held up a thumb and Groves did the same, grinning. Then the sub-lieutenant was all serious concentration again.

Redman spoke to *Violent*. 'Contact eight hundred yards. Dead ahead. My course two-one-two. Cease asdic transmissions. Take station for "creeping" attack. Approach at eight knots.'

'Altering course now and reducing speed,' came Jackie Dixon's cheerful voice. All ships of the group had practised the 'creeping attack'. Only once before had Redman used it in action. Then he'd been the attacking ship. Now his was the directing ship.

'Bearing two-oh-five – range seven hundred. Closing slowly,' came from the asdic's bridge-speaker. Lofty Groves's voice was calm. He rarely got excited. He was the best ASCO

Redman had ever had.

'Steer two-oh-five,' Redman ordered. There was no need to report the contact to Mountsey. He'd be listening to the TBS chat.

Redman saw that *Violent* was now on a converging course. He turned to Pownall. 'Get radar to report *Violent*'s range and bearing at each minute.'

Immediately came the first report – range 1500 yards – bearing 163 degrees. On *Violent*'s bridge Jackie Dixon was conning his ship on to a course which would put *Violent* immediately ahead of *Vengeful* in the shortest possible time.

Now that *Violent* was no longer making asdic transmissions the U-boat would not hear her and her slow speed of approach on an astern bearing meant that the destroyer's propeller noises would be drowned by the U-boat's. The submarine would still hear *Vengeful*'s transmissions, but since the distance between the U-boat and Redman's ship was opening the submarine would not take evasive action. That would only come when and if the range closed and the U-boat commander heard the destroyer's speed increase for the run-in to a depth-charge attack. With a 'creeping attack' that wouldn't happen and the U-boat commander, 300 to 400 feet down and blind, would have no means of knowing that an attack was taking place.

A stream of ranges and bearings came to Redman from the asdic cabinet. The range was opening slowly – what he wanted – and the submarine was making slight alterations of course, evidently keeping to deep water. Redman decided that the U-boat commander was either a very cool type, or his boat's wake and the noise of her own propellers were masking *Vengeful*'s asdic transmissions. Most probably, he concluded, the German, aware that the range was opening, believed the destroyer had lost contact.

The asdic cabinet reported the range to be one thousand yards. Redman adjusted *Vengeful*'s speed to keep that constant. To port, *Violent* was closing in. Only four hundred yards to go. On the bridge-speaker the note of the asdic transmissions changed and became confused before resolving into a series of double echoes. Redman frowned, the knot in his stomach tightening as he waited for Groves's report.

It came after what seemed a long time. 'Bearing one-nine-oh . . . drawing left . . . range steady. She released a

29

*pillenwerfer* just before altering, sir. We've sorted out the double echoes.'

'Well done,' said Redman. 'We heard something funny going on.

A *pillenwerfer* was a decoy used by U-boats to throw off a pursuer . . . a canister which released a stream of bubbles to reflect an asdic transmission in much the same way as the U-boat itself. Experienced operators were quick to detect the absence of change in range and bearing.

'Steer one-nine-oh,' the captain ordered, and gave the new course to *Violent*. From the chart-table Pownall called, 'He's heading for the Inner Sound, sir. West of Raasay.'

'Good. He's either cunning or plain stupid.'

'There's thirty fathoms in the Sound, sir. Close inshore. Perhaps he'll bottom there. It's steep-to.'

Raasay was twelve miles ahead. At six knots the U-boat needed at least two hours to make it submerged. Redman hoped to deal with it well before that. It was 1503. The light was going under a dark sky with low cloud and continuous rain. Light was not essential, asdics and radar were independent of it, but it helped enormously in a 'creeping attack'. The quicker they could get on with that the better.

A figure in oilskins came to the bridge and stood behind him. 'Cup of hot cocoa, sir?'

Redman turned and saw Topcutt pouring steaming cocoa from a jug. 'It'll drive away the cold, sir.'

'Thank you, Topcutt. You shouldn't have troubled this early.'

The able-seaman's expression conveyed polite disagreement, but he said, 'Yes, sir,' and left the bridge.

Pownall said, '*Violent*'s range three hundred, bearing one-one-oh, sir.'

'Good.' Redman's voice was steady in spite of the tension. 'That'll do. She'll be in station within ten minutes.'

He switched on the ship's broadcast and spoke to the crew. 'We're in firm contact with a U-boat. *Violent* will be in station within ten minutes. We'll carry out a "creeping attack" and catch him with his pants down.'

Those ten minutes seemed long ones to the men in both ships but eventually *Violent* was in station, directly ahead of *Vengeful*, and the attack began. Maintaining his distance from the U-boat at a thousand yards, Redman conned

*Violent* up the U-boat's track, the asdic cabinet giving the submarine's range and bearing, while Pownall repeated *Violent*'s range and bearing by radar. Suspense built up on *Vengeful's* bridge as the destroyer ahead crept slowly, silently, unheard, along the U-boat's track.

Redman passed the final distances to Jackie Dixon. 'One hundred yards to go . . . fifty . . . twenty-five . . .' The time intervals could be measured in seconds but they seemed to take infinitely longer as if the attack were paced by a watch that had stopped. Now *Violent* was over the U-boat, the German commander, oblivious of her presence, hearing at best only the *ping* of *Vengeful*'s asdic – still a thousand yards away and thus no threat – held his course.

But Redman had to get *Violent* ahead of the submarine to allow time for her depth-charges to reach the U-boat's depth. Then the German would steer directly into the pattern Jackie Dixon was about to release.

At last *Violent* was ahead of the U-boat. 'Fifteen yards . . . twenty yards . . .' On Redman's hands, clenched on the bridge rail, the knuckles showed white. He repeated the ranges to Jackie Dixon: 'Thirty yards . . . forty . . .' The moment had come. 'Fire!' he ordered, and hoped his voice didn't sound to others as much of a croak as it did to him.

In the rain and mist ahead he could see the shadowy outline of *Violent*, and the wind brought down the dull *rumph* of her depth-charge throwers as the twenty-six charges, fired in calculated sequence, left the throwers and chutes.

The tension on *Vengeful*'s bridge was like that before a free-kick in the penalty area at a cup final. It was released with sudden violence as sea, ships and air shook and trembled, great columns of water mushrooming skywards with a thunderous roar. It was as if the ocean-bed had erupted in a series of primeval explosions.

Showers of sparks came from *Violent's* funnel as she was shaken by the waterhammer of her own charges. Seconds ticked away. Groves's voice sounded on the loudspeaker; calm, matter of fact. 'We're picking up sounds of the U-boat breaking up, sir.'

The guns' crews were disappointed. Not for them the high excitement of a U-boat surfacing in the turbulent water of the depth-charge explosions. *Violent's* pattern must have torn the submarine open, to flood and sink it like a stone, its crew bewildered in their death agony.

For the next ten minutes *Violent* and *Vengeful* pinged away at the wreck of the U-boat until they had a good navigational fix. A slick of diesel oil had formed on the surface and was spreading downwind. There was little debris. Splinters of wood, some papers and dead fish. Before they left to rejoin, Jackie Dixon reported the picking up of flesh which his doctor had identified as human lung tissue. Redman felt faintly sick. Now that the excitement of the hunt was over he was no longer elated but tired and worried, thinking of the problems of the oncoming night. But there were things to be done. First he congratulated *Violent,* then over *Vengeful*'s broadcast he spoke to his own ship's company. 'It was a first-class attack and reflects great credit on every man in the ship. Thanks to *Vengeful* and *Violent* the Fifty-Seventh Escort Group has chalked up the first U-boat kill for convoy JW 137. Well done.'

Next he went to the asdic cabinet and congratulated Groves and his operators – 'If there's a better A/S team in the Western Approaches, I'd like to meet it,' he said. After that he gave a pat on the back to Petty Officer Blandy who'd manned the radar throughout the attack.

Redman wrote out a signal to C-in-C Western Approaches, repeated to Captain (D) Greenock and the senior officer of escorts in *Bluebird,* reporting the sinking. He gave it to the yeoman. 'Tell the W/T office to get that off as soon as possible.'

Later, when *Vengeful* and *Violent* were rejoining the group at twenty-three knots and were once more within TBS range of *Bluebird,* Mountsey's voice sounded on the bridge-speaker. 'Well done, *Vengeful* and *Violent*. Neat but not gaudy.'

The *gaudy* sounded like *gory* and Redman shivered as he pictured the lung tissue floating in a bucket of sea water. With remarkable speed, signals of congratulation came in from the Commander-in-Chief, Western Approaches, from the Vice-Admiral in *Fidelix,* and from Captain (D) Greenock.

Later, when the first-lieutenant congratulated him, Redman said, 'Funny how warmly one's congratulated for killing people.'

'For killing *Germans,* sir,' corrected Strong with his broken-nosed smile. Mistaking the captain's irony for humour, he did not know how much his remark had distressed Redman. But the ship's company had no inhibitions. They were jubilant, excited. It was the ship's first success in a 'creeping attack' and its third U-boat ever. It had been a quick, clean kill. A great start to what lay ahead. Completely unexpected. Like a goal immediately after the kick-off.


## CHAPTER FOUR


Daylight came shortly before nine o'clock, pale and hesitant under fast-moving clouds, drenching rain and poor visibility. Big seas, white-crested, rolled in from the west, and life on board *Vengeful* resumed its norm of discomfort.

Redman had spent most of the night on the bridge helping the convoy form, ushering laggards into their appointed places, closing ships showing lights or badly out of station, encouraging, coaxing and threatening by loud-hailer. Twice he'd gone to the sea-cabin to snatch a rest only to be called back to the bridge by false alarms: once when the officer-of-the-watch called him for a contact which turned out to be a shoal of fish, and the other when Pownall blundered.

It was not until the early hours of morning that *Vengeful* settled down in station on the port bow of the convoy.

The light grew stronger and the rain lifted momentarily. For the first time the convoy could be seen from *Vengeful*'s bridge. An armada covering ten square miles, its hard core the eight columns of merchant ships, around them the escorts: frigates and corvettes in close station, destroyers and sloops farther out; the commodore's pennant flying from the leading ship in the third column; the fleet oiler boxed in the centre, the rescue ship astern.

Redman lay on the bunk in the sea-cabin adjoining the wheelhouse one deck below the bridge. He wore his clothes but for the duffel coat and cap. The cabin door led into the wheelhouse and was latched open, a drawn curtain giving scant privacy. Grey daylight showed through the small porthole above the bunk, the only other illumination was a dim red lamp in the light socket. During the hours of darkness it protected his night vision. It was not enough to read by for any length of time and he found it depressing. Above his pillow the bridge voice-pipe loomed like the mouth of a trumpet.

Real sleep was seldom possible. There was a steady flow of sound from the bridge above: the insistent *ping* of the asdic, the orders given by the officer-of-the-watch, reports by look-outs, the asdic and radar operators, the plot and signal-men. In the wheelhouse the quartermaster and telegraph-man were within eight feet of him. He heard the wheel and engine orders they repeated and their muttered conversation. They were not supposed to talk while on duty but this was asking too much of young men. Only if they raised their voices would he shout, 'pipe down'. A period of silence would follow and then, believing he'd gone off to sleep, they'd begin whispering and muttering again. They did not realize that the captain's faculties were attuned to his responsibility. He never did really sleep. His sub-conscious missed little.

There was a folding wash-basin in the cabin, two drawers under the bunk, a diminutive cupboard and a stool. All that an area of eight by four-and-a-half feet could take. It was known in the wardroom as the 'dog-box'. It was here when he was not on the bridge that he lived, ate and rested while at sea. The nearest lavatory was three decks down. Since the time taken to cover that distance and to remove and replace Arctic clothing was unacceptable to a captain whose ship was engaged in an operation where alarms were frequent, he cultivated constipation as assiduously as a monk did absti-nence. For lesser requirements there was a communal bucket at the back of the bridge. Here again there were problems. To be slow when temperatures were well below freezing was to invite frostbite on a delicate organ.

Since real sleep was almost impossible he regarded his bunk as a place of rest. Sometimes, tired and exhausted, he would fall into fitful broken sleep, but an undisturbed hour was rare.

While he was resting he was thinking, which was about all he could do. Not like sleeping, when a man dreamt and somehow recharged his reserves of nervous energy. Mostly his thoughts were about the U-boat they'd sunk the afternoon before. It had been a good attack. Both ships and their specialist teams had done their jobs with remarkable efficiency. Nothing had gone wrong on an occasion when much could. But Redman had a vivid imagination and before long thoughts of the U-boat crew dying began to worry him. The sudden, inexplicable, devastating explosions from that lethal pattern; the pressure hull collapsing; the lights going out; the horrific sound of sea flooding in; the screams of dying men, the agony of bursting lungs. All this made a dreadful picture and soured the sense of achievement he might otherwise have felt. He imagined that no one else in *Vengeful* was troubled by these thoughts and he felt somehow diminished. When he'd congratulated the ship's company on the broadcast, and afterwards Groves and Blandy, he knew he was playing a part. Saying what had to be said, giving praise where it had to be given, aware that behind the façade lay reservations and scruples which his officers and men would not understand because there hadn't been a Marianne and a Hans in their lives. When at last his thoughts broke away from the sunken U-boat he thought of Pownall's mistake.

It had happened soon after the watchers changed at four in the morning. Redman had been in his sea-cabin for less than thirty minutes when he was woken from sleep, his first for eighteen hours. It was Pownall's voice booming in his ear.

'Forebridge – captain, sir,' came down the voice-pipe. 'Contact green oh-four-oh. Range twelve hundred. Altering to bearing for pounce attack.'

'Coming up,' was Redman's instant reply. As he went through the wheelhouse he heard the alarm bells and the quartermaster repeating Pownall's orders. 'Starboard twenty, one-eight-oh revolutions, sir.'

Racing up the ladder to the bridge he felt the build-up of vibration as *Vengeful*'s speed increased. He couldn't see properly because his eyes were not yet attuned to the dark, but on getting to the bridge he at once compared the range and bearing of the asdic contact with the visual presentation on the PPI. 'Get radar to check along that asdic bearing,' he snapped.

Pownall did. The radar operator replied, 'Bearing oh-five-two, range seven hundred, surface ship, closing rapidly.' The asdic cabinet's report at that moment was much the same, the operator adding. 'Target drawing left. Extent and HE look like a surface ship, sir.' It was Collins, the best HSD in *Vengeful*.

Redman ordered, 'Hard-a-port,' and told the asdic cabinet to disregard the contact and resume normal sweep. Later, when he'd steadied *Vengeful* on a safe course, tense and angry, he turned on Pownall. 'That was a careless mistake,' he said. 'You were attacking one of the merchant ships in convoy.'

Pownall was silent, trying to work out how the mistake had occurred. Visibility was down to a few hundred yards and he'd lost concentration at a critical moment. Why? There wasn't time to think out the answer to that one. The Old Man was obviously bloody angry and he had to say something. 'She was badly out of station, sir.'

'I know she was,' replied Redman. 'But that was no reason to attack her. You were within a mile of the port wing column. You knew you had a line of ships to starboard. If you'd been watching the PPI you'd have seen what was happening.' He paused, waiting for Pownall to answer. But the navigating officer was silent.

Though he couldn't see his face, Redman glared at him. 'Why didn't you check the A/S contact with radar at once?'

In the dark Pownall, who had a quick temper, shook off his feelings by kicking the compass pedestal. 'I'm sorry, sir,' he said. 'It was careless of me. But she sheered out of line and I . . .' He gave up. There just wasn't a workable excuse.

Redman, frustrated by broken sleep and the knowledge that they'd been close to disaster, wasn't prepared to let go. 'It was a damned *stupid* mistake, Pownall. We'd have looked bloody silly if we'd rammed her.'

Between the evidence of his own failure and Redman's nagging, Pownall was working himself into a silent rage. He knew it was no good arguing but he objected to being ticked off in front of the yeoman, the signalman, the look-outs – and no doubt the men in the wheelhouse, and the radar and asdic operators who'd probably heard it all through their voice-pipes.

Redman, on the other hand, quickly cooled down. He regretted his display of temper. Anger was something a captain shouldn't give way to. Unfair to the subordinate who couldn't answer back. Nor should he have admonished Pownall within hearing of the men on the bridge. That could

36

have waited for another occasion. Pownall was a competent officer. His attention had wandered momentarily. These things happened quickly. It had been a long day for him too. No point in destroying his self-confidence. Redman forced a note of friendliness in his voice. 'Right, Pilot. Take over. Get her back into station.'

When he was annoyed with the navigating officer he called him 'Pownall' – on other occasions 'Pilot'. Pownall knew this and normally it amused him. But not at that moment. When Redman had left the bridge, Pownall, confused and humiliated, had once more kicked the compass pedestal before taking steps to get *Vengeful* back into station. That done he returned to the problem of how he'd made such an ass of himself. At last he remembered.

He'd been thinking of Elizabeth. Elizabeth at the dance at the Wrennery the night before they'd sailed from the Clyde. He'd had a good deal to drink and it had seemed the moment to let her know what was on his mind so he'd proposed. She'd laughed as if it were very funny. Then, when she saw she'd hurt him, she was contrite. 'I'm terribly sorry, James, I thought you knew.'

'Knew what?'

'There's someone else. Surely I told you.'

'You didn't as it happens. Who is he?'

'It'd just be a name to you. He's in the Army. Eleventh Hussars. Somewhere in Europe.'

'Interesting,' he said. 'Are you going to marry him?'

She laughed. 'Yes. I'm afraid you must think I'm a wicked woman. But life has to go on. Hasn't it?'

He did, and it did. In the six months on and off that he'd known her – most of that time he'd been at sea – this was the first he'd heard of the Army. He took her hand. 'Let's have a drink . . . to celebrate your . . . what is the word?'

'Betrothal,' she suggested, looking at him sideways to see how he was taking it.

Yes. That was it. Thinking about Elizabeth. He hadn't looked at the PPI for minutes on end. Bloody fool.

So it was her fault. He'd tell her that next time in harbour. Kiss her forgiveness – she was a nice girl – and take her down to Rothesay for a weekend. Then there'd be real news for the Eleventh Hussar to whom she no doubt wrote despondent letters about the dullness of life on the Clyde and how she couldn't wait until he got back. Which was all too true. And she probably couldn't wait until *Vengeful* got back either. So there might be someone else. Who? wondered Pownall, with a dismal sense of being irrational. Jealousy, after all, was the Eleventh Hussar's prerogative.

The difference between *Vengeful*'s wardroom at sea and in harbour was considerable. At sea pictures, books and other things which could move were taken down and stowed away, fiddles were put on the dining table, and the cloth was dampened to stop crockery sliding. The Charlie Noble was not lit, and from the leaking joints of heaters the smell of steam competed with odours from the pantry. All in all it was a cheerless place in rough weather, sparsely populated, its few inhabitants unusually quiet. Well back in the stern over the propellers, it was far from comfortable.

Shortly before one o'clock on the second day out from Loch Ewe only Wilson, Sutton the doctor, and the two midshipmen were present, the others being on watch or asleep. The Maltese messmen moved between the pantry and the table they were preparing for lunch. A midshipman was asleep, wedged in a corner of the settee. Another was reading a magazine.

The doctor, who had never been on a Russian convoy, was questioning Wilson. Finding the answers discouraging, he changed the subject.

'Tell me about the captain,' he said.

'How d'you mean?'

'What's he like?'

'All right. I suppose we're lucky to have him. Some can be bastards.'

'He's a dug-out, isn't he?' The doctor pulled at his ear.

'Yes. He left the service in '38. Went into the family business. Wine importers or something like that. When this brawl began he was called up.'

'Has he spent much time at sea?'

'All of it, I think, except for courses. Corvettes and frigates first. He lost the last one. Torpedoed in the Western Approaches. After that he had a spell in hospital being put together again. Then he came here.'

The destroyer rolled heavily, the doctor paused, his eyes on the porthole where the top of a sea slapped and splattered into foam. 'He's a bachelor, isn't he?'

Wilson looked at his watch then at the pantry hatch. 'Roll on lunch time. Sorry,' he said, turning back to the doctor. 'You were saying?'

'Is the captain married?'

Wilson shook his head. 'No little woman waiting at home for the Old Man.'

'The girl in the silver frame. On his desk?'

'We don't know. Big mystery. She's never been seen near the ship. Number One once asked the Old Man. After several drinks. All he got was a dirty look, so he reckoned he'd boobed. We've inquired tactfully of Topcutt who's been with him for years. Old Toppy looks mournful and says, "The captain's private life is no business of mine. Nor'n of yours, sir." So we've given up.'

'Girl-friend, I expect,' said the doctor. 'Not my business anyway. But when I go to his cabin I don't like looking him straight in the face. Weak of me, I know. He frightens me.' The doctor's pale eyes were apologetic. 'So I look at her. Easy on the eye, isn't she?'

'Smashing.' Wilson looked across to the wardroom table again. 'Oh, come on, Malta,' he muttered. 'Fill the blasted trough.'

The doctor waited for the ship to come back from a sudden lurch to port. 'What's he like at sea?'

Wilson stared at him. 'You're very nosey about him, aren't you, Doc?'

'Not really. But he's the kingpin around here and I'm the new boy; rather like wanting to know what the Head's like when you go to your first big school.'

'Well. He's okay. Gets a bit ratty at times when things go wrong. Not surprising really. Doesn't get much sleep. Tired, I expect.'

'He is,' said the doctor.

Wilson yawned, shook his wrist and held the watch to his ear. 'How d'you know?'

'I'm a doctor.'

'Yes. I suppose so. I mean I'd forgotten that. I'm sure you're a doctor.'

'Very good of you,' said the doctor. 'One likes to be sure.' He leant forward. 'But seriously. When did he last have a decent rest?'

Wilson poked at his forehead with a forefinger and frowned. 'Well. Let's see. He missed the last one and . . .'

'The last one?'

'Our last boiler clean and leave period. Shortage of escorts. We had to do two quick trips to Iceland. Then take an assault ship down to Gib. Don't ask me why. There was no war going on when we were there ten days ago. We reckoned a Wren must have caught her tit in the cipher machine and mutilated the destination group. We loved her for that. The sun. So warm, you know.'

The doctor wasn't to be shaken off. 'When *was* the last leave period?'

'About eight weeks ago for the starboard watch. Eleven for the port. That's me.'

'You mean the captain hasn't had a decent sleep for eight or eleven weeks?'

Wilson got up. 'Thank God, Carana,' he said to the messman. 'I thought there was a catering strike.' He looked at the doctor absentmindedly. 'Not as bad as that. We've had eight to ten days in harbour in the last couple of months. He gets his head down then. Unless he's ashore on a thrash.'

'Good heavens.' The doctor stood up, the sleeping midshipman began to stir. 'No wonder.'

'No wonder what?'

'Nothing. I was just thinking.'

'Oh, Christ,' said Wilson. 'Here comes that conceited bastard Pownall. Stand by for *les bons mots*.'


Shortly before dark that evening the radar buzzer sounded on the bridge. Redman went to the voice-pipe. 'Forebridge – radar.'

'Radar – forebridge.' It was Petty Officer Blandy's voice. 'Captain, sir. Numerous blips on green one-six-nine, twenty-six thousand yards.'

Redman looked at his watch. 'Good, Blandy. That'll be the Home Fleet destroyers with the escort carrier and cruiser. Coming up from Scapa Flow. Due to join at 1425.'

Blandy knew this. That was why he was in the radar hut helping the operator. Normally he only manned the set in action, his principal duty being its maintenance.

Before long the TBS speaker was alive with exchanges

between the Vice-Admiral, the senior officers of escorts, and the commodore of the convoy.

Daylight had all but gone when the carrier and the cruiser screened by the Home Fleet destroyers came up from astern at high speed, their bows throwing clouds of white spray into the air, their grey hulls glistening wet in the twilight. *Fidelix* the escort carrier and *Northampton* the heavy cruiser took station in the 'box' in the centre of the convoy. Two Home Fleet destroyers fell in astern of them, the rest of the flotilla forming a fighting screen round the convoy. The corvettes and frigates continued to provide the close anti-submarine screen, while *Bluebird*, *Vengeful*, *Violent* and the other ships of the Fifty-Seventh Escort Group proceeded at twenty knots to form the outer screen, eight miles ahead of the convoy.

When at last they were in station nothing could be seen from *Vengeful* but a blanket of darkness, thickened by storms of rain and sleet. The ship seemed alone on an empty sea, but the pips of light flowing and fading like fireflies on the PPI revealed the position of the convoy and its escorts. To the officer-of-the-watch these presented an intelligible picture: *Violent* a mile and a half on *Vengeful*'s starboard beam, beyond her a long line of ships steaming abreast – the outer screen.

The TBS crackled again on *Vengeful*'s bridge: it was *Bluebird* passing orders for the night: mean course 012 degrees, speed 12 knots, zig-zag diagram 31a, convoy's speed of advance 9 knots.

Cupido brought the captain's meal at 1930. It came in a straw-lined wooden carrier, purpose made. But the journey from the wardroom galley on the quarterdeck, along the length of the iron deck and up three ladders to the sea-cabin on a cold December night – with the Faeroes astern to port, the temperature close to freezing and icy spray and sleet sweeping the ship – was too much for it. So the captain's hot meal arrived, as usual, cold. Redman, against all reason, invariably attributed this to inefficiency, if not bloody-mindedness, on Cupido's part, whereas Cupido did his best to keep the meal hot, fighting his way along the upper deck in all weathers, sometimes falling and spilling the carrier's contents.

Then he'd go back to the galley for more. There he was abused by the cook for clumsiness and at the other end by the captain for being late. Cupido, having long since realized he couldn't win, accepted his misfortune with a stoicism which bordered on the heroic. He never defended himself, never apologised.

Unless there was an alarm of some sort, the moment Redman looked forward to at sea arrived at about 2000 when, an unpalatable meal finished, he would ask the officer-of-the-watch to let the engineer-officer know that he would like to see him. This was the signal for Emlyn Lloyd to arrive in the sea-cabin. The two men would discuss the day's events, its problems and highlights, and then the ritual would begin.

'Care for a game, Chiefy?'

'Well now. And that's a good idea,' was the Welshman's invariable reply.

Redman would unfold the small chessboard with its pegged pieces, and they would sit side by side on the bunk, the board between them, considering their moves by the dim light of the red lamp. The stake never varied, a Mars Bar, the day's nutty ration, and it was the winner's privilege to bisect it neatly, passing half to the loser.

Redman usually won if it had been a bad day for him, if there had been problems and things had gone wrong; whereas the engineer officer won on the others. It was some time before Redman suspected that this was no accident. Emlyn Lloyd was the soul of kindness, perhaps the warmest-hearted man in the ship, and Redman felt that in letting him win, the Welshman was trying to make up for the troubles of the day. Though he disliked the privilege, he never complained.

When the first-lieutenant wrote up the logbook at 2000 that night he recorded the wind as south-west, force 6; sea and swell westerly, 6; air temperature 38°F; sea temperature 42°F; sky overcast, cloud ten-tenths, ceiling low, visibility poor; rain and sleet frequent.

With wind and sea astern, or on either quarter depending upon the leg of the zig-zag, the ship laboured heavily, a sliding corkscrewing motion. Resigned to these conditions, her company settled down to another night of acute discomfort. Because they'd done these journeys before they knew that what they were experiencing now was mild compared with what was to come.

## CHAPTER FIVE

To the accompaniment of strong winds shrieking through rigging and never-ending movement in rough seas, the convoy and its escorts made steady progress, plodding on doggedly to the north. To starboard, two hundred and fifty miles away, lay the west coast of Norway; to port Jan Mayen Island and Greenland.

In the early hours of the third day the convoy crossed the Arctic circle in a south-westerly gale. It blew itself out fifteen hours later and was followed by a blizzard from the north-east. Snow lay like a shroud upon the ships and their escorts. Next day the wind changed again, backing to the north-west and blowing with unremitting fury, the spray thrown up by plunging bows freezing on upperworks and rigging to swell them with ice.

The nights grew longer as convoy JW 137 reached into high northern latitudes and by the fifth day the sun had ceased to rise. Other than a brief period of twilight between ten and noon, black darkness prevailed throughout the twenty-four hours. With air temperatures now twenty and thirty degrees below freezing the men on *Vengeful*'s upperdeck – watchkeepers, signalmen, lookouts, guns' crews, depth-charge and 'hedgehog'[1] mortar parties – wore Arctic clothing: anorak suits with fur-lined hoods, the men's gloved hands inside mittens which hung from their necks. Binoculars and other metallic objects could not be touched with bare hands for fear of frostbite.

[1] The *hedgehog* was a multiple mortar which threw missiles ahead of the ship. These exploded when they struck a submerged submarine and sank it.

The battle now joined was not against the formal enemy but the Arctic winter. Its purpose was to keep guns, depth-charge chutes and throwers, the 'hedgehog', searchlights, radar aerials and other weapons and equipment serviceable.

Working in darkness, the ship pitching and rolling, *Vengeful*'s crew fought with picks and steamhoses at ice which threatened the stability of the ship and the efficiency of its weapons. It was a continuous struggle which they could not have won but for rigid maintenance routines and the steam-jackets and lagging around gun mountings and other moving parts.

There were other problems: thermal layers formed in the sea at different depths, with widely varying temperatures. These deflected the asdic beams with which escorts hunted submarines, providing a protective blanket under which a U-boat could dive knowing that it would be immune from detection. Though gales and blizzards, storms of snow and sleet, freezing cold, a cloud ceiling which never lifted more than a few hundred feet, and almost continuous darkness imposed great hardships on the men, they protected the convoy by screening it from observation and making opera-tions by enemy aircraft impossible and for submarines ex-tremely difficult. This, however, did not please the Vice-Admiral who with large forces at his disposal was looking for a fight . . . *to seek out and destroy the enemy wherever possible*. But it made the passage of the convoy safer and this was welcomed by many, particularly the crews of mer-chant ships who suspected that they were likely to be on the receiving end of any serious encounter with the enemy.

A man who was deeply disappointed at the lack of contact with U-boats was Lieutenant Sunley in *Vengeful*. Quiet, dedicated, immensely skilful in handling the ship's HF/DF apparatus, Sunley and his operators listened in vain for a B-Bar message. So-called because of the unchanging charac-teristics of its prefix group, it would not only have told Sunley that the convoy had been sighted but he would have got a directional bearing of the U-boat transmitting it. Other ships in the group would also get its HF/DF bearings and by exchanging them the position of the submarine could be plotted. But no B-Bar message came and Sunley and his men prayed for better weather.

So convoy JW 137 with its load of tanks and aircraft, guns and ammunition for Russia's Eastern Front, pushed northwards. There were the customary alarms: depth-charge attacks took place suddenly and without warning, usually on asdic contacts which turned out to be shoals of fish; a US Liberty ship's cargo shifted in the north-easterly gale and she fell out of the convoy while a frigate stood by until the list had been righted by pumping and flooding ballast tanks. Then they began a long stern chase to catch up.

On several occasions ships lost contact and had to be shepherded back into station by units of the close escort.

After one of these, *Vengeful* heard a corvette reporting by TBS the loss of a seaman overboard in heavy seas. The brief exchanges which followed told of the failure of the rescue attempt. Men died quickly in Arctic waters.

On the afternoon of 5th December, the convoy then five days out from Loch Ewe, the first major alteration of course for navigational purposes was made. It was a forty-five degree turn to starboard and it put Bear Island ahead, distant 370 miles. It maintained the distance from the Norwegian coast — and therefore the distance of the nearest enemy airfields and submarine bases – at about 250 miles, and it left the Vice-Admiral's options open. He could, depending upon weather and enemy action, pass north or south of Bear Island as JW 137 made its easting towards the Barents Sea.

It was known throughout the convoy that the critical phase of the journey had begun. In *Vengeful*, morale was high notwithstanding the daunting weather and miserable living conditions, particularly on the messdecks under the fo'c'sle, which were seldom less than inches deep in icy water. Here men tried to sleep in hammocks which performed incredible gyrations, or sit on benches to eat at tables which tilted bizarrely and without warning. It was difficult to remain dry. The heat which came from steam radiators and the bunching together of many bodies in confined spaces was scarcely enough to keep warm.

Morale in *Vengeful* was normally high. It was a reflection of the confidence which the captain and first-lieutenant showed in the ship's company and the fighting efficiency of the ship. Despite occasional moans about the conditions under which they lived, the men responded to this confidence. On the 5th December, as the convoy altered course towards Bear Island, *Vengeful*'s morale was particularly high for they had already notched up their first kill. Her crew knew that but for *Violent* which had shared in the hunt of the U-boat outside Loch Ewe, the convoy had made no contact with the enemy. This gave *Vengeful*'s men a sense of superiority, of being ready to take on successfully anything which might come along. Like the Vice-Admiral, they were looking for a fight.

Pitching and rolling, the wind screeching through ice-covered rigging, convoy JW 137 pressed on to the north: thirty-five merchant ships, twenty-six warships, 275,000 tons of war supplies and close on 10,000 men committed to this twentieth-century odyssey in the perpetual night of Arctic winter.

## CHAPTER SIX

'Forebridge – captain, sir,' the first-lieutenant's call from the voice-pipe above Redman's pillow awakened him from brief sleep.

'What is it, Number One?'

'*Bluebird* has an A/S contact.'

'Right. I'm coming up.' He rolled off the bunk, steadied himself against the movement of the ship, frowning through red light at the ice on the inside of the porthole. Wedging himself against the wash-basin, he picked up night-glasses and mittens and pulled the anorak hood over his head. As he made for the bridge he was thinking not of *Bluebird*'s A/S contact but of the lump of ice. It was an old enemy. Despite attempts by the dockyard, the rubber seal round the port-hole still remained defective and a jet of icy air came through when the wind blew. In the Arctic the moist air froze and within a short time an ice lump formed on the inside of the porthole. At a certain stage, caught between the warmer temperature of the sea-cabin and the freezing air outside, the lump stabilised and effectively sealed the leak. For this reason Redman had instructed Cupido to leave it alone.

A lump of ice so close to his body was a physical and psychological irritant, but it was better than a jet of icy air. For these reasons the ice lump had over the last two convoys become the subject of a love-hate relationship.

Redman, eyes not yet accustomed to the dark, got to the bridge by feel and instinct. Once there he made for the PPI. The first-lieutenant, standing next to it, anticipated his question. '*Chaffinch* is investigating with *Bluebird*, sir.'

'Who's on the TBS?'

A voice in the darkness said, 'Me, sir. Burrows.' It was the yeoman of signals.

'Close to one thousand yards, *Chaffinch*.' Ginger Mountsey's voice sounded on the bridge-speaker.

'Will do. Bearing two-eight-eight, thirteen hundred yards,' came the disembodied reply.

Redman said, 'They'll never hold an A/S contact in this weather.'

'No, sir,' agreed the first-lieutenant.

They waited in semi-darkness seeing nothing but the glowing and fading pips of light on the PPI, listening to the brief exchanges between the ships two and three miles away to starboard. It was early morning and the luminous dial of Redman's watch showed the time to be almost half past four. Wind and sea had moderated and the motion of the ship had become less violent in the two hours since he'd last been on the bridge. The sky was overcast but the ceiling had lifted and there were breaks in the clouds ahead. It was no longer snowing.

'Weather's improved, Number One.'

'It has, sir. Not for long, I imagine.'

'*Fidelix* should be flying off aircraft in this half-light.'

'Yes, sir.'

Ginger Mountsey's voice came in again. 'Target classified non-sub. Resume station *Chaffinch*. Sorry to have troubled you. Over and out.'

'Not at all,' replied *Chaffinch*. 'The pleasure was ours.'

Redman said, 'I'd like a fiver for every shoal of fish that's murdered my sleep.'

'Bad luck, sir.' The first-lieutenant was as cheerful as always. 'Probably won't happen again for some time.'

Redman grunted, depends what you mean by 'some time', he thought. He stood silent, his mind empty, watching the Aurora Borealis, its curtain-like drapes in constant movement, opening and closing, one colour succeeding another, filling the northern sky with radiant movement.

'Beautiful, isn't it?'

'Sir?' The first-lieutenant was at the PPI watching *Bluebird* and *Chaffinch* get back into station.

'The northern lights. Aurora Borealis to you.'

'Oh, yes, sir. Marvellous to see them again, isn't it? Always bucks one up.'

Redman decided once more that the first-lieutenant, though extremely capable, was still adolescent. An enthusiastic schoolboy. For him the war was a game, romantic and exciting. The first-lieutenant, on the other hand, was thinking that he didn't much like the wheeze in the captain's throat and wondering what caused it. In his view the captain took life too seriously. Of course he was tired and had a lot of responsibility, but good humour helped. The first-lieutenant always made a determined effort to be cheerful when he spoke to him, though often he didn't feel as cheerful as he sounded.

Redman said, 'Yeoman. No need for you to stay up here. Get your head down while you can.'

'Aye, aye, sir. Thank you, sir.' The yeoman took off the TBS headset, hung it up, spoke to the signalman-of-the-watch, and left the bridge.

Redman had a high opinion of the yeoman. If any man in the ship was indispensable it was Burrows. He knew the signal manual backwards, not only the purport of the signals but the manoeuvres associated with their execution. If a forming or disposing signal were received the yeoman knew precisely the action required on *Vengeful*'s bridge. With considered tact he would convey this to the officer-of-the-watch, or even to the captain.

'I think that'll mean altering to port and increasing to twenty knots, won't it, sir?' he'd say, putting the facts he knew in the form of a question, inferring that he was seeking not giving information.

Burrows was important to Redman for quite another reason. The captain thought he saw in Burrows his last yeoman, Patterson. It was as if the dead man had been reincarnated. They were so much alike in looks and character. Dark friendly eyes, calm and collected, men who could always be depended upon. Redman was conscious of a debt to Patterson which he could never repay, and for this he tried to make amends in his relations with Burrows.

When he got back on to his bunk and closed his eyes he knew he would not sleep. His mind was now too full of Patterson. What had long since become an obsession had been triggered off by the yeoman's 'thank you, sir.' It was an unnecessary remark. If anything a little un-Servicelike, but it was in Burrows's nature to express gratitude for the consideration the captain showed him.

Redman took a deep breath, turned on his side and the pictures began to form. 'Thank you, sir' had been Patterson's last words before he died.

That night, two years earlier, Redman had been in his sea-cabin, somewhere between sleep and consciousness, when the explosion came. The torpedo had struck the frigate beneath the bridge, wrecking among other things the bridge superstructure and the sea-cabin. It was a winter's night with headwind and sea, some five hundred miles west of Rockall. The ship sank quickly, before any alarm signal could be given. Redman had heard and felt the violence of the explosion but he must have lost consciousness almost immediately for the next thing he knew he was in the water. It was a night of intense darkness and his one instinct had been to get away from the sinking frigate before the depth-charge pattern in the stern, set shallow and primed ready for dropping, exploded. He was vaguely conscious of other men in the water, and at times, from the tops of seas, he could see the dim flicker of red survivor lights. They seemed far away, but he decided to make for them. First he found the mouthpiece of his Mae West and blew into it until the life-saving belt was inflated. It was then, when he tried to swim, that he found he could not use his legs. Why, he did not know, but he was conscious of numbing pain when he tried.

Though he could see nothing he could taste and smell the

oil fuel in the water and wondered if, when the depth-charges exploded, the oil would burn. But no explosion came and he knew then that the gunner (T) and depth-charge party must have withdrawn the primers immediately after the torpedo struck. The oil fuel had flattened the wave crests, leaving only the swell. He was slimy with fuel and knew he must get away from it. But he couldn't move. He came over the top of a sea, slid down the slope and something in the water bumped into him. It was a wooden grating from the frigate's compass platform. He grabbed it and found he could get his head and shoulders clear of the water with its aid. This increased his chances of survival. He didn't rate them high because he was not wearing a survivor's light and he was weak. The damage to his legs, or perhaps his spine, was sapping his strength. A voice called somewhere in the darkness, upwind, not far away.

'Captain here,' Redman shouted back against the wind. 'Who's that?'

'Patterson, sir.' The broken voice was weak.

'You all right, yeoman?' Redman knew he couldn't be, but the question had to be asked.

'Can't move, sir . . .' There was a gurgling sound. 'Can't keep . . . head . . . out water.' More sound, spitting and retching. 'You . . . all right . . . sir?'

Again Redman tried to use his legs, this time to paddle in Patterson's direction. But they wouldn't respond and the pain was considerable. 'My legs have gone, yeoman. Can't move.' It was a laboured sentence because the wind, the oily sea splashing over him, and his weakness made communication difficult. He wondered if he could hold the grating with one hand and paddle towards the yeoman with the other. 'I've a grating here, yeoman,' he called. 'I'll try to reach you.' It took a long time to say that and much effort. Some of it had to be repeated because the yeoman didn't answer and Redman needed to hear his voice again to check direction. The yeoman, like Redman, had no survivor's light. He sounded as if he were fifty yards away.

'Can't you answer, yeoman?' he shouted. 'For God's sake man, try. I don't know where you are.' That, too, took a lot of saying.

There was a longish pause. After it Patterson's voice came

downwind, hoarser, weaker, more broken. 'Thank you . . . sir.'

Redman spat out a mouthful of sea and oil, inhaled deeply, changed his grip on the grating and pushed it round so that it was facing in Patterson's direction. He struck out with his free hand, paddling in icy water which he could feel but not see. But it was a hopeless floundering, a meaningless thrashing of the sea, and he could not tell in the darkness if he was making headway. His calls to Patterson were no longer answered.

Quite suddenly Redman gave up. He didn't know for how long he'd tried or how hard he'd tried, but he remembered deciding he'd made an effort and could do no more. Afterwards, as the obsession grew, he believed he could have done more, shown greater resolution. His legs had been weak, not his arms and shoulders.

Afterwards, lying in hospital through drab timeless days, and in the months that followed, the conviction grew that he'd given in too easily. He might have saved Patterson. He did not think he'd tried really hard. Perhaps he'd not wanted to reach the yeoman for fear the grating could not support them both. He remembered thinking about that at the time. Had it influenced him? How much was real, how much fantasy? He didn't know. He compared his feeble efforts with those of Hans on the glacier above Crans-sur-Sierre. Hans, a stranger, had struggled for hours in a blizzard, alone, just as Redman had been alone after the sinking. But Hans had refused to give up and in the end he'd succeeded. That was why Redman was alive.

To him those last words of Patterson's were a reproach: 'Thank you – sir.' Thank you for what?

Redman turned over and re-wedged himself between bunk-board and bulkhead.

He felt wretched and miserable and prayed that sleep would come to deaden his thoughts.

It was the best part of an hour before the first-lieutenant's voice woke him once more from fitful sleep.

'Forebridge – captain, sir.'

'What is it, Number One?'

'*Fidelix* reports bandits one, bearing two-three-oh, thirty miles, fifteen hundred feet. She's turning into wind now to fly off aircraft to intercept.'

'Sound the alarm. I'm coming up.'

'Aye, aye, sir.'

As Redman made for the bridge the alarm bells sounded a series of shorts and longs and sleepy men stumbled and groped through the darkness to their anti-aircraft stations. The first lieutenant standing at the bridge screen was silhouetted against the distant glow of the northern lights. Redman moved up alongside him. Not long afterwards the yeoman arrived, then Pownall. The midshipman-of-the-watch, Bowrie, was standing by the radar phone.

Redman said, 'Our two-nine-one on to that aircraft yet, Number One?' The 291 radar was used for the detection and tracking of aircraft.

'Not yet, sir. Just outside maximum range, I think.'

'Jerry'll be shadowing by radar. Not likely to close the range while he can keep contact.' Redman cleared his throat. 'Better weather was bound to attract our chums. Expect Jerry's using the cloud base for cover.'

Pownall's voice came out of the darkness. He was passing instructions to the pilot. The buzzer from the radar hut sounded. The midshipman reported that 291 radar had picked up the enemy aircraft. He passed the bearing, range and height to gun positions. The TBS bridge-speaker crackled with voice messages between *Fidelix,* her attendant destroyers, the senior officers of the escort groups, and the commodore of the convoy.

'*Fidelix* reports two Wildcat fighters and four Avengers airborne, sir,' said the yeoman.

Redman said, 'Good,' and looked astern into the black sky knowing he would see nothing, but imagining them there.

The Wildcats would be climbing to intercept the shadower while the Avengers carried out anti-submarine patrols over thousands of square miles around the convoy. Since the convoy had been sighted, it was vital to put down surfaced U-boats anywhere in the vicinity. The Avengers would search in the dark with airborne radar, ready to attack with depth-charges and rockets. Surfaced U-boats would be listening for radar transmissions with search-receivers, so it would be a cat-and-dog hunt in the icy darkness of an Arctic winter.

On *Vengeful*'s bridge they could hear the fighter-direction officer in *Fidelix* vectoring the Wildcats on to the German shadower. The cloud ceiling was fifteen hundred feet and the shadower had disappeared into it, moving from west to east across the convoy's port quarter, putting himself between the Norwegian coast and the convoy, keeping to the darkest quarter of the sky, one eye firmly on his escape route. His chances of getting away now would depend on how long it took the Wildcats to find him.

Bowrie's voice broke into Redman's thoughts. 'Radar 291 reports f-fighters closing bandit f-fast. Distance apart t-twelve miles.'

'Good.' Redman cheered up. 'Hope they get him quick.' Soon afterwards the yeoman said, '*Fidelix* has intercepted bandits' sighting report to base.'

Redman was silent. There was nothing to say. They all knew it would happen and what it meant. The position, course and speed of convoy JW 137 was now known to the German High Command. Action would follow. Quickly, while the break in the weather lasted. Torpedo-bombers would soon be rolling down runways on German airbases along the Norwegian coast, some of them less than three hundred miles away. U-boat patrol lines between Bear Island and the North Cape – one hundred and ninety miles ahead – and off the Kola Inlet would be alerted.

Redman said, 'It won't be long now, Number One.'

'Yes, sir.' The first-lieutenant sounded pleased. 'Nice to have a go at them again.'

'Time, Pownall?' Redman asked.

'0613, sir.'

Redman stood at the bridge-screen steadying himself against the movement of the ship, looking into the darkness astern, wondering what the next twenty-four hours would bring. Not sleep, that was certain.

The sound of the fighter-direction officer's voice was becoming familiar. He had a North-American accent. Canadian, thought Redman. The FDO was guiding the Wildcats on to their targets. His directions were clear and explicit, no trace of excitement, no sense of urgency, a man absorbed in the technicalities of what he was doing, the instruments he was watching. It was evident that the Germans were now aware of the fighters. It had become a stern chase but the reconnaissance plane was no match for the Wildcats. They were overhauling rapidly.

Redman wondered what was going on in the minds of the German aircrew. Were they still thinking 'it can't happen to us', or had they realised that it was about to and resigned themselves to entering their particular Valhalla?

Not long afterwards they heard the Wildcat pilots reporting contact. Seconds dragged by on *Vengeful*'s bridge, the men there straining their attention for the next report. Broken disembodied chatter came from the fighter pilots. 'He's on bloody fire . . . starboard engine,' said one voice. There was a pause. 'I'm following him down . . .' said another. 'Jesus! We've really got the bastards . . .'

Then the fighter-direction officer was telling them to cool it and giving them a 'well done' all in the same breath. Redman thought again of the German aircrew. How long did it take to fall two thousand feet? Could they bale out? What was the point? They knew they couldn't last in Arctic water and there was no hope of rescue. Better stay in the thing until it hit the sea and broke up. But it was on fire. Was the urge to jump irresistible? What sort of things went on in a man's mind? Could he rationalise such a situation or did it resolve itself in unadulterated terror? The yeoman's voice broke into his thoughts. '*Fidelix* reports enemy aircraft shot down, sir.'

'Well done.' Redman said it with humility. He was thinking of the Fleet Air Arm sub-lieutenants in the billiard-room in Greenock.

The first-lieutenant was saying something. '. . . or shall we remain closed up, sir?'

Redman said, 'No. Let them carry on now. Get what rest they can. The party'll begin in earnest soon.'

The signal from *Fidelix* announcing the shooting down of the German shadower was followed by one ordering an alteration of course – forty-five degrees to port. This diversion opened the distance between the Norwegian coast and the convoy and, if maintained, would take the ships north of Bear Island. How far north would depend upon what came from an Avenger aircraft, call-sign *Red Three*, sent to report on the ice-edge, usually to the north of the island in mid-winter. When the weather closed in again, which was likely

54

at any time, the Vice-Admiral could, at the moment of his choosing, order a ninety-degree-wheel to starboard. This would take JW 137 well south of the island.

In considering these tactics he had in mind that sooner or later enemy aircraft would report the convoy's new course to the German High Command. There, he hoped, they would conclude that the convoy intended to pass north of Bear Island and move the bulk of the U-boat patrol line accordingly. In that case it would be less likely to intercept JW 137 if it passed to the southward. The success of this plan depended upon a number of imponderables, of which the weather was by no means the least.

But the Vice-Admiral's options remained open. He could, according to circumstances, pass north or south of Bear Island. The decision need not be made for at least another twelve hours. If during that time the convoy was not again sighted by the enemy, it might well pay to take the northern route.

## CHAPTER SEVEN

Soon after the shooting down of the reconnaissance plane, two more shadowers arrived on the scene. Having found the convoy the German High Command was determined not to lose it while the weather lasted.

This time, however, *Fidelix* had four fighters in the air covering the sector nearest the Norwegian coast and the new arrivals were shot down before they could make sighting reports. Thus the diversionary routing was still unknown to the enemy. It was a secret the Vice-Admiral was anxious to preserve. An attack by torpedo-bombers was imminent. Every minute the convoy spent on the diversionary course made the enemy's task more difficult. *Fidelix*'s meteorological officer had warned that the lull in the weather would break at any moment. *Red Three,* sent to reconnoitre the ice-edge, had reported a gale moving south-west over Bear Island. The message had followed her report that the ice-edge was well to the north of the island.

This news confronted the Vice-Admiral with a difficult

decision. Should *Fidelix* recover her aircraft now or keep them airborne in the hope of intercepting an enemy air attack well clear of the convoy? To delay recovery too long might entail the loss of aircraft and their crews. He took a calculated risk – waited twenty minutes then gave the order to recover. *Fidelix* set about her task.

On *Vengeful*'s bridge the TBS and VHF loud speakers relayed a series of laconic messages between returning aircraft, the escort carrier and her attendant destroyers. A running if cryptic commentary.

'God knows how they find the carrier,' said Redman, looking into the wintry darkness. 'Let alone land on it.'

The first-lieutenant said, 'Jolly good, aren't they, sir?'

Redman smiled. The remark was typical of the first-lieutenant. It belonged more to rugger and cricket than the bridge of a destroyer. 'Yes, they are,' he said.

An urgent voice sounded on the bridge-speaker. 'Alarm! *Moonbeam*. Alarm! Wildcat overboard port side.'

'Roger,' came the reply. 'Proceeding.'

*Moonbeam* was the call-sign of one of the two destroyers stationed close astern of the escort carrier for rescue work while aircraft were being flown off or recovered. The exchanges which followed told of difficulties. The Wildcat pilot was apparently unable to move, the aircraft was sinking, and semi-darkness was complicating the rescue operation.

'Aircraft now against my lee side,' said a voice from *Moonbeam*. 'Men on lifelines trying to get pilot out, but aircraft sinking fast.'

'Roger.'

A long pause followed. Redman peered astern. Nothing could be seen, but somewhere in the gloom of Arctic morning a man was fighting for his life. Redman could picture the scene only too vividly. The frantic attempts of rescuers hampered by Arctic clothing, a rolling ship and twenty degrees of frost. Men with life-lines round their waists struggling in icy water to extricate the trapped, partially stunned, pilot.

A few minutes later *Moonbeam* called *Fidelix*. 'Wildcat has sunk. Pilot lost. Regret rescue attempt unsuccessful.'

'Resume your station, *Moonbeam*,' replied the anonymous voice in the carrier.

56

There was no time for requiems, for messages of explanation and sympathy. The patrolling Avengers had still to be recovered, wind and sea were rising, and there were telltale flurries of snow.

Three of the four Avengers were recovered but there was no sign of *Red Three*. No word had come from her since she'd reported on the ice-edge and weather north of Bear Island. It was more than an hour later that the VHF loudspeaker on *Vengeful*'s bridge relayed repeated calls from *Red Three* to *Fidelix*. These were answered by the carrier, but the Avenger was not receiving *Fidelix*'s VHF signals due either to a defect in the aircraft's VHF receiver or the weather. This posed a tragic but not unfamiliar problem. If *Fidelix* switched to long-range VHF, German tracking stations on the Norwegian coast would pick up the signals and by means of cross-bearings plot the position of the convoy. The secret of the diversionary routing would be out. The Vice-Admiral had to decide between risking the lives of the Avenger's aircrew or hazarding the convoy. In a sense the decision made itself. No action could be taken which might help the enemy intercept JW 137. The Avenger and its crew would have to get within short-range VHF of the convoy unaided or come down in the cold wastes of the Arctic.

Getting no response to its calls, the distant voice in *Red Three*, a very young one it sounded to Redman, took on a note of desperation.

'We're lost, and cannot read you,' it said. 'Please give us a bearing on W/T frequency.'

The Avenger carried a telegraphist/air gunner and powerful W/T equipment. Technically, *Fidelix* could have switched to *Red Three*'s W/T frequency and thus have enabled the lost aircraft to obtain the vital bearing, but to do so would have given away the position of the convoy. *Red Three*'s only hope now was to carry out a square search. If fuel and weather permitted she might find the convoy.

On three more occasions the calls for help were repeated. The last message was abbreviated. 'Please answer,' pleaded the worried young voice. 'Just one quick bearing. No more.'

Tension had been building up in Redman, his imagination stretched by tired nerves. The last message was too much for him. 'For Christ's sake.' He struck the bridge-screen with his gloved fist. 'For Christ's sake. This bloody war.' With that he left the bridge, on it a shocked first-lieutenant. He, too, had been upset by the Avenger's messages, but one just didn't give way to that sort of emotion. It was bad for the men on the bridge. It was the captain's duty to set an example of resolution. After all, reflected the first-lieutenant, we're at war. Addressing no one in particular, he remarked with a note of cheerfulness he didn't feel. 'Well. We've shot down three of theirs. And they *now* don't know where JW 137 is.'

'Yes, sir,' agreed the yeoman respectfully. The signalman-of-the-watch added under his breath, 'Nor do the poor bastards in *Red Three*.'

The attack by the German torpedo-bombers did not material-ise, but the gale did. It came with sudden violence from the north-east bringing snowstorms which so reduced visibility that ships in the convoy had difficulty in seeing their next ahead. JW 137 was now steaming almost directly into wind and sea and its speed of advance was down to four knots.

Throughout that day the gale blew relentlessly and storms of snow and sleet deepened the Arctic darkness, laying a screen over the convoy which protected it from attacks by bombers or submarines.

In the escort carrier's wardroom absence of the Wildcat pilot and the crew of *Red Three* was noticed but not remarked upon.

At 1915 that evening the Vice-Admiral ordered an alteration of course to the south-east and the convoy performed a ninety-degree wheel to starboard. Under normal conditions this was a difficult manoeuvre for merchant ships at night. In a north-easterly blizzard in Arctic darkness, with the master of each ship struggling to keep contact with his next ahead, the problems were magnified many times. Unlike their escorts, the merchant ships were without radar.

Nevertheless the wheel was successful, the close escorts shepherding back into station those ships which lost contact, and convoy JW 137 settled down on its new course. It would take the convoy sixty miles south of Bear Island which lay just over one hundred miles to the north-east.

With the gale now on its port beam, JW 137 staggered

and rolled through freezing darkness towards the Barents Sea.

The alteration of course was not without its vicissitudes for *Vengeful*. As port wing ship she was on the outside of the turn and had to sweep round in a wide arc, increasing speed to keep in station with the other ships of the outer screen. This involved taking a considerable battering from the weather: seas had jumped the breakwaters and flooded her messdecks forward; in the engine-room an artificer (ERA) had been struck on the head by a fire extinguisher jerked from its rack by violent movement; and the flash screen to B gun, the forward four-inch, had been buckled by a heavy sea.

After the first-lieutenant had reported that the fighting efficiency of the ship was not impaired, and the doctor that the ERA was in the sick bay with concussion, Redman went down to his sea-cabin.

But *Vengeful*'s wild rolling and pitching made rest, let alone sleep, impossible. To stay in the bunk he had to curl up, lie on his side and wedge himself between bunkboard and bulkhead. This required an exertion of pressure which could not be maintained asleep so, dog-tired, he gave up the unequal struggle, got off the bunk, pulled the anorak hood over his head and went to the bridge where the first-lieutenant and Groves were on watch.

'Can't sleep in this,' he explained.

'Bloody, isn't it, sir.' The first-lieutenant was customarily cheerful.

Redman grunted and they were silent for a time, together in the darkness, holding on to the bridge-rail, sheltering as best they could from snow, sleet and douches of freezing spray which swept the ship. Behind them the wind shrieked through the rigging, a continuous piercing shrill of such intensity that it hurt the eardrums and inhibited speech.

They stood by the PPI, the first-lieutenant at times ordering adjustments of course and speed to keep *Vengeful* in station. Groves, the sub-lieutenant, was at one of the spinning clear-view screens looking ahead into a wall of darkness where he saw only the pictures of his thoughts. They were of his last leave and a land girl in Somerset. He was reliving those days, part romantic, part erotic, worrying and wondering. Wondering if she was thinking of him, what she was doing at that moment, trying to remember her smile and the sound of her voice. Wondering if she was being faithful and worrying about that. There was a lot of competition. The farm where she worked was near a US Air Force base. She used to tease him with stories of crazy parties with glamorous US fighter pilots. She would imply enough to make him jealous, then protest that infidelity was something of which she was incapable. He wondered if she didn't protest too much.

The first-lieutenant, too, was thinking of a girl: Susan, a third-officer Wren in Greenock, who came from Blandford in Dorset where his family lived. He had wanted to tell the captain of their plans and this seemed the moment, even if it did mean having to more or less shout the news.

'We're announcing our engagement next time in, sir,' he said.

'Who's we?'

'Susan and me, sir.'

'Susan?' said Redman doubtfully. 'Which Susan?'

'Susan Blake. The girl in FOIC's cypher office.'

'Ah. You mean Susie. The dark girl with grey eyes and nice teeth.'

The first-lieutenant thought she had a lot more than grey eyes and nice teeth but he said, 'Yes. That's her, sir.'

'Too good-looking for you, Number One.'

'D'you really think so, sir?' The darkness hid the first-lieutenant's lop-sided grin.

'Yes, I do. Can't imagine what she sees in you.'

'She thinks I'm fabulous, sir.'

'You must have shot her a hell of a line, Number One.'

'I did, sir. Terrific one.'

There was another silence. Redman felt his way across to the chart-table, thrust his head and shoulders in under the canvas screen and switched on the light. He was not looking at the chart. It was an excuse to break off the conversation. He wanted to be alone with his thoughts. Later he switched off the light and stood at the bridge-screen, away from the PPI. The first-lieutenant's news had taken his thoughts back over the years to Marianne.

# CHAPTER EIGHT

It was in Avignon, having finished his work in the Languedoc, that Redman decided to go to Paris. There had been a business excuse, but the real reason was a sudden irrational desire to see Marianne. He telephoned his uncle, said he'd completed the tour of the Languedoc vineyards and would return via Paris where he would look up Lefevre the wineshipper. He'd added that he'd like to take a few days' leave there. His uncle had agreed and the next day Redman caught the train for Paris.

He'd not seen Marianne since the summer of 1938 when she and Hans had stayed at his aunt's house in East Horsley. It had been a splendid week. He'd liked Hans and found his sister attractive. He and the girl enjoyed the same things, shared the same tastes. Like long rambling walks through Ranmore Forest and along the rim of the downs, a preference for the country as against the town, for comedy rather than tragedy. They talked endlessly, laughed a lot, he helped her over stiles and fences, held her hand and kissed her when the opportunity occurred, which was not often because Hans was so often there. Redman was much aware of the difference in their ages: she nineteen, he twenty-nine. For this reason, though she attracted him, he'd not taken her seriously. Afterwards they'd exchanged letters at increasingly long intervals and in time he'd accepted that she was nothing more to him than a friend abroad. A foreign girl he liked.

At the end of the year she'd written to suggest he might spend a week at her parents' house outside Frankfurt. Hans would be there. But it had not been possible. Redman had only recently left the Royal Navy to go into his uncle's wine business and there was little prospect of getting to Germany at that time. In any event he was no admirer of the Third Reich and the idea of visiting Germany – much as he liked Marianne and Hans – was distasteful.

That Christmas she wrote to say she was going to Paris in the New Year to study art. She gave him an address. Asked him to write when he had time.

He'd not warned her that he was coming and her surprise when she saw him that afternoon waiting at the gates of the Ecole des Beaux Arts was unfeigned and delightful. She'd left a group of chattering students and rushed across the courtyard calling, 'Francis, Francis,' as if she feared he'd not seen her. When she reached him she panted, 'What are you doing here?' Her eyes were wide with amazement.

He'd laughed. Explained that he'd come to Paris to see her, and she'd said, 'Is that true? Do you really mean that?' And he'd said, 'Yes, of course I do.' She'd taken his hand and squeezed it affectionately. 'Oh, that's marvellous. I'm so happy.'

The few days of leave had run into a week and might well have been more but for a caustic telegram from his uncle. The time in Paris had been the happiest he'd ever known. By the third day he realised he was in love and life took on a new dimension. In the mornings and afternoons he would explore the Left Bank in a leisurely unplanned way. Always they would meet for lunch, most often at a little restaurant near the wrought-iron gates at the foot of the Rue des Beaux Arts. After lunch she would return to the art school and they would meet again in the later afternoon at the Café Royale in the Place St Germain. Each night they would sample a new restaurant. Usually she made the choice, and it would be small and inexpensive but the food good. 'We students know where to go,' she would explain. 'We have to. We cannot afford the other places.'

Lovely lazy spring days followed each other all too quickly and, inevitably, what was for Redman an idyllic existence had to end. He remembered every moment of the day before his departure. They'd walked down the Boulevard St Germain arm in arm, past the Odéon Métro station, the Seine out of sight on their left. She was strangely quiet and when they crossed streets and he took her hand she clasped his tightly as if afraid to let it go. It was a warm evening in late April. Trees not yet in leaf stood gaunt and bare against grey buildings. 'They need only a tricolor to make an Utrillo,' she'd said. 'Yes,' he replied. 'Nature's catching up.'

She made a moue. 'You know what I mean, you awkward Englishman.'

They'd gone into a bistro and he'd ordered a Pernod and she citron and perrier water. She remained silent and preoccupied. He chided her and she smiled, looking at him with limpid affectionate eyes. 'Don't worry. It's nothing.' She squeezed his hand to reassure him. 'Let's move on. I feel restless.'

So they'd strolled on, turned left into the Boul' Miche and gone down to the Place St Michel. They'd looked at displays in the little *journal* kiosks and played a game, guessing the number of countries represented by the papers and periodicals on display, then counting them. She'd taken him into the Church of St Séverin, and they'd wandered about its beautiful ambulatory, discussed the stained-glass window beyond the altar. Why was it cubist whereas all the other windows were orthodox theological? They had seen people praying in the chapels. Wondered about them. The sad young woman. What was she praying for? Sick child? Erring husband? And the old woman? Perhaps easier to guess in her case. He remembered the quiet rather humble mood in which he and Marianne had left the church because they'd had nothing in particular to pray for. It was a gorgeous spring evening and they were in love.

Later Marianne complained that she was tired and they'd gone to a little restaurant off the Rue St Séverin, attracted there by stands of lobsters, prawns and mussels glistening under the light of a street lamp. Inside it was dim, and flickering ships' lanterns, fishermen's nets, glass buoys, cork floats and ropework gave it character. They'd eaten fish soup and mussels, drunk Muscadet, and talked in subdued voices, touching each other, sometimes laughing, sometimes sighing.

When the bill came she was shocked. 'I don't like to see money thrown about like that,' she'd said. There was so much poverty. Did he not know? Realize that it was wrong? He'd learnt in that week that she was a radical. Filled with compassion, eager to change society, to remove the inequalities. He argued for the status quo but had to give up. He could get nowhere. On this they were too far apart. His thinking had been conditioned by Dartmouth and seventeen years in the Royal Navy. 'You are a Junker,' she'd said, eyes flashing, nose wrinkling in disapproval. 'You believe in the status quo. In class distinction.'

He shook his head. 'Your trouble, Marianne, is an overdose of Left Bank ideology.' At that point they'd decided not to spoil their last evening together.

The meal finished, they'd gone down to the Pont St Michel and walked back along the Seine, stopping at the print stalls on the Quai des Grands Augustins, chatting to the owners. They moved on and there was another long silence when neither said what was on their minds. To-morrow would be the last day.

At ten o'clock she began to shiver and complain of the cold. Said she was tired. They took a taxi to the Rue des Beaux Arts. It stopped outside the small apartment house in which she had a room. He paid it off and for a moment they stood on the pavement looking at each other.

She asked him if he'd like to see her room. She'd never done that before. On other nights he'd taken her to the front door and she would fish in her bag for a key. Then she'd unlock the door and, very tenderly, they would say good night. He would kiss her and she would go in, turning and waving before running upstairs.

He would walk a few blocks, then take a taxi or the Métro back to his hotel off the Place Vendôme. Before falling asleep he would think of the time they'd spent together during the day. He would go over everything they'd said and done and make mental notes of things she'd said which, in retrospect, were not clear.

Once they were sitting on a bench in the grounds of the Church of St Germain-des-Prés. It was a quiet peaceful place. Little lawns and flower-beds, chestnut trees putting out tentative leaves, tangled ivy on old stone walls beyond which traffic rolled unceasingly down the boulevard. He questioned her about something she'd said the night before.

'You read into these things meanings which were never there,' she said. 'Then you question me as if you were full of suspicion. As if I had done wrong.' She frowned and her cornflower blue eyes regarded him seriously.

'It isn't that,' he said. 'I *do* think over things you've said. They interest me. Then sometimes I wonder what you meant. The next day I ask you. It's nothing more than that.'

'For example?'

'Like yesterday when I asked if you loved me and you said, "Give me time. How can I know?" And now I've just asked you what you meant by "How can I know?" You see,

I'm so sure I love you, I wonder why you had to say "How can I know?" '

She touched his arm and smiled, looked round quickly, kissed him. 'I *think* I love you, Francis. But I have never been in love, so how can I know if this really is love? This is why I want time. Do you not understand?'

But on that last night it had been different. Without affectation or embarrassment she'd said, 'Would you like to see my room?' and he'd said, 'Yes, I would.' They'd gone up the narrow creaking staircase together, synchronising their footsteps, laughing at each other with their eyes.

She'd put down her things, given him the only chair, and made coffee on a hot-plate. They sat and talked and drank it, and afterwards he took her in his arms and kissed and caressed her and lifted her on to the bed. She'd not protested when he undressed her and afterwards she lay there and he saw how finely she was made, her arms crossed to conceal small breasts, her head turned away in a gesture of modesty.

He asked her if she'd made love before. Quietly, seriously, she said, 'Yes.' His surprise had shown because he'd not expected that reply. He was a man with little experience of women, naïve and idealistic in his beliefs about them. Most of his adult life had been spent at sea, much of it on the China and West Indies stations. There had been the usual flirtations and an unsuccessful affair with a married woman. Nothing more.

Marianne had seen his surprise. 'You are worried?'

He said, 'I suppose I'm surprised. You're so young.' She'd sighed. 'It was an affair. A married man. A few months only. Then it was finished. I realise now it was nothing. I was not in love. It was sex. This attraction can be very strong you know.' She'd looked at him appealingly. 'Please. Not one of your interrogations. It finished long ago.'

He'd laughed at that and undressed and then he was holding her in his arms, experiencing the delicious excitement of their nakedness. All of her was warm and firm and supple. He told her so and she interrupted the sentence by closing his mouth with hers. They caressed and explored each other's bodies and finally made love. He found her intensely passionate. Responsive beyond anything he'd imagined.

Afterwards they lay in each other's arms, absorbed in their love. He said, 'I was rough. Did I hurt you?' She'd shaken her head and smiled and said, 'No. You are very gentle.' He leant over her and covered her neck and shoulders with kisses. 'I love you,' he said. And she replied, 'Me too. I love you.' The words seemed small and inadequate for an emotion so deeply felt, but there were no others that would not have sounded affected. It was love of a kind he'd not experienced before and as the hours passed he became sad, reluctant to leave her for he'd wanted that time and feeling to remain for always.

When he left he said, 'Remember. We meet tomorrow at five at the Royale. Don't be late. It will be our last night in Paris together.' And she had said, 'No. I won't be late. I promise.'

Back in the hotel that night he'd had little sleep. His mind was disturbed. Not only was he in love but they had made love and he knew he was committed.

Tomorrow they would say good-bye. What should he do? War was coming. She was German. He was on the emergency list of the Royal Navy and would certainly be called up. It was an impossible moment in time to propose marriage or to make plans that could be meaningful. And she was only nineteen.

Worrying about what he should do, what he should say, he fell asleep, his problem unsolved.

He found a table on the balcony at the Royale from which he could look out over the Place St Germain-des-Prés and see the pavement up which she would come from the art school. This would be their last meeting for a long time. If war came they might never meet again. The problem with which he had fallen asleep remained unresolved. What should he do? How could he explain things to her in such a way that it did not sound as if he were trying to back out? Should he damn the consequences, forget the imponderables, propose? It was the only decent thing to do. But was it remotely practical? Might it not be grossly unfair to her. To find herself newly married in a country at war with her own?

Confused, hopelessly undecided, he tossed a coin. Heads he'd propose. Tails he wouldn't. It came down heads. But he hadn't decided whether it was to be sudden death or the best of three. Again he tossed. Tails. On the third toss it landed on the floor. Heads again. Two heads in favour of proposing. But it was not a fair toss, he decided. It had landed on the floor. At last he acknowledged that the absurd gamble was bogus. He'd already made up his mind not to propose. Commonsense was overwhelmingly against it. This was something which could wait. War *might* not come. Then he'd be free to propose and she'd be older and more able to decide for herself. He was not proud of his decision. Knew it was weak-kneed. It didn't help either that her brother was Hans, the man who'd saved his life in the mountains above Crans-sur-Sierre. And to have seduced his rescuer's sister seemed a strange way of showing gratitude.

Unhappy and diminished he drank his coffee looking across the Place to the pavement up which she would come. Time went by. It was a quarter-past five. She was already fifteen minutes late. That was unlike her. He felt a mixture of irritation and concern. Moments later he saw her in the crowd coming up the pavement, then waiting with them at the corner. It was the peak hour. The traffic was heavy. In an interval she saw him and waved. He held up his wrist, pointed at his watch, thumping the table in mock anger. He saw her worried frown and instantly regretted what he'd done. In the next brief traffic lull she rushed across against the baton of the gendarme: his whistle shrilled and he waved her back. But it was too late. Behind the autobus in front of which she'd crossed a car came up fast. There was the shriek of brakes, the squeal of tyres, and a body cartwheeled into the air. The traffic halted. A knot of people gathered. Someone ran to a telephone. Redman raced down the stairs across the boulevard and broke through the ring of people. He saw her crumpled body, the face white and lifeless, blood trickling from her mouth and nostrils. The gendarme kneeling at her side looked up, shook his head. 'Elle est morte,' he'd said with heavy finality.

And so had ended a sublime week. He knew immediately, and the years after confirmed that knowledge, that his life would never be the same, that the burden on his conscience would be too great. What had happened affected him fundamentally. He became a changed man.

He had welcomed the war as a means from escape from the tragedy with which he had to live. But it had not worked out like that. The agony of remorse remained. He remembered only that Marianne had meant more to him than anyone he'd ever known, that he had been responsible for her death, that he'd cheated the fall of a coin, and that her brother had saved his life.

It seemed to him a multiple betrayal.


CHAPTER NINE


A few hours before the Vice-Admiral ordered the alteration of course to the south-east, the German High Command transmitted an urgent message to U-boats on the Bear Island and Kola Inlet patrol lines. It gave the last known position, course and speed of convoy JW 137 and continued: *Convoy's course at* 0610 *suggests intention pass south of Bear Island, but northerly passage more likely in view prevailing weather and enemy's knowledge that convoy's course and position known to us.* The signal ordered four U-boats to stations north of Bear Island, leaving four on an extended patrol line between the island and the North Cape. The main force of fifteen U-boats was concentrated on the patrol line outside the Kola Inlet. An additional submarine, U-0117, was on passage from Trondheim to reinforce it.

The High Command's signal concluded: *estimated time of arrival of convoy off Kola Inlet, midnight to early hours tenth December.*

The High Command's signal was intercepted by the Admiralty, deciphered and passed to the Vice-Admiral in *Fidelix*, together with an appreciation of the situation. The contents of this signal were unknown to the German High Command for although the Admiralty's message had been intercepted, a new British cipher was being used which defied all attempts by Department B, the German Navy's cryptographic section, to break it. The position given by the Germans was forty miles in error and the course was still that reported by the shadowing aircraft at 0610. The German conclusion that the

68

northerly passage was more likely was based on interception by them of *Red Three*'s message that the ice-edge was well to the north of Bear Island. This was precisely what the Vice-Admiral had hoped for. The double bluff had succeeded. The German High Command had been forced to split its already thin Bear Island patrol line. There were now only four U-boats between Bear Island and the North Cape, a distance of close on two hundred miles, and their chances of sighting the convoy on its southerly route were comparatively remote in that weather. As the Vice-Admiral could not break wireless silence without giving away the convoy's position, the Admiralty signal went unacknowledged. This was the cause of some disappointment to German tracking stations on the Norwegian coast but not to their High Command which knew, as did Whitehall and the Vice-Admiral, that the U-boats' main effort would be reserved for JW 137's arrival off the Kola Inlet.

Next day the convoy passed south of Bear Island in the late evening. Not that the time made any apparent difference. The north-easterly gale had persisted, with its storms of snow and sleet and all-enveloping darkness. By morning it was clear that the Bear Island patrol line had been evaded, and during the next forty-eight hours nothing of consequence happened. There were the usual alarms, asdic contacts, pounce attacks, depth-charge explosions, and echoes which dispersed to be later classified as 'fish' or 'doubtful' or 'non-sub.' Sometimes these were followed by alterations of course in case the 'doubtful' *had* been a submarine but, notwithstanding, JW 137 steamed on, a storm-swept armada averaging six and a half knots now that sea and wind were no longer ahead.

There was the continuing problem of ice, and ships' companies were kept busy breaking it away from equipment and superstructures. There were other problems. *Violent* reported that her sub-lieutenant had left the bridge on being relieved at the end of the middle-watch and had not been seen since, despite a search of the ship. It was presumed that he'd been swept over the side while making his way aft in heavy weather.

There were, too, less serious problems. A US Liberty ship using a shaded blue lamp passed a message to her nearest escort, the corvette *Cape Castle*: *Fireman McGafferty has not passed water for two days. In great pain. We have no doctor. Please advise. Urgent.*

The corvette didn't carry a doctor so she discussed Fireman McGafferty's problem by TBS with the nearest Home Fleet destroyer. Having obtained her doctor's opinion, *Cape Castle* signalled the Liberty ship: *Place McGafferty in bath, raise water temperature steadily and stand clear.*

An hour later the Liberty ship signalled *Cape Castle*: *Many thanks. Worked fine. McGafferty's bladder now empty.*

The corvette replied: *Splendid. Delighted to have been of assistance.*


During the early hours of the 8th December the north-easterly gale blew itself out. A period of calm followed but snow and sleet persisted and *Fidelix* could not operate her aircraft. This was not only a source of considerable frustra- tion to the Vice-Admiral, but complicated the task of the escorts as JW 137 was within air reconnaissance range of the Kola Inlet and a good deal closer to the U-boat patrol line. On the other hand, the Vice-Admiral knew that the Germans were equally hamstrung by the weather for as long as it lasted there would be no danger of enemy air attack.

Soon after midday the lull in the weather broke and a south-westerly gale blew off the Norwegian coast, less than one hundred and fifty miles away, bringing with it more snow. But it lacked the ferocity of its predecessor. Wind and sea force 7 were now on the convoy's starboard beam. The ships rolled heavily but shipped little water.

In the first dog-watch the Vice-Admiral ordered a major alteration of course, this time to the south-east. JW 137 was now on its last leg, heading for the Kola Inlet some two hundred and ten miles distant. Allowing for the various courses the convoy would steer on its final approach along swept channels through minefields, the distance was closer to two hundred and fifty miles. But the Vice-Admiral and his escort commanders knew that the U-boat patrol line was probably no more than one hundred and thirty to one hundred and fifty miles ahead. The most dangerous phase of the journey had begun. Tension built up in escort ships and merchantmen.

The new course put the south-westerly gale on the convoy's starboard bow and reduced its speed of advance to five knots. Unpleasant as this gale was, it blew with less violence than the north-easterly which had preceded it, but *Vengeful* and her consorts on the outer screen had resumed zig-zagging. This made life more uncomfortable, if anything, than on the previous course.


## CHAPTER TEN

Korvettenkapitän Johan August Kleber, commander of U-0117, stood in the forepart of the horseshoe bridge surmounting the conning-tower. He was secured by a steel belt to the superstructure, as was Leutnant zur See Schaffenhauser, the officer-of-the-watch, and the seamen doing bridge duty. The submarine was running on the surface on an easterly course, the south-westerly gale on her starboard quarter. From time to time the small bridge flooded as she wallowed and sliced through steep following seas. The men wore rubber diving suits, heavy woollens and submarine jerseys under them, and felt-lined seaboots. But it was difficult to keep warm and because of the numbing cold they stamped their feet, swung their arms and struck their chests with gloved hands to keep up circulation. Drips of moisture on eyebrows and beards froze quickly despite eye masks and anti-frost grease on their faces.

There was nothing to be seen on this stormy night. It was more a matter of feeling and sensing. Feeling the gale, the continuous drenching of near-frozen salt water, the brush of snow and the sting of sleet, each man bracing himself against the violence of the boat's motion. In some respects the submarine rode the weather better than a surface ship, for other than the forward conning-tower and after gun-platform she offered little obstruction to the sea which foamed and curled about the whale-like steel hull. Only one sound challenged the noise of wind and sea and that was the metallic thunder of the U-boat's diesels.

Kleber disliked intensely the discomfort he and his crew had to endure, but he was in good spirits. In the first place he was grateful for the weather, bad though it was. The gale brought heavy snow swept off the Norwegian coast, and that and almost total darkness throughout each day ensured freedom from enemy aircraft. He was grateful, too, for the signal from High Command giving the estimated position, course and speed of an Allied convoy sighted by a reconnaissance aircraft. His boat, U-0117, was on passage from Trondheim to join the patrol line off the Kola Inlet and he was looking forward to action. It had come sooner than he'd anticipated. Until the signal from High Command there had been no reports of a convoy en route to Russia. As it was, U-0117 would be in time to take part in the operation to intercept it and the weather was right for what he had in mind. He and his navigating officer, Dieter Leuner, had plotted the position of the convoy and its probable courses north and south of Bear Island. Whichever was taken, they had concluded that U-0117 would arrive off the Kola Inlet a few hours ahead of the enemy. Kleber had already altered course some fifteen degrees to the north in the faint hope of making contact with the convoy before it reached the patrol line. If he succeeded in this he should, in that weather, be able to shadow it without undue risk.

Kleber, fair and athletic with a strong face, was a cheerful extrovert with a good brain and sound nerves. But he had been too long out of the war for his liking. Early in 1943 he'd got his first command, and during the first eight months of that year proved himself to be an outstanding U-boat commander. He had sunk over 100,000 tons of enemy shipping before he was unexpectedly removed from the struggle, the victim of a severe wound during an air-raid on Lorient where his boat was based. His spine was damaged and for some time it was thought he would never again be fit for active service. But he fought against the disability with characteristic determination and recovered. Highly thought of in the German U-boat arm he was, both because of the injury and his excellent record, attached to a training flotilla in the Baltic. That took him to Danzig where he became a senior instructor responsible for working up new U-boats and their crews and later, with the changing fortunes of war, to Oslo.

Kleber was not happy with the training appointment which he regarded as non-combatant, but he was intelligent enough to realize that it had probably saved his life. Most of his contemporaries who had remained at sea in U-boats after the autumn of 1943 had not survived.

The German Naval Command allowed Kleber to return to sea in September 1944 because the war had reached a stage where U-boat successes were badly needed. It was felt that the presence and skill of such a seasoned commander would boost morale and secure results. This had already proved correct for U-0117, now on her second patrol under his command, had on the first in the course of a prolonged attack on a Russian convoy sunk a frigate and two merchant ships. His self-confidence, his aggression, his willingness to take risks, had won for him the unquestioned loyalty of officers and men and this had contributed much to the boat's success. The former captain whom Kleber had relieved had had no such successes. Over-cautious, he had lost the confidence and respect of his crew. They had been glad to exchange him for a man whose name and reputation stood high in the U-boat service.

The son of a patrician family with its roots in East Prussia, Kleber made no secret of his opinion that Hitler was an upstart leading the German people to destruction. But it was his custom to simplify complex issues and he had no doubt where his own duty lay: Germany was at war, he was an officer in the German Navy; for him there was no other choice but to devote his skill and energy to the service of his country. This he did with single-minded determination.

Kleber's parents had been killed in an air-raid in 1943. His marriage shortly before the war to Helga Kuschke, a young lecturer in sociology at Heidelberg, had been a short-lived affair. While his parents had ascribed its break-up to the war, Kleber suspected the fault was his.

The exigencies of war decreed that when he was not at sea or on leave most of his time was spent in Brest and Lorient, the Atlantic U-boat bases. There he had been involved in brief but intense encounters with other women. Though Helga knew nothing of these they worried him, for he felt that in some intangible way they damaged his relationship with her. Moreover, they were lapses from standards of behaviour to which he attached some importance. There was a powerful streak of Calvinist puritanism in Johan Kleber.

It had not occurred to him that, in the circumstances of

war, adherence to those standards was scarcely possible for a man of his boundless energy, high spirits and zest for living.

As it happened, the real reason for the failure of his marriage had nothing to do with amorous adventures in France. It lay in Kleber's character and was well described in a letter from his wife to her mother shortly before the marriage broke up.

*Everything Hans does he does well. He sets the highest standards, not only for himself but for others. He is a perfectionist. This he cannot help for he was born that way. But it is not really a virtue. Others – and I am one – find difficulty in living up to the standards he imposes. Because of this he makes me feel a failure in many things. The way I run the house. How I dress. My looks, my figure. How I manage on the money he allows me – and my own money! I have to keep detailed accounts. Hans checks them. He says he does this to help me. So that I may know where the money goes. As if I didn't without writing it all down.*

*I think I am still fond of him, or much that is him. But not so much that I am prepared to lose my personality in his. To become a sort of ersatz Hans. I prefer to be myself, inferior maybe, and to have some sort of life of my own. Fortunately we have no children and we are young. Now is the time to make the break, however difficult it may be.*

To those who knew Hans Kleber well – and they were mostly the officers and men with whom he had served in the U-boat arm – this might have seemed a harsh judgment. In fact it was, in most respects, closer to the truth than they would have cared to acknowledge, for the characteristics of which Helga complained fitted in well with the requirements of naval discipline.

Be that as it may, it was this absence of family ties which at times introduced an element of recklessness into his decisions and explained his willingness to take risks where others refrained.

Conditions on U-0117's small bridge were difficult in the extreme. There was not only the high wind, the seas driving in on them through the unprotected after side of the bridge, and the cold to compete with, but so much spray, snow and sleet in the air that the lenses of night glasses and eye masks frosted soon after they were cleared. Despite these difficulties, Kleber found running on the surface at high speed exhilarating. And the prolonged surface run ensured that the submarine's batteries received a handsome charge, which was important for what lay ahead. Another advantage of being surfaced was that fresh air swept through the boat clearing away the sickly stench of decaying food, grease, diesel oil, chlorine gas and human sweat.

Inside the boat conditions were deplorable on these Arctic patrols. It was not only the foul air but the humidity; water dripped everywhere; verdigris formed on exposed metal surfaces; bedding, clothing, charts, sailing directions and naval manuals became damp and mildewed. Kleber had nothing but admiration for the stoicism with which his men endured their lot, and the fact that their morale was high was all the more remarkable since the Allies now had the upper hand in the war against U-boats; a fact well known throughout the U-boat service.

U-0117 had been running on the surface on passage from Trondheim for over forty-eight hours. During this time she had sighted nothing, the weather having been uniformly bad. Periodically Kleber had dived the boat to free it of ice on the superstructure and external armament, and to check the trim. The temperature of the sea was several degrees above freezing, whereas the air temperature was twenty to thirty degrees below.

'*Das Boot arbeitet hart in dieser See* . . . the boat works hard in this weather,' Kleber remarked to Schaffenhauser the sub-lieutenant with whom he stood shoulder to shoulder in the darkness, gripping the rail below the bridge screen. 'But it's refreshing to be travelling on the surface. And we make good speed. At least thirteen knots.'

Schaffenhauser said, '*Jawohl, Herr Kapitän.*' While he agreed they were making good speed, he preferred to be submerged. For all the smells of foul air, mildew and dampness – and added discomfort when they used the *Schnorchel* in bad weather, when men gasped for oxygen and suffered from bouts of nausea as seas closed the float on the air intake valve – for all that he felt more secure submerged. On the surface he was uncomfortably aware of the air threat. One felt naked and exposed. The sudden swoop from above, the brilliance of flares dropped by attacking aircraft, the accuracy of their depth-charging and rocket fire. It was good to have a hundred metres or so of sea above you, with thermal layers to protect the boat from searching asdic beams.

But Schaffenhauser mentioned none of this to Kapitän-leutnant Kleber who had a zest for action and seemed to thrive on discomfort and danger. Schaffenhauser thought a lot of the captain and did not wish to lose his esteem.

As if he were reading the young man's thoughts, Kleber said, 'Only another hundred and twenty miles to the patrol line, Schaffenhauser. That's about nine hours. We'll have to submerge then if this gale lets up and visibility improves. The air will become too busy.'

'Yes, *Herr Kapitän*.' Schaffenhauser hoped that the weather would break and that they would have to submerge even sooner.

'It's not the Russian Catalinas that worry me,' said Kleber. 'It's the British carrier aircraft which do the damage. They are the professionals.'

'At what point do we join the patrol line, *Herr Kapitän*?'

'At the centre. Opposite the entrance to the Inlet. The Russians have swept a passage through the minefields there. The convoy must use it eventually. It is for us to get in our attack early, while they still have some distance to go.'

There was silence after that. Eventually Kleber said, 'Wind and sea seem to have eased a little. Not much, but I hope no more.'

'No more, *Herr Kapitän*?'

'Yes. Bad weather protects us. And once we're on the patrol line we are fifteen U-boats. I want to try once again a high-speed down-wind surface attack. As we used to in the Atlantic in 'forty-two and 'forty-three.'

Schaffenhauser was silent. The captain had a great reputation and he hesitated to question his views. But everyone in U-boats knew that the enemy's new radar had made 'wolf-pack' attacks suicidal. Such tactics had long since been abandoned. He said, 'Yes, *Herr Kapitän*. But there was nothing like the high density of enemy escorts then, was there? And their radar direction-finding equipment was not as sophisticated as today.'

Kleber laughed with easy confidence. 'Of course. You are

right. It was not so difficult then, I admit. But you know in this sort of weather we are free from attack by aircraft and they are undoubtedly the U-boat's greatest menace. Secondly, under these conditions of bad visibility, attacking downwind, if you are bold and aggressive, you can penetrate the escort screens, get your torpedoes off and dive under the protective thermal layers. These we did not have in the Atlantic.'

'Do you really think those tactics would still work, *Herr Kapitän*? These Russian convoys have an outer screen of destroyers. It has to be penetrated first.'

'Yes. I accept that, but I believe it can be done. I have given much thought to it. Of course the weather must be right and that is why I regret the possibility that the gale might moderate too soon. But remember this tactic has not been used for a long time. We must get an early sighting, create a diversion to dilute the escort force, concentrate quickly, dive deep in advance of the outer screen and let it pass over us while we sit under thermal layers. Afterwards we surface close to the convoy in the up-wind position. Then, with the element of surprise, we inflict heavy losses.'

Schaffenhauser was beginning to find Kleber's enthusiasm infectious. 'Yes, *Herr Kapitän*,' he said. 'I see the possibilities. It is an exciting idea.'

Kleber corrected him. 'It is more than that. It is a sound tactical plan. I discussed it in detail with the Flag Officer, U-boats, Group North, as soon as I joined the flotilla. At the start he said "under no circumstances". But in time I convinced him.'

'What did he say then, *Herr Kapitän*?'

'He agreed that if conditions were right it would be worth trying.' Kleber did not add that he and the Flag Officer had formulated tactical plans for putting his ideas into operation under varying conditions, that each plan had been given a code letter, and that copies were in the hands of all U-boat commanders on the patrol line.

Instead Kleber shrugged his shoulders and said, 'But this gale must continue.'

'I think it will, *Herr Kapitän*.'

'Good. I see you are an optimist, Schaffenhauser. The right approach to war.' He struck the young man lightly on the shoulder. 'We shall see what the next twelve hours bring.'

Periodically Kleber stopped engines and swung U-0117 to port or starboard to check with radar, search-receivers and hydrophones for a surface ship astern. It was a routine safety precaution. He did not expect to make any contact at that time and in that weather.

A few minutes before 0603 he gave the order to dive to one hundred metres. He intended keeping U-0117 submerged for fifteen to twenty minutes to melt the snow and ice on the conning-tower and anti-aircraft guns, and catch a trim for the action which lay ahead. However, a defect in the *Schnorchel* housing gear, a broken cable, kept U-0117 submerged for almost an hour longer than Kleber had planned.

When Ulrich Heuser the engineer-officer reported the defect remedied, Kleber, impatient at the delay, gave the order to surface. Soon after surfacing he swung the boat to port and starboard and stopped engines. Almost immediately the buzzer from the control-room sounded and Ausfeld's urgent call came up the voice-pipe. 'Faint radar impulses on search-receiver port astern sector. Nothing on hydrophones.' Ausfeld was the warrant officer responsible for radio, radar and other electronic equipment.

'*Gut*,' said Kleber, '*Geben Sie klar Schiff zum Gefecht* . . . sound the action alarm.'

Wedged in the corner of the wardroom settee, Terence O'Brien braced himself against *Vengeful*'s corkscrewing – a combined pitch and roll which made a ride in a roller-coaster seem like a vicar's tea-party. 'My point,' he said, 'is that war should not be taken too seriously.'

Wilson, sea-booted and sweatered, wedged in another corner, said, 'Good point, but our problem's weather not war.'

'Don't take either too seriously.'

The wardroom dropped thirty feet into the trough of a sea, slewed right then left, the stern shuddering as it hit the sea and the propellers bit into the water. O'Brien, who'd been thrown off the settee, re-wedged himself. 'As I was saying . . .'

'Quite,' said Pownall, raising a quizzical eyebrow. 'You usually are.'

'Am I now, Pownall?' said O'Brien. 'Please to explain.' He was wearing a red ski-ing jersey with a yellow-and-white scarf, his ginger hair and beard equally untidy.

'Making war,' said Pownall with assumed severity, 'is a serious business. Skill, intelligence, dedication, thorough training and a highly professional approach are necessary. Qualities which, I'm bound to say, you wavy-navy's lack.'

'D'ye hear that now,' said O'Brien. 'The man's insulting us.'

'Of course,' said Wilson. 'He's RN. One keeps forgetting.'

'You mean he does it for the money.' O'Brien looked at Pownall with new interest.

'Precisely,' said Wilson. 'Whereas we RNVR's do it for fun. You know. Like cricket – the Gentlemen and the Players.'

The first-lieutenant came into the wardroom, a burly figure, his anorak powdered with snow. He pulled back the hood, took off his gloves and put his hands on the steam-heater. 'Bloody cold outside.'

'No more than seasonal,' said Pownall.

The first-lieutenant shouted, 'Pantry!'

The messman appeared. 'Sir?'

'What's for breakfast, Guilio? I'm hungry.'

'Porridge, mutton and potatoes, sir. And bacon and eggs.'

The first-lieutenant groaned. 'Not that stringy mutton with those awful blobs of fat?'

'Yes, sir.'

'Must we have them, Guilio?'

'Yes, sir. Arctic diet. Admiralty orders.'

The doctor put down the periodical he'd been looking at. 'Fatty diet keeps up body heat, Number One. Most people actually feel the need for fat in the Arctic winter.'

'Hear, hear,' said Wilson.

'Well, actually I don't,' said the first-lieutenant.

Pownall said, 'Can't often agree with Wilson, but on this I do.'

'Anyone on the bridge?' inquired O'Brien.

'The Old Man, Groves and Rogers,' said the first-lieutenant. 'Satisfy you?'

'In the Irish Navy we'd make do with one. I suppose

we're an unusually talented people.'

'The Old Man wants as many of us as possible to have a good meal now. The next twenty-four hours are likely to be busy.'

'Well indeed and that is depressing news,' said O'Brien. Pownall frowned his disapproval. 'O'Brien doesn't like our professional approach to war, Number One.'

'Too bad.' The first-lieutenant sneezed, then blew his nose. 'Hope we get some action on this last leg. Not a sausage since those recces were shot down three days ago.'

'So boring,' agreed Pownall. 'Like pleasure cruising.'

'Round the bay for a bob,' said the first-lieutenant.

O'Brien scratched his already dishevelled hair and stared at the first-lieutenant. 'D'you really mean to say you *want* action, Number One?'

'Good God, O'Brien. Of course I do. That's what we're here for.'

'No,' said Wilson. 'With respect. We're here to get JW 137 to Murmansk in one piece. No action, no sinkings. Object achieved. Plenty action, plenty sinkings. Object not achieved. It's as simple as that.'

'Rubbish,' said the first-lieutenant. 'Main object of the operation is to seek out and destroy the enemy.'

'I'm all for a quiet life,' said O'Brien. 'Action means getting hurt.'

'No wonder Ireland lost at Twickenham in your year.'

'I was a reserve. If I'd played we'd have won.'

'We ought to have a trade union, a joint one, with Jerry,' suggested Wilson. 'Job demarkation. They undertake not to interfere with the convoy. We undertake not to bugger about with their U-boats and aircraft. Only sensible way to fight a war.'

'That's a fine Christian sentiment,' said O'Brien. 'Couldn't have put it better meself.'

'That,' said Pownall thinking of something else, 'no one would dispute.' He looked at the wardroom clock – 0807. His estimate of the time of arrival at the U-boat patrol line was 1600. He decided he didn't feel very hungry.

Guilio wobbled in from the pantry doing a balancing act with a tray. But the suddenness of *Vengeful's* roll to port defeated him. It was as if the ship had fallen down the side of a steep hill. The dishes fell and splintered and he skidded on something slippery, ending up on the settee next to the first-lieutenant. 'Sorry, sir. It was the roll.'

The first-lieutenant gave him a friendly pat. 'Bad luck, Guilio. You can't win 'em all.'

The Maltese rose unsteadily to his feet. 'I'll clean up that lot, sir, and get some . . .'

The action alarm bells drowned the rest of the sentence.


## CHAPTER ELEVEN


The first-lieutenant, athletic by disposition, timed himself from the first moment of hearing the action alarm to his arrival on *Vengeful's* bridge. He did this by counting the seconds as he made his way along the iron deck and up three steel ladders in slippery reeling darkness. Twenty-seven seconds, he noted, as he ranged up alongside the captain. Not bad under those conditions. He'd done it in thirteen in fair weather on a good day.

'First-lieutenant here, sir.' His breath came in short gasps.

'Good,' said Redman. 'We've a radar contact. Very small blip. Doesn't show on the PPI. Too much wave-clutter.'

Redman spoke into a voice-pipe. 'Forebridge-radar. Captain here. What d'you make of it now, Blandy?'

'Still showing intermittently, sir. Very small. Green oh-oh-eight, eight thousand yards.'

'Good man. Keep on to it . . .'

Redman spoke next to the plot. 'What's the target doing?'

'Mean course oh-nine-five, sir. Moving from starboard to port, speed about twelve knots. Bearing one-seven-three.'

'Good,' said Redman. 'Steer one-five-oh.'

Pownall passed the order by voice-pipe to the quarter-master in the wheelhouse.

'Yeoman,' called Redman. 'Inform *Bluebird* we have a radar contact classified submarine bearing one-seven-three, range eight thousand yards.'

'Aye, aye, sir.' The yeoman passed the message by TBS. Almost immediately the bridge loudspeaker relayed *Bluebird's* reply. '*Vengeful* and *Violent* detach at once to investigate.'

Redman took *Violent* under his orders and having instructed both ships to cease A/S transmissions and house their asdic domes he increased speed to sixteen knots, all that could be managed safely without incurring weather damage. *Vengeful*'s plot having confirmed the target's course as slightly south of east, Redman, with *Violent* a mile away on his starboard beam, altered course to intercept, bringing the target on to the starboard bow.

On the bridge-speaker they heard *Fidelix*'s signal to the convoy away from the direction of the radar contact. The Vice-Admiral was taking no chances.

*Vengeful* and *Violent* plunged through a dark fury of wind and sea, sheets of spray sweeping their bridges, bows scooping solid water each time they dipped into a head sea, frozen spray cutting razor-like into the faces of men in exposed positions. Guns' crews, searchlight and depth-charge parties and those on the bridge sheltered as best they could, wondering how long the misery would last, sceptical as always of finding anything to attack at the end of it.

Redman, fighting against the smarting of tired eyes, concentrated on the PPI. A dark shape moved up alongside him. 'Who is it?' he snapped.

'Topcutt, sir. Hot cocoa, sir.' He passed a mug to the captain and from the folds of a woollen shawl produced a jug and poured the cocoa.

Redman said, 'Thank you, Topcutt. You're a marvel.'

The able-seaman made a strange noise, a mixture of embarrassment and pleasure, and disappeared into the darkness. Redman, confirming mentally his long-held belief that the best people in the world were the humble ones, concentrated once more on the PPI and the reports coming in from radar and the plot. At 7000 yards *Violent* picked up the contact and confirmed *Vengeful*'s classification of 'submarine'.

Apart from the risk of damaging the asdic dome by steaming fast into a head sea, Redman had ordered its raising and stopped A/S transmissions because submarines could hear *pings* at considerable distances. If the submarine they were hunting heard their radar transmissions increase in volume it would certainly dive, in which case the chances of attacking it in bad weather would be so slight as hardly to exist at all. On the other hand, there was just a chance in poor visibility of getting reasonably close if the weather sufficiently hampered the U-boat's search-receiver. Redman was aware, however, that *Vengeful* and *Violent*'s prime task was to put the U-boat down before it picked up the convoy and made a sighting report. The nearer the destroyers got to the submarine, the more effectively they would achieve this, even if only by random depth-charging.

His optimism was short lived. At 5000 yards both ships lost contact, the blip disappeared from radar screens and operators reported 'lost contact'.

Redman ordered an A/S search of the estimated diving position but nothing resulted. It was like looking for the proverbial needle in a haystack. The submarine was somewhere there, he had no doubt, sitting safely under a temperature layer, running dead slow on her electric motors. The problem was where?

Loss of radar contact and failure of the A/S search was reported to *Bluebird*. Ginger Mountsey ordered *Vengeful* and *Violent* to remain in the diving area for another thirty minutes and to 'warm it up'. The A/S search was continued, both ships dropping depth-charges at irregular intervals. Some, at least, Redman hoped, would be near enough to frighten the U-boat into remaining submerged for some time.

In *Fidelix's* operations-room the Vice-Admiral was discussing the problem with the staff-officer operations, Rory McLeod.

'We know that a U-boat dived here,' he pointed to the position on the plot with a pencil, 'at about 0820. What was her distance from the convoy then?'

There was a pause. Cockburn, the navigating and plotting officer, said, 'Twelve miles, sir.'

'But she was about five to six thousand yards from *Vengeful* and *Violent* when she dived,' said the Vice-Admiral. 'Now – was that a routine dive or had she picked up radar transmissions on her search-receiver?'

'I would assume the latter, sir,' said the S.O.O.

'So would I,' said the Vice-Admiral. 'And unless he's an idiot the U-boat commander will conclude there's a convoy somewhere in the sector from which his search-receiver picked up radar signals. U-boat commanders are *not* idiots so we must assume that before long he'll make a sighting report.' The Vice-Admiral pursed his lips. 'What he *won't* know is that we've made an emergency turn.'

The SOO said, 'He'll be able to give an approximate position of the convoy at 0820. Since aircraft can't operate in this weather I don't think that's going to help the enemy all that much, sir.'

'No. But it will help the Kola patrol line. The last sighting report the German High Command had was that made on the sixth by the reconnaissance aircraft we shot down. They'll be more than happy to up-date the position of JW 137.'

The S.O.O. nodded bleakly.

The Vice-Admiral blew his nose before looking at the plot again. 'Well, we shall have to wait for a B-Bar message. If that doesn't come within the next couple of hours I shall be more than surprised.' He looked round at his officers with bright challenging eyes. There wasn't any sign of disagreement.

The convoy's emergency turn to port increased the time it took *Vengeful* and *Violent* to get back on to the outer screen. When at last they had, and things seemed to have settled down, Redman climbed on to the bunk in the sea-cabin, stared moodily at the ice on the porthole, the lump shining ruby red in the reflection of the cabin's light. He pulled the damp crumpled Admiralty blankets over his clothed body, screwed his head into a cold knobbly pillow and closed his eyes. He was conscious only of wondering when sleep would come and how long it would last . . .

A nurse was leaning over the bed, a young girl with flaxen hair, a high complexion and wistful blue eyes. She was very beautiful he decided. So lovely that he wanted to touch her to see if she was real, but he couldn't move. She was tidying the bed, smiling in a familiar way as if they shared a secret, and he smelt the mixture of perfume and young womanhood and knew he wanted her. It was warm in the ward. Shafts of sunlight came through the windows near his bed and a gentle breeze ruffled the curtains. He felt relaxed, at peace with the world. The injection, he decided, must have been responsible for his euphoria.

What was that she was saying? He tried to concentrate. '. . . and you must rest. Sleep as much as you like. The longer the better. We won't disturb you.'

'Will you be here when I wake up?' It was, he knew, a

tremendously important question. Waiting for her reply he felt insecure, frightened of being alone.

She didn't answer and when he turned his head he saw she was not a nurse but Marianne. She wore a blue smock, patterned with paint stains. She said nothing, just looked at him in a strange way, then left the ward. He called after her but realised she couldn't hear because of the wheeziness in his voice. He sighed and lay back in bed, feeling the cool white sheets and the warm breeze coming in through the window. Presently his sadness went and the euphoric feeling returned because he was tired and knew he could sleep and that when he woke she would be there. She would never desert him. She had said that in Paris.

It would be like . . .

Pownall's voice came cold and urgent through the voice-pipe above the pillow. 'Forebridge – captain, sir.'

'What is it, Pownall?'

'*Camden Castle* reports U.S.S. *John F. Adams* stopped with ruptured main steam pipe. She is standing by her.'

'Poor devils,' said Redman. 'Rather them than us.'

'Yes, sir.'

Redman lay back on the bunk watching the ice-hump in silent misery. He looked at the time. It was nearly twenty-three minutes since *Vengeful* and *Violent* had got back into station. His exhaustion was compounded by the struggle to breathe. His eyes smarted and were heavy with tiredness.

Oh God, let me sleep, he muttered. Let me sleep and not dream.

'Radar impulses gaining in strength, *Herr Kapitän*.' It was Ausfeld on the voice-pipe. 'Starboard astern sector, estimated range six thousand metres, closing.'

Kleber said, 'Good.' He stood for a moment looking back into the dark tumult of wind and sea, knowing that somewhere out there enemy destroyers had picked up U-0117 on radar and were hunting him. Exultation overlaid instinctive fear, for he knew they must be the vanguard of the convoy bound for the Kola Inlet.

'Clear the bridge!' he called, and in one motion pressed the diving-alarm and spoke into the voice-pipe. 'Take her down to sixty metres, chief.'

Ulrich Heuser's deep voice came back at once, 'Sixty

metres, *Herr Kapitän.*'

As Schaffenhauser and the lookouts went through the upper hatch Kleber shut off the bridge voice-pipe and took a last look round. Then he followed, shutting the hatch behind him and ramming home the clips. Next he went through the lower hatch, Schaffenhauser shut it and clipped it fast. The diving-alarm blared above the piercing hiss of air escaping from the ballast tanks as they flooded, and U-0117's bows dipped down for the dive. Before long the boat had left the steep seas of the surface and the motion steadied as she went deeper. The noisy clatter of diesels had given way to the rhythmic hum of electric motors and ventilating fans, and the boat was free from vibration.

Standing at the small chart-table where Dieter Leuner was marking the diving position, Kleber thought about the relative ranges and bearings of U-0117, the hunting destroyers and the convoy ahead of which they must have been steaming. It was important to have a clear mental picture of what was happening on the surface.

From Heuser, standing behind the planesmen watching the depth gauges, came sharp orders as he sought to maintain the desired angle of dive. 'Sixty metres, *Herr Kapitän,*' he reported, levelling off the trim.

'Hold her there, chief,' said Kleber. 'Steer one-one-zero. Revolutions for four knots. Silent running. Prepare for depth-charging.' Kleber had altered the submarine's course twenty degrees to starboard to reduce the noise interference of its own propellers on the hydrophones.

Ausfeld soon reported. 'Propeller noises – destroyers – bearing green one-three-zero to one-four-zero. Estimated range five thousand metres.'

'Any *pings*?'

'Not yet, *Herr Kapitän.*'

Kleber knew that if there were he'd probably have heard them himself. They were usually audible in the boat, even at fairly long range. There wasn't a man in the control-room who wasn't listening for them.

Kurt Rathfelder, the executive officer, reported the stern tube ready for firing an acoustic torpedo.

Kleber shook his head, strong white teeth showing between open lips. 'We are going to find and shadow that convoy, Rathfelder. If we attack now the destroyers will *know* we are

here. As it is they think we are, but they have no certainty.'
He looked at the chart again. It was damp and mildewed, difficult to mark with a pencil without damaging the paper. From the diving position, Dieter Leuner had laid off the range and bearing of the propeller noises. In that weather, decided Kleber, destroyers would not do much more than fourteen to fifteen knots, and they would be steering a converging course to intercept him. He did some mental arithmetic: within the next ten to fifteen minutes the enemy should have the submarine within asdic range. When Ausfeld reported hearing *pings* they'd dive deeper. There was plenty of water. The chart showed 250 to 300 metres.

Kleber's arithmetic was good. Twenty minutes later Ausfeld reported asdic *pings*. Soon they could be heard without difficulty in the control-room.

'Take her down to one hundred and forty metres, chief.'

'One hundred and forty metres, *Herr Kapitän.*'

The submarine tilted bow down as the men on the hydroplanes responded to Heuser's orders.

Kleber called Ausfeld. 'Let me know when the *pings* are lost.'

The eyes of the men were focused on the dials, gauges, tell-tales and valves which reflected the subdued light in the control-room. The only sounds apart from cryptic orders and reports were the low hum of the electric motors at slow speed, the faint scratch of instrument styluses, the dripping of water which had condensed on the inside of the hull, and the *pings* which came at regular intervals like the tick of some sinister metronome. Ventilating fans and other auxiliary machinery and instruments not needed had been switched off.

At a depth of 130 metres the *pings* faded and were lost. The destroyers' ranges were estimated at between 1500 and 1800 metres. Kleber knew that the submarine had passed under a temperature layer which was deflecting the asdic beams. He knew too that the destroyers would depthcharge the estimated diving position and at once took steps to get away from it. 'Emergency full ahead together,' he ordered. 'Hard-a-port.'

The hum of the electric motors rose to a higher pitch and the boat heeled over as her bows swung to port.

'Steer zero-two-zero,' said Kleber.

The temperature layer not only deflected asdic beams but

muffled the sound of the enemy's propellers so that bearings and ranges became difficult to obtain. But Ausfeld's hydrophone operator was able to give them very approximately and this was of some assistance.

Three minutes later the first depth-charge explosions were heard astern and to starboard. Not long afterwards a slight hammer effect was felt as compression waves struck the submarine.

'At least eight hundred metres.' Kleber's confident smile reassured the men in the control-room. '*Die Tommies mussen es schon besser machen, wenn sie uns die Angst eintreiben wollen* . . . the Tommies will have to do a lot better than that if they want to worry us.' He decided to keep U-0117 on her course and maintain maximum submerged speed for another ten minutes.

For the next half-hour depth-charging occurred at irregular intervals. They were single, sometimes double explosions. The closest was estimated at 500 metres. Kleber knew that the destroyers had lost contact and were depth-charging at random to keep him submerged while the convoy altered course. He imagined it would have made an emergency turn away from his reported position. As each depth-charge exploded, Dieter Leuner plotted the approximate position given by the hydrophone operator. When the explosions ceased Kleber looked at the chart, considered the various possibilities and made his decision.

Fifteen minutes later he took U-0117 above the temperature layer to 50 metres. Before long Ausfeld had again picked up propellers' noises. They were to the north-east, estimated range 9000 to 10,000 metres, opening. Kleber realised the destroyers must have abandoned the search soon after the last depth-charge explosion. Now they would be returning to their screening positions in front of the convoy. When the propeller noises could no longer be heard, Kleber brought U-0117 to the surface.

The course steered by the destroyers, estimated by Ausfeld, suggested that the convoy's emergency turn had been to port. Kleber set course to the eastward to overtake, keeping to windward.

Once again U-0117 was running at high speed on the surface. The moderate south-westerly gale blew now from astern. Conditions on the small horseshoe bridge were incredibly uncomfortable as the submarine slithered and wallowed through heavy seas. Snow and sleet storms followed each each other with monotonous regularity, and despite the feeble Arctic twilight of forenoon, visibility was rarely above five hundred metres.

It was almost two hours later that Ausfeld reported faint radar impulses fine on the port bow. Kleber at once reduced speed. With diesels throttled back to seven and a half knots, U-0117, astern and up-wind of the convoy, settled down to shadowing, her search-receiver just able to hold the multiplicity of distant radar impulses at maximum range. Kleber counted on the submarine's silhouette, trimmed well down, being too small a target for the escorts' radar in those seas.

At 1017, having established the approximate course of the convoy, Kleber made his sighting report to the Naval High Command. It was an unusual signal in some respects. When Whitehall intercepted and deciphered it, it appeared to be a weather report, albeit with curious features.

The signal evidently gave the U-boat's position co-ordinates but in a new style cipher group, and the name or word KLEBER in plain language appeared before the penultimate group which gave the time of origin. The message ended with XXXX instead of the customary cipher group representing the U-boat's call-sign. Though of a minor nature, these were departures from the standard form used for weather reports by German U-boats. Cipher officers in Whitehall could not decide the significance of the variations, and the four Xs defied rational explanation. The cipher groups thought to be the position co-ordinates could not be broken, but they were presumed to be based upon bearings from German radio beacons along the Norwegian coast.

In all other respects the message's form and content, and the transmission frequency, was that normally used for weather reporting by U-boats. Whitehall had, of course, no means of knowing that this *ruse de guerre* was an essential part of Plan X, agreed by Kleber with the Flag Officer, U-boats, Group North.

As soon as Kleber's message was received in the operations room at Trondheim, Plan X was put into operation. In accordance with custom, the convoy was, for reference purposes, named after the U-boat commander who had sighted it.

Thus JW 137 became known to the German High Command as *Kleber's Convoy*.

## CHAPTER TWELVE

The brass-rimmed clock on the bulkhead of *Vengeful*'s HF/DF office showed 1017 when Leading-Telegraphist Blades, the operator on watch, heard a ground-wave signal transmitted by a U-boat. His hands flew to the tuning controls of the receivers in front of him and with almost imperceptible movements he amplified the signal, checked its frequency and read off the bearing. That done he immediately broadcast to all escort vessels by TBS – remote controlled from his desk – the bearing and series number of the B-Bar message.

For every second of every hour of every day since leaving Loch Ewe, Blades and his fellow operators – there were three of them – had sat in the minute office under the quarter-deck taking turns to watch their receivers and listen for a ground-wave transmission on the frequencies used by U-boats. They had done this in conditions of the utmost discomfort but they had been trained to identify such signals instantly, for speed was imperative. A U-boat's sighting report took under thirty seconds to transmit. Now, at last, one had come.

At the twenty-third second after picking up the signal, his vital task completed, Blades pressed the buzzer which sounded on the bridge, in the chart-room beside the plotting table, and in Lieutenant Sunley's cabin. All who heard it knew that *Vengeful* had picked up a B-Bar message from a U-boat.

Within minutes escorts had exchanged HF/DF bearings and plotted the submarine's position. They did not, of course, know that this was U-0117, commanded by Kapitänleutnant Johan August Kleber, though they suspected that KLEBER was the captain's name. Nor did Kleber know that his boat's position had been plotted for its message had

90

been transmitted on an ultra-high frequency: one which the Germans believed the British could not use for direction-finding purposes, a belief which persisted until the end of the war.

Once the U-boat's signals had been deciphered, the U-boat tracking-room in Whitehall lost no time in passing its contents to the Vice-Admiral in *Fidelix*. Describing it as *apparently a weather report*, Whitehall drew attention to its unusual features. The Vice-Admiral did not acknowledge the signal because he intended maintaining wireless silence until the position of JW 137 was, beyond all doubt, known to the enemy.

In *Fidelix*'s operations-room the Vice-Admiral discussed the signal with his staff-officer-operations, Rory McLeod, and the navigator, Lieutenant-Commander Cockburn.

'What are the facts?' he asked, proceeding at once to answer the rhetorical question. 'This morning *Vengeful* and *Violent* closed to within five thousand yards of a radar contact, classified submarine. At that range they lost contact. The submarine had dived. The time was 0820. No A/S contact was made so the U-boat was presumably sitting under a temperature layer or conditions were too bad for A/S.'

The Vice-Admiral leant over the plotting table where a stylus scratched the flagship's course on to a moving sheet. He turned to the radar displays. Pips of light glowing and fading showed the position of the ships in the convoy, the cruiser, the oiler, the corvettes and frigates of the close escort, the Home Fleet destroyers inside the close screen, the escort destroyers and sloops of the outer screen, the little rescue ship astern and the host of merchant ships . . . an abstract picture of JW 137 plodding through the long Arctic night, rolling and plunging on its way to the Kola Inlet.

'We completed the wheel to port soon after 0840. That left the U-boat to the south-west of us.' The Vice-Admiral pulled at his chin with forefinger and thumb. 'About two hours later – at 1017 to be precise – a B-Bar message was picked up which puts the U-boat there.' With his thumb he indicated the position on the plot. 'Because they were nearest the bearing, and since they can steam upwind faster than any of the other escorts, we detached two Home Fleet destroyers to put him down. But they failed to make contact. Radar or otherwise. The U-boat must have dived immediately after transmitting the B-Bar.'

'Standard practice, sir,' said Cockburn. The Vice-Admiral eyed him keenly wondering what innuendo lay behind the remark. It was not for nothing that the navigator was called 'Cocky' in the wardroom.

'Sensible chap,' said Rory McLeod. 'He wants to stay alive.'

'Confounded nuisance not being able to operate aircraft in this weather.' The Vice-Admiral growled his annoyance. 'Then we get this.' He held up the Whitehall signal giving the contents of the B-Bar message. 'They describe it as *apparently* a weather report. It describes the weather we're experiencing with considerable accuracy – and we know that U-boats do transmit weather reports. But it has these unusual features. KLEBER could be the name of the commanding officer, I suppose, or a code name for the U-boat. But the four Xs? Any ideas, gentlemen?'

Cockburn shook his head. Rory McLeod said, 'They may have some cipher significance, sir. An indicator group, perhaps. Who knows?'

'Quite,' said the Vice-Admiral. 'I, for one, don't. Nor does Whitehall. And now the sixty-four dollar question. Is this weather reporter the U-boat that *Vengeful* and *Violent* put down earlier, or another fellow?'

Rory McLeod said, 'From the plot I would think it's likely to be the same boat, sir. It has travelled in our general direction between its 0820 and 1017 positions.'

'In that case one would expect the B-Bar message to have been a sighting report not a weather report.'

'Yes, sir,' said the navigator. 'Unless . . .'

'Unless what, Cockburn?'

'Unless the U-boat was unaware of *Vengeful* and *Violent* when it dived at 0820. Could be a U-boat on passage to Kola, making routine dives and transmitting weather reports.'

'Unlikely,' said the Vice-Admiral, shaking his head. 'Even in this weather, if his search-receiver was in trouble I'd have thought his hydrophones would have picked up propeller noises.' He paused to gather his thoughts. 'We've not altered course since the B-Bar message because the one we're steering is taking the convoy away from the U-boat. I believe that to be a sensible decision. And in favour of your point, Cockburn, we do know that a weather report has been made but apparently no sighting report.'

'I take it, sir,' said Rory McLeod, 'that when and if a sighting report is made there'll be the usual W/T chatter between the German High Command and the U-boats on the Kola patrol line. They'll acknowledge as they always do, and we'll get huff-duff bearings and plot their positions.'

'Yes,' said the Vice-Admiral, who'd been about to say the same thing. 'Thank heavens for their tendency to chatter. When they do we shall have something to go on. Now, gentlemen, I think I'd like to get back to the bridge.'

The fifteen U-boats on the patrol line outside the Kola Inlet were disposed along a shallow arc, its highest point south of the Skolpen Bank, its extremities opposite Vardo Point in the West and Voroni Rocks in the East. The arc was a little over one hundred miles long and its average distance offshore ranged from thirty to fifty miles. The U-boats which manned it were about seven miles apart.

The Murman coast was particularly suitable for *Schnorchel* boats and the three U-boats not on the surface when the High Command's XXXX signal was made at 1020 were submerged and schnorkelling. Since a radio antennae was raised with the *Schnorchel* mast all submarines on the patrol line read the signal.

U-0153 was one of three submerged at that time. Her captain, Willi Schluss, was more than ready to accept the discomfort this entailed in return for the security offered by fourteen metres of water over the submarine. Conditions in the boat were unpleasant, and though they were in the lee of the land the weather offshore was decidedly rough. On top of the usual misery of a dark, dripping and humid interior, the *Schnorchel* float which controlled the air-intake valve was at times covered by seas which closed it. The shutting off of fresh air resulted in the diesel intakes sucking oxygen from the interior of the boat, creating a sudden vacuum which made men gasp for breath, suffer severe headaches and attacks of nausea.

Hugo Kolb, the engineer-officer, was one of those who did little to conceal his contempt for the captain's tendency to *Schnorchel* when the boat could have been surfaced. *'Er will wohl ewig leben* . . . he wants to live for ever,' said Kolb, a Nazi zealot with pale blue eyes and a bullet-shaped head. Obermaschinist Zeck, his second-in-command, nodded in silent agreement.

'God knows how he ever became captain of a U-boat,' said Kolb.

Ivory teeth and the whites of large eyes against a grease-stained face gave Zeck the appearance of a white man made-up to look like a Negro. 'We get killed pretty quickly these days,' he said. 'The young and inexperienced have to be used.'

Kolb frowned. 'Youth and inexperience cannot be helped, but Schluss is a coward.'

Zeck, who took a realistic view of life and longed for a peace which would take him home to his wife and children in Westphalia, said, 'Well, if he succeeds we too will live for ever, so why complain, *Herr Ingenieur.*' Having said that he smiled discreetly to indicate that the remark was not meant seriously. He knew Kolb would not approve and had no wish to offend him.

Kolb's eyes flashed. 'That is not the point. We are here to fight the enemy. To serve the Fuehrer and the Reich. Not to see how long we can survive. The chances of making a sighting are good on the surface. There we can make proper use of the search-receiver. Maybe even see something in the semi-twilight. But submerged with the *schnorkel.*' He spat expressively.

'You are right, *Herr Ingenieur*. But Kapitänleutnant Schluss commands the boat. His orders must be obeyed.'

'We shall see,' said Kolb darkly. 'Wait until we get back to Trondheim.'

'*Falls wir zurückkommen* . . . if we get back,' murmured Zeck to himself. The obermaschinist had his doubts.

As Willi Schluss read the High Command's 1020 signal he shivered and his intestines knotted painfully. It was not un-expected. U-0153 had already intercepted Kleber's 1017 weather report. It had caused Schluss the greatest anxiety. The four Xs and the use of the commander's name in place of the submarine's call-sign meant that a convoy had been sighted. Now the High Command was ordering the attack.

Worse still, it was to be led by Kleber. Schluss was an imaginative, apprehensive young man, on his first patrol in command. The high rate of mortality among U-boat crews had necessitated more and more men like him who had neither the experience nor the courage and resolve for the job, being given command of new construction.

Because he was intelligent and quick to learn he had done well in training flotillas in the Baltic and in Oslo Fjord. It was on his performance there that he had been given command of U-0153. But his lack of aggression, his uncertainty and nervousness had soon become apparent to the crew, and the morale of these young men, themselves sadly lacking in experience, had suffered. Tension between the captain and Kolb the engineering officer, an older and more experienced U-boat man, permeated U-0153. She was an unhappy boat.

Schluss, small, dark, bookish, introverted, came from Karlsruhe. He had been studying economics in Berlin when war came. An intellectual liberal with compassion for peoples of all races and creeds, he had long believed in the futility of war. To find himself involved in one was a traumatic experience. His dislike of a dogmatic Hitlerised father, a minor party official, had not helped. Willi Schluss, at home on leave, or in barracks or afloat, was an unhappy young man with no belief in the justice of the cause he was obliged to fight for. Originally trained for surface vessels, he had spent most of his time in the *Gneisenau,* first in Brest and afterwards in Kiel and the Baltic. Later when the decision was made to run down the crews of surface ships he had, with thousands of others, been drafted into the submarine service. There he had done his best, but it was an impoverished best. His heart was not in the job.

After he had re-read the High Command's signal for the third time, Schluss opened the safe in which the confidential books were kept. From it he took a bundle of envelopes marked '*Streng geheim* . . . top secret'. They were held together by an elastic band. He thumbed through these until he came to one marked *Plan X.* In the small nook off the control-room which was his cabin he pulled the curtain and with trembling fingers opened the envelope. As he read his fears increased, his mouth dried, and he suffered an attack of dizziness. He had not until that moment known the details of *Plan X.*

It involved a concentration of submarines in a surface attack at high speed: the old *Rudeltaktik* . . . 'wolf-pack' tactic long-since discarded because of crippling losses inflicted on these packs by enemy escort forces after mid-1943.

'It's incredible,' he mumbled to himself in subdued hysteria. 'These Russian convoys are the most heavily escorted ever known. A pack attack on the surface . . . Why . . . it's . . . it's asking us to commit suicide. It's mad. That's what it is.' His eyes filled with tears. He fought them back, dried his eyes and concentrated once again on the secret orders.

*Plan X,* read in conjunction with High Command's 1020 signal, required the eight U-boats on the western arc of the Kola patrol line to concentrate on the shadowing U-boat – Kleber's in this instance – the position of which was given. The concentration of *Gruppe Kleber,* as it was now known in the operations-room at Trondheim, should be completed by 1530.

That, decided Schluss after a stint on the chart-table in the control-room, gave U-0153 a little under five hours to get into position.

In terms of *Plan X* the shadowing U-boat's 'weather reports' gave – in a new code – the convoy's position, course and speed at each transmission and would serve as beacon signals, to be re-transmitted by High Command to ensure reception.

The plan also provided that the seven U-boats on the eastern arc of the patrol line – referred to as *Gruppe Osten* – were to concentrate on a position indicated by a cipher group in the High Command signal. The special code attached to *Plan X* showed this position to be north-west of the Skolpen Bank. The purpose of the Skolpen concentration was to lure escorts away from the convoy and to act as support and back-stop to *Gruppe Kleber.*

The U-boats of *Kruppe Osten* in executing *Plan X* were to acknowledge all High Command signals and report their positions on each occasion . . . *but they were to make two reports*: one upon receipt of the signal, the other at irregular intervals between fifteen and twenty-five minutes after its receipt – and two different call-signs were to be used so that the signals would appear to have come from two different U-boats. This *ruse de guerre* would lead the enemy to believe that there were fourteen U-boats in the Skolpen concentration, only one less than the total of fifteen on the Kola patrol line.

The eight U-boats of *Gruppe Kleber* on the other hand were *not* to acknowledge High Command signals once embarked upon the execution of *Plan X*. They were to maintain radio silence while making their approach to Kleber's position from the southward, keeping outside radar range of the convoy's escort force. Captains of U-boats were reminded that their search-receivers would pick up enemy radar transmissions well outside the range at which the enemy's radar could detect submarines, particularly in bad weather. As each boat of *Gruppe Kleber* reached the concentration area it was to trim down, steer the course and speed ordered by High Command, and await a signal from Kleber to commence the attack.

The method of attack would vary, depending upon the circumstances at the time. There were many refinements and alternatives and a code word for each. For example, *KLEBER* repeated twice, followed by *CLOSING DOWN* repeated twice, would require the U-boats to dive, seek the protection of temperature layers and allow escort screens to pass over. Thereafter they were to surface astern of the escorts and attack the convoy. It was probable, recorded *Plan X*, that most enemy escorts would by that time be disposed on the opposite side of the convoy, having been diverted there by signals from *Gruppe Osten* on the north-west rim of the Skolpen Bank.

Schluss had observed in the preface to the operational orders that *Plan X* would only be ordered when weather conditions were regarded as favourable – and only if they were such that enemy aircraft could not operate. Since the U-boats would have the advantage of weather and surprise, read the preface, it should be possible to saturate the diluted escort force and inflict heavy losses on the convoy.

If the signal to attack had not come from Kleber within fifteen minutes of the time laid down for completion of concentration – given at 1530 in High Command's 1020 signal – all U-boats were to attack independently. Under certain circumstances, depending upon the movements of the convoy, Kleber was permitted to order the attack before completion of concentration. *Gruppe Osten* was to concentrate upon attacking the escorts diverted to the Skolpen Bank.

The High Command's orders noted that the attack was to be pressed home with *hartnäckiger Kühnheit* . . . relentless daring. Fine words, thought Willi Schluss, if one is a staff officer ashore writing the orders. For the U-boat crews in *Gruppe Kleber* he believed them to be a death sentence.

The operational orders ended with, *Having read Plan X and High Command's signal ordering its execution, you are to proceed at maximum surface speed to the point of concentration.*

Willi Schluss decided that some delay might be advantageous so he re-read *Plan X* slowly and carefully, becoming more and more unhappy as he did so. The knowledge that Kleber was to lead the attack made of his already considerable fears a mindless terror.

Korvettenkapitän Johan August Kleber had been chief instructor in the flotilla in which Willi Schluss had trained. They had met again only two months ago in Trondheim when U-0153 had joined Group North and Kleber had come on board to welcome the new arrival.

Reminded of that occasion, Willi Schluss took a snapshot from his wallet and looked at it sadly. Three officers on the bridge of U-0153, taken on a rare day of winter sunshine in Trondheim Fjord. Willi Schluss, characteristically glum, on the left. Kleber, tall, handsome and smiling, in the centre. Rathfelder on the right. He, too, was smiling. God knows why, thought Willi Schluss. There was nothing to smile about. Schluss knew Kleber only too well. One of the few surviving aces. Noted for his outstanding courage and determination, readiness to accept risks, almost reckless daring. Qualities Schluss regarded with profound misgiving.

'Oh God,' he thought in silent misery. 'Why does it have to be him?'

Pale, emotionally upset, he pulled aside the curtain and went into the control-room. With the conviction that he was about to commit an act of immolation involving all in U-0153, he gave the order to surface.

# CHAPTER THIRTEEN

Having transmitted the *XXXX* sighting report at 1017, Kleber in U-0117 continued to shadow JW137 using the search-receiver to keep in touch while remaining outside the range at which the escorts' radar could detect the submarine.

Semi-twilight in the forenoon, a condition not far removed from the darkness, lasted for about two hours, but low cloud, constant storms of snow, sleet and flying spray kept visibility down to under a thousand metres. The moderate south-westerly gale persisted. Kleber, estimating its strength at force six, was satisfied that under prevailing weather conditions there was no danger from enemy aircraft.

That the German High Command agreed was evident when Ausfeld reported receipt of its 1020 signal to the Kola patrol line. Schaffenhauser, whose duties included those of cipher officer, put the message through the cipher machine and handed it to the captain. Not that Kleber was in any doubt as to its contents. Principal author of *Plan X* and originator of the sighting report, he knew what it would contain – but for one item, the time by which concentration should be completed. He knew that already the fifteen U-boats off the Kola Inlet would be proceeding to their stations at maximum speed, seven of them making for the north-western rim of the Skolpen Bank, the remaining eight heading for him.

Having handed over the bridge watch to Rathfelder he went down to the chart-table in the control-room. Salt water dripped from his rubber suit, the flesh on his hands and face was numb with cold, but his spirits were high.

Dieter Leuner, third watch officer and navigator, had already plotted the positions of the U-boats off Kola, the estimated position of the convoy, U-0117's position – obtained by cross-bearings from German radio beacons on the Norwegian coast – and the concentration area north-west of the Skolpen Bank.

Those in the control-room, realising that the time for action was approaching, watched silently as Kleber worked on the chart with pencil, dividers and parallel rulers. When he'd finished he turned to Dieter Leuner. 'The eight boats of the western sector – *Gruppe Kleber* – are on average eighty miles from us. We keep station on the convoy and make seven knots with wind and sea on the starboard quarter.' He paused, taking another look at the chart. '*Gruppe Kleber*, keeping to the southward during the approach, will have the weather on the port bow. I estimate they cannot make more than ten or eleven knots steaming into it. Agreed?'

'Yes, *Herr Kapitän*. And that will be hard going.'

'So, allowing for the westerly current, our combined speeds will be eighteen to nineteen knots. Distance to go for the U-boats, depending upon their position on the patrol line, fifty to ninety miles. It's now 1025 hours. The nearest should reach us by 1300. The farthest by 1500.'

Dieter Leuner leant over the chart, checking the captain's calculations. 'Yes, *Herr Kapitän*. If those assumptions are correct, that is so.'

'And High Command orders concentration to be completed by 1530 hours. So we have a time margin. Small, but enough.' Kleber slapped the navigating officer on the back. '*Nun beginnt der Spass* . . . and then the fun starts, Dieter.'

Dieter Leuner was not sure about the fun, but Kleber's confident smile confirmed his belief, shared by the men in the control-room, that they had a first-rate captain. A man who liked a fight and whose record showed he knew how to handle one.

Ausfeld reported by voice-pipe from the sound-room. 'Radar impulses gaining in strength. Estimated range of nearest, twelve thousand metres.'

'So,' said Kleber. 'We are too close. Their radar has tracked us down. More efficient than it used to be. Now they send destroyers to make us submerge.'

'Thank God for temperature layers,' said Dieter Leuner.

Kleber called Ausfeld by voice-pipe. 'Let me know when the range is eight thousand metres.' He turned back to Leuner. 'We'll dive then. Get under a layer and make five knots submerged. Steer the same course as the convoy. We'll drop astern. Later we'll surface and catch up without difficulty.' The flashing white teeth and brilliant smile were reassuring. 'In the meantime prepare for depth-charging. I don't suppose it'll be any more accurate than the last lot.' He had raised his voice so that all in the control-room should hear. Kleber knew a great deal about morale building.

Whitehall intercepted the High Command's 1020 signal to the Kola patrol line and before long its contents were deciphered. But the Admiralty was little wiser than it had been after interception of the first signal – now referred to as the *KLEBER* weather report – made by a U-boat at 1017 that forenoon in a position twelve miles south-west of convoy JW 137.

Substantially the High Command's signal was a repetition of the *KLEBER* signal – ostensibly the High Command was re-transmitting the weather report to all U-boats in the area. But there were certain differences. The still unbreakable cipher groups, believed to be position co-ordinates, were now preceded by the words *Gruppe Osten,* two new cipher groups – also unbreakable – appeared and the four Xs were followed by *KLEBER* and the High Command's call-sign.

The Admiralty and the escorts to convoy JW 137 intercepted acknowledgments by the U-boats off Kola – fifteen in all – their HF/DF bearings were noted, exchanged between escorts and plotted. Thus, within a few minutes, the positions of all fifteen U-boats were known to the Admiralty, to the Vice-Admiral in *Fidelix* and to the escorts.

It was noted that no signal of acknowledgment came from the area in which the U-boat which had sent the *KLEBER* weather report was known to be.

While the officers in the U-boat tracking-room at the Admiralty, and in *Fidelix*'s operations-room, were analysing and weighing the contents of the *KLEBER* weather report and the High Command's 1020 signal, Redman in *Vengeful* was looking at both with a mixture of shock and incredulity. It wasn't the import of the signals which worried him. It was the name *KLEBER*.

Could it possibly be Hans? Redman knew that he'd worked in his father's legal practice in Frankfurt before the war and that he'd been a keen yachtsman. Once, light-heartedly, knowing that Redman served in the Royal Navy, Hans had said, 'If there's a war I think I'll try for the navy. I don't fancy marching or flying.'

Redman had said, 'Well, don't get in my way if you do.

I'd hate to sink you.'

They'd laughed. Redman had added, seriously, 'Let's hope there won't be a war,' and the subject was changed for it was one they avoided.

Remembering this, he frowned at the signal in disbelief. It couldn't be Hans. It was not an unusual name in Germany. He remembered once having asked trunk inquiries for the Klebers' telephone number. 'There are a number of Klebers in Frankfurt,' the London operator had interrupted. 'Five with those initials. Give me the address, please.'

No, he decided, handing the signal-board back to the yeoman, it was highly improbable. Hans could, after all, have gone into the *Reichswehr* or the *Luftwaffe*. More likely, in fact, for they were bigger services. Anyway, there were probably dozens of Klebers in the German Navy, particularly since its swamping by reserves.

But the nagging doubt remained, and while he leant over the chart-table watching Pownall plot the position of the Kola U-boats, he thought once again of that day in the mountains above Crans-sur-Sierre.

Redman breathed deeply, the Alpine air diffusing rivulets of cold sweat through his body. The profile of mountains, range upon range, fell back in perspective marking the horizon with pale serrated ridges. The slopes below, their extremities lost in mist, were buttressed with snow-laden rock, their flanks enfolding blue-green glaciers. Wisps of snow spiralled from distant peaks, church bells echoed up from the valley, the sun shone warm and reassuring.

He looked at his watch. Nine o'clock on Sunday morning. In the valley the Swiss were paying homage to their God, while the handful of visitors were probably still in their beds. The mountains, the fresh spring snow and crystalline air were remote from the world below. A sublime landscape, he seemed to be the only figure in it.

Narrowing his eyes against the glare he looked down the slopes. Ski-ing conditions seemed perfect despite small puffs of cloud low in the valley. The breeze would soon disperse them. The slopes, steep and difficult, were new to him and it was their reputation that had brought him there. Sampling the unknown, pitting his skill against danger. These things attracted him.

He bent down to adjust the safety release bindings, checking the calibrations: *leicht, mittel, hart*. He eased the bindings slightly: a broken leg on a deserted slope could mean disaster at that season when blizzards came with little warning, freezing an immobile body, concealing it until the summer thaw. He stood up, adjusted his goggles, ran the skis back and forth to clear their undersides of packed ice, and pushed off.

Ski-ing down the slopes he avoided the moguls with quick showy turns, gauging the quality of the new snow. At the bottom he flung fast round a shoulder of the mountain to find a narrow pass, a sharp rise in its crutch. He schussed down the last stretch, crouching, taking the shock of impact with angled knees, shooting into the air with a vigorous kick as he reached the crest. Landing beyond it, he swung in his skis, stopping urgently in his tracks, churning up a flurry of snow.

Below him lay the descent the locals called '*das Geschützrohr*' – 'the gun barrel'. The piste was exceptionally steep, barely passable. The sharp upward curving sides gave the impression of a blinding white tunnel, its edges deep in snow while the piste itself – or what he had presumed to be the piste – had been swept clean by the wind. Its ice ridges and moguls glistened menacingly and less than two hundred metres down its length it melted into cloud. Redman realised that visibility there would be no more than a score of feet.

He looked back up the mountainside. Most of it was hidden by the shoulder round which he'd come. It was unlikely that anyone would be following, that day or any other. He reproached himself for his foolhardiness. Two eagles circling above a distant valley reminded him of vultures and he shivered. The drifts and icy confines of 'the gun barrel' made it impossible to traverse. If he schussed, it could be years later before he emerged, deep frozen, from the bottom of a glacier. But he had to do something. He couldn't stay there. For a moment he wondered if he was dramatising the situation, then decided he wasn't. Sobered by fear, he pushed off, skis parted, crouched down, sticks under arms, speed building up until he was deafened by the wind.

Crashing over ridges and tumuli he tried hard to keep his legs supple, but was thrown through the air with increasing violence. Then, without warning, he was in the clouds plummeting through misty oblivion, only his reflexes saving him from baling out. The ground appeared from nowhere, rushing up to meet him, ramming his knees into his body. Again he was flung into the air. Fighting to keep the skis parallel, bracing himself for impact, he landed heavily on hard-packed snow. Miraculously he was still on his feet and free of that frightening speed.

The fog thinned. Ahead he saw a ledge, beyond it a clear drop. With fierce energy he attempted a turn but there was hard ice under the skis. For the third time he was thrown through the air. He hit the ice and his body seemed to burst. Enormous forces wrenched his legs from under him, his arms flailed, and a yellow light exploded behind his eyes.

It seemed he was stumbling through a dark forest and had come suddenly upon a clearing for the light was dazzling. It was a cold hostile world in which he found himself – a world filled with pain and blood-stained snow. Frightened, he attempted to make for the forest again but could not move.

Later he became aware of a dark shape above him, hands gripping, a man's voice. Absurdly loud.

Kleber traversed the snow slowly savouring the crisp Alpine air. He stopped above '*das Geschützrohr*' and slipped up his goggles. Resting on his sticks, he examined the ski tracks. They were fresh. Someone had gone down there recently.

He looked down the long narrow chute, its end shrouded in mist. It was well named. Expert though he was he would not tackle it alone. He'd been down once, the year before, with Max Weinhardt, chief instructor and leader of the mountain rescue team. It had been an exciting experience. But Weinhardt knew the safe route and had led. He'd explained the danger before they started. '*Das Geschützrohr*' had a lethal piste at its lower end, a steep hump, eight metres high. In bad visibility a skier unfamiliar with the chute would go straight over the hump to find a sharp ledge beneath it, below that a glacier. It was not large, but laced with edges, clefts and crevasses, and there was little snow. Once on it, the chances of survival for an injured man were small.

He pulled down his goggles, was about to move on, when the mist eddied and cleared from the foot of the chute. Below it he saw the glacier and frowned in disbelief. The body on it, grotesquely sprawled, must be the lone skier whose tracks he'd just examined.

After a moment of indecision he set off down the chute, ski-ing carefully, controlling his speed, and when he reached the hump, climbing it with special care. He went up its steep side, edged round the shoulder avoiding the jutting rock ledge, working his way cautiously on to the glacier. He was well aware of the risks he was taking. But since boyhood danger had drawn him. It was not bravery. It was a compulsion. The attraction of that which was to be feared. A challenge to skill and manhood.

Slowly, painstakingly, he worked his way down past the crevasse until he reached the body. It lay sprawled on blood-spattered ice, broken skis around it. He bent down, felt the skier's heart and pulse. He couldn't have been there long. When Kleber removed the injured man's snow goggles he recognised him. It was the Englishman. They were staying at the same hotel. He'd been there for only a few days. Kleber and his sister Marianne had spoken to him once at the bar. A calm, taciturn man with brooding eyes and a firm mouth. Afterwards Marianne had said she thought him attractive. 'I like these strong silent men.' She laughed mischievously. 'You never know what they're thinking.'

'I do, Marianne, when they look at you.'

'Go on,' she said. 'You've a nasty mind.'

'I know human nature,' he protested.

'Your own,' she said. 'Not everybody's.'

Kleber worked on the Englishman, examining him with strong, gentle hands. There was an abrasion on the back of the skull. He was bleeding from nose and mouth, and a leg and wrist were broken.

'*Mein Gott,*' Kleber muttered. '*Mein Freund, Sie machen es einen schwer* . . . you are certainly a problem, my friend.' He shook the man gently but got no response. He slapped his face. The Englishman groaned. Later he opened his eyes and said, 'Oh, Christ!'

Kleber smiled reassuringly. 'Don't worry. It's all right. I'll get you out of here.'

The man turned his head, looked back up the glacier and

105

frowned. He could not comprehend what had happened. How he'd got there? The German explained. The Englishman shook his head. He remembered nothing of ski-ing down. But he did recognise the stranger. The tall fair German from the hotel. The man with the good-looking sister. He was appalled at the risks his rescuer must have taken to reach him on the glacier. How would he get out of it? He asked him.

The German said, 'Save your strength. You're going to need it all.' He looked round sizing up the glacier. 'Wait,' he said. 'I do first a reconnaissance. To find the route down.' He moved away. The Englishman dozed off. He was awakened by someone shaking him. It was the German again. 'It is only another two hundred metres to the end of the glacier,' he said. 'After that an easy slope with good snow.'

Kleber shed his skis and helped the Englishman to his feet, supporting him with an arm around his waist, the injured man's arm round his neck. But it didn't work. The broken leg baulked any carrying techniques, the Englishman groaning, cursing, apologising. At last Kleber decided there was nothing for it but to carry him on his back.

It was an arduous, precarious journey. The man was heavy and it had to be done in short spurts. Twenty yards at a time. Then a rest. After each stint the German would go back to fetch his skis and sticks. Then he would pick up his human bundle and struggle forward again. The surface of the glacier was treacherous; Kleber slipped at times and fell, and the Englishman would cry out with pain. It took two hours to reach the bottom of the slope. By then Kleber was near to exhaustion.

He found a comparatively sheltered place against the flank of a buttress, beneath a rock overhang. He propped the man in a corner, gave him slab chocolate and biscuits, and sat down next to him to rest. Later he said, 'I go now for help. The weather is good. Don't worry. I will be back with men and a stretcher. But move the limbs as much as possible. To keep the circulation going. Yes?'

'I'll try.' Redman looked at the German, shaking his head, his face lined with pain. 'You shouldn't have risked your neck for me.'

'You would have done the same. It is not so much.'

With sudden formality the Englishman said, 'My name is

106

Francis Redman.'

The German bowed. 'Mine is Hans Kleber.'

They shook hands as if to seal the introduction. Kleber said, '*Auf wiedersehen*. I'll be back soon.'

He was as good as his word, but 'soon' proved to be many hours later.

That night Redman found himself in a warm bed in a small hospital in the valley, leg and wrist in splints and plaster, head bandaged and a pretty Swiss nurse leaning over him. 'How do you feel?' she asked.

'Marvellous,' he said, and fell into a deep sleep.


# CHAPTER FOURTEEN


About an hour after enemy destroyers had forced U-0117 to dive for the second time that morning, Kleber brought her to the surface and set off in pursuit of the convoy, driving down-wind at high speed.

The time was 1139.

Maintaining the last-known course of the convoy the submarine had made good four miles while submerged. In that time Kleber estimated the convoy to have travelled six or seven miles allowing for the westerly current. Before diving U-0117 had been keeping station up-wind of JW 137, ten to twelve miles on its starboard quarter.

Not long after surfacing Ausfeld reported, 'Faint radar impulses between red zero-one-zero and zero-two-five. Estimated range twenty-seven thousand metres.'

'*Ausgezeichnet* . . . splendid, Ausfeld. Who is operating the search-receiver?' Kleber had to raise his voice and shout down the voice-pipe to make himself heard above the howl of the wind and the buffeting of the seas.

'I am, *Herr Kapitän*. Now we have found the convoy I hand over to Haben the watchkeeper.'

'It should be called Ausfeld's convoy, not mine,' shouted Kleber.

'You joke, *Herr Kapitän*. I do only my best.'

'A very good best.' Kleber turned to Rathfelder. 'By heavens, it's freezing. My hands and feet are numb. Go

107

down and get some hot soup into your body. When you're back, I'll do the same.'

By noon Kleber had closed to within eleven miles of JW 137. Now he put U-0117 broad on the convoy's starboard quarter, maintaining the up-wind position. The U-boat was trimmed well down. A virtually impossible radar target for escorts at that range. The convoy was still steering the course it had been on when U-0117 was last forced to dive. For the time being there was no need for a further shadowing report.

The clock over the chart-table showed 1227.

At 1120, an hour after its first message to the Kola patrol line, the German High Command made a further signal. It was intercepted by the Admiralty and this time Whitehall found it to be a conventional operational signal ordering all U-boats of *Gruppe Osten* to report their positions. In the next half-hour the Admiralty intercepted B-Bar signals from fourteen U-boats. The HF/DF equipped escorts to JW 137 had already picked these up and plotted the positions of the submarines.

In the operations-room in *Fidelix* and in the U-boat tracking-room in Whitehall, the movements of the Kola U-boats were being studied and analysed. In the time that had elapsed between their responses to the High Command's two signals, the 'fourteen' submarines had steered courses between north and north-west, and had travelled distances varying from ten to fifteen miles.

Although the courses steered were not convergent, they indicated a general movement towards the north-western extremity of the Skolpen Bank.

The Vice-Admiral examined the plot closely before moving across to the chart of the Murman coast and the radar displays.

'Well,' he said to his operations-officer, Rory McLeod. 'At this stage I'd say their tactical plan is to concentrate to the north-west of the Skolpen Bank. They know the minefield's there and that's important for two reasons. One, they are aware that our present course takes us to the Bank. I imagine they assume – and it's a reasonable assumption – that we'll close it within the next six to seven hours. Then we

108

shall have to decide whether to pass north or south of the minefield. By concentrating on the north-western rim of the Bank they cover either route.'

From under bushy eyebrows the Vice-Admiral's sun-wrinkled eyes switched from Rory McLeod to Cockburn, the navigating officer. 'Agree with that?'

'Yes, sir,' they said in unison. McLeod added, 'You said the enemy's knowledge of this minefield on the Skolpen Bank was important for two reasons. You mentioned the first. What was the second, sir?'

'The second's pretty obvious. Look.' The Vice-Admiral pointed to the plot. 'They've split into two groups. One, of six U-boats, is evidently steering to pass to the west of the minefield. The other eight are on courses to the east of it. If they didn't know there was a minefield there they'd be taking the shortest route. In other words they'd be steering convergent courses. I may be wrong. When the High Command next asks for their positions we'll know.'

'And in the meantime, sir?' McLeod watched the Vice-Admiral closely.

'We hold on. Allowing a surfaced U-boat eleven or twelve knots in this weather – and that's generous – I doubt if those with the least distance to go can get into position much before 1400. Those with farthest to go, before 1530. If we maintain this course, we'll be all of thirty miles west of the Skolpen Bank by 1530. Provided nothing crops up in the meantime, that will be the moment to make our decision. By then we'll have a pretty good idea where our friends are and what they're up to.'

He looked at the chart again. 'You've done the staff course, McLeod. D'you go along with my rather potted appreciation of the situation?'

McLeod grinned. 'Entirely, sir. Only sorry I can't produce folios of beautifully typed appreciations as we did at Greenwich. You know, sir: *Courses of action open to the enemy. Enemy's probable course of action . . .'*

'Etcetera,' interrupted the Vice-Admiral who was an ex-submariner. 'Good mental discipline that, but I'm all for looking at the chart and the weather and asking what I'd do if I were the enemy.'

Cockburn then mumbled something under his breath.

'What was that?' challenged the Vice-Admiral.

'Nothing, sir. I was just thinking.'

'H'm.' The Vice-Admiral looking at him speculatively. 'If you always mumble when you think you should see a doctor.'

Rory McLeod saved the situation. 'It's clear that we're being shadowed, sir. '

The Vice-Admiral swung round as if shifting guns to a new target. 'Of course we are, my dear chap, and it's pretty obvious it's our friend *KLEBER,* the phony weather reporter. His so-called weather report has been the only B-Bar transmission this forenoon. It was retransmitted soon afterwards by the German High Command. Now we know that the Kola patrol line is concentrating ahead of us. So much for that weather report.' The Vice-Admiral snorted.

'But the weather reports are remarkably accurate, sir,' said McLeod. 'Nothing phony about them in that sense.'

'They are and that's puzzling. But there's something odd about those signals. The *KLEBER* and the four Xs and those unbreakable cypher groups. They probably tie up with something else to make a sighting report. I'm pretty certain of that.' He blew his nose loudly. 'Or have you gentlemen alternative suggestions?'

'As you say, sir. If there's another shadower we'd have picked up his B-Bar sighting report,' said McLeod.

'Good old staff course,' said the Vice-Admiral. 'It gets you there in the end.' He drew in his lips, puffed out his cheeks and frowned. 'This damned weather. If we could fly off aircraft there wouldn't be a surfaced U-boat within a hundred miles.'

'Yes, sir,' said the navigating officer, anxious to make amends. 'I couldn't agree more.'

The Vice-Admiral glared at him.

The U-boat tracking-room in Whitehall had reached much the same conclusions as the Vice-Admiral. There, too, it had been decided to await further information of U-boat movements before coming to explicit conclusions.

The timid knock repeated several times roused Redman from half sleep. 'What is it?' he said.

'Me, sir.' The curtain was pulled aside and Cupido stood

wedged in the doorway of the sea-cabin, his drawn face unnaturally red in the gleam of the cabin light. To Redman there was something Mephistophelean about the bony forehead, high cheek bones and sunken eyes. He did not know, nor for that matter did the steward, that Cupido was suffering from a gastric ulcer. Cupido had not taken his troubles to the doctor. To him it was just a gnawing pain, the turn of a knife in his bowels. Something he'd been getting on these journeys to Russia. Couldn't eat much without feeling sick afterwards. He'd put it down to indigestion. Meals were at irregular times because the ship's company was so often closed up at action stations. Mostly false alarms. He blamed no one. It was just a fact of life.

For several reasons Cupido evinced in Redman feelings of hostility. The young steward breathed garlic at him; the meals he brought to the sea-cabin which should have been hot were almost invariably cold; and he so often looked scruffy. He did now, standing in the doorway, a grey woollen balaclava over his head, a piece of spunyarn tied round the waist of his watch-coat from which buttons were missing, his seaboots several sizes too large. He dripped water like a dog fresh from a stream. Powdered snow on his eyebrows gave him the appearance of a bedraggled Father Christmas. One hand held the doorframe, steadying him against the movement of the ship, the other clutched the food-carrier.

'Your lunch, sir,' said Cupido apologetically.

Redman looked at the cabin clock, got off the bunk, stood back to make room. Cupido came into the cabin, put the food-carrier on the deck, pulled the small folding table from the bulkhead.

'Where's your picking-up harness, Cupido?'

'Under me watch-coat, sir.'

Redman frowned at the food-carrier.

'What is it today?' The hoarse, toneless voice was the measure of the captain's exhaustion.

'Mutton, french beans and potatoes, sir. Steam pudding and treacle. And coffee, sir.' Cupido opened the carrier, took from it the plates of food, the cup, coffee pot and cutlery, and set them into the fiddles on the table.

Redman looked at the food doubtfully, felt it with the back of his hand. First the meat and vegetables, then the steamed pudding and finally the coffee jug. He frowned at Cupido through red-rimmed eyes. 'Lukewarm to cold as usual.'

'Sorry, sir,' said Cupido, adding under his breath. 'Do me best.'

Redman shook his head, tightened his lips, said nothing. Cupido feared him most when he was like that.

The steward sighed, gathered and steadied himself, took a last sad look at the captain and staggered into the wheel-house. There the combination of an exaggerated pitch and roll threw him against the man at the wheel. 'Watch it, cock,' said the quartermaster. 'You'll sink the bloody ship.'

The bows of U-0153 plunged into a head sea. A great wave leapt from the darkness, swept down the casing and broke against the conning-tower, its crest cascading on to the small bridge.

But for the steel belts which secured them to the super-structure, Willi Schluss, Emil Meyer the executive officer, and the bridge dutymen would have been swept over the side. The icy water drained away and Schluss, gripping the rail inside the bridge screen, gasped for breath. Through the voice-pipe he spoke to Brückner the navigating officer in the control-room. '*Wieviel Fahrt machen wir* . . . what speed are we doing?'

'*Zehn Knoten, Herr Kapitän.*'

'Ten knots! Too much for this weather. Reduce to revolutions for eight knots.'

'Eight knots?' Brückner's incredulity travelled up the voice-pipe.

'Yes. Conditions are impossible up here.'

But for the darkness Willi Schluss would have seen the near frozen face of the executive officer beside him crease into a painful smile. Emil Meyer knew that Hugo Kolb in the engine-room would reduce to the revolutions ordered but later, without the captain's authority, he would slowly increase them again. Brückner – like most of the officers, he was in league with Kolb – would, as he had just done, understate the speed by a couple of knots when the captain next complained. And he certainly would complain, re-flected Meyer. He was a frightened little man. *Of course* conditions on the bridge were impossible. What did he expect them to be when a submarine drove hard into a force 7 Arctic gale. But this was war. Not a training exercise in the Baltic.

Emil Meyer knew that Schluss had set a course ten degrees farther to the southward than Brückner reported as necessary to reach *KLEBER*'s position. Brückner had objected but Schluss reprimanded him, pointing out that *Plan X* stressed the need to keep well to the southward in making the approach.

Brückner protested that the course he'd given already allowed for that. Schluss, with some sharpness, had reminded Brückner who was in command.

For his part Willi Schluss, though he suspected that his officers operated some sort of cabal against him, felt relieved though only temporarily. If he could delay the approach of the submarine sufficiently, they might not be able to reach Kleber's convoy by 1530, the time set by High Command for completion of the concentration. With luck U-0153 could still be too late for the battle.

Chief Petty Officer Barnes, *Vengeful's* coxswain and senior CPO, knocked on the open door of the first-lieutenant's cabin. The first-lieutenant looked up. 'Come in, coxswain.'

The coxswain brandished the manilla file and book he was carrying. 'Defaulters and requestmen, sir.'

'Good – or rather bad. What have we got?'

'Nothing much, sir. Mostly requestmen. A few defaulters.'

The first-lieutenant leant back in his chair and regarded the coxswain with a friendly smile. Barnes was a first-class chief-petty-officer, the most important cog in the upper deck's non-commissioned wheel, the smooth operation of which was so vital to the life of the ship.

'One awkward case, sir. AB Farley. We can stand him over until tomorrow if you wish. We'll be in harbour then.'

The first-lieutenant groaned. 'Not him again. What's he been up to this time? Peeing into a messmate's seaboot last week, wasn't it. Taken short in the night and hadn't time to make the heads.'

'Yes, sir. That's what he said.' The coxswain's expression conveyed his disbelief of Farley's defence. 'Bit more difficult this time, sir. He's come up against Petty Officer Tanner again.'

The first-lieutenant frowned. 'Petty Officer Tanner charged him last time. You don't think . . .' He hesitated. 'You don't think Tanner has it in for him, do you?'

'No, sir. Loot'nant O'Brien is Farley's divisional officer. He'll bear me out, sir. It's just Farley. Got a chip on his shoulder, sir. Looks for trouble.'

The first-lieutenant sighed. 'I expect you're right. Tanner's a good petty officer. What happened?'

'Well, sir. It begun Monday. Down in the seamen's mess-deck. Petty Officer Tanner tells Farley to get a bucket and scrubber and brighten up the mess-table.'

'Farley was cook of the mess that day, was he?'

'Yes, sir.' The coxswain shuffled the papers in the file and cleared his throat. 'Well, then, sir, Farley doesn't say anything. Just makes this objectionable noise.'

'What sort of objectionable noise, coxswain?'

'Passes wind, sir.'

'In other words, Farley farted.'

'Yes, sir.'

'But that's not an offence, coxswain.'

'The way he did was, sir. There were witnesses. Men on the messdeck. Watch below. Long and deliberate, they said it was.'

'I don't really see how anyone can decide that a fart is deliberate, coxswain. Even if it's long.'

'That's not all, sir.'

'After the first one, sir . . .' The coxswain looked pained. '. . . after that Petty Officer Tanner says, "Watch it, Farley. I'm not standing for that." Farley doesn't answer. Just lets off another long one again, sir.'

'Must have had a lot of wind stored up somewhere, coxswain.'

'Must have, sir. He does it twice more after that. Four times in all. Each time Petty Officer Tanner speaks to him. Deliberate, sir. Doesn't say a word. Just passes wind.'

The first-lieutenant was thoughtful. 'Remarkable achievement. I must talk to the doctor about it sometime. What's he charged with, coxswain?'

'Well, sir. Petty Officer Tanner laid a charge of dumb insolence.'

The first-lieutenant shook his head. 'Won't wash. I mean

114

he wasn't exactly dumb and anyway that was scrubbed from K.R. and A.I.[1] years ago. You know that, coxswain.'

'That's what I told Petty Officer Tanner, sir.'

'So what's the charge?'

The coxswain thumbed the file of papers, swaying from side to side to counter the movement of the ship. 'Conduct prejudicial to the maintenance of good order and . . .'

The end of his sentence was drowned by the action alarm bells.


## CHAPTER FIFTEEN


The echoes became blurred and faint, the extent of target grew rapidly and then faded until there was nothing. From the asdic cabinet Lofty Groves reported, 'Shoal of fish, sir.' *Vengeful*'s action alarm had turned out to be, like so many before, a false one.

Redman said, 'Resume normal sweep,' adding for the benefit of no one in particular, 'Damn and blast the bloody fish.' To the yeoman he said, 'Inform *Bluebird* that the contact was non-sub.' He turned to the first-lieutenant. 'Secure, Number One. Resume normal war cruising stations. See that all hands get a hot meal as soon as possible. We've a busy time coming.'

The first-lieutenant said, 'Aye, aye, sir,' but he thought, for God's sake – as if I hadn't already thought of that.

To Pownall, who was officer-of-the-watch, Redman said, 'She's yours, pilot. Take her back into station.'

Pownall said, 'Aye, aye, sir,' and went to the compass platform.

Redman stood at a clear-view screen gazing into the darkness ahead. Not that he could see anything, but he could think. He was nearer to exhaustion than he realised. Lack of sleep, attacks of bronchial asthma and a nagging headache were wearing him down and his thoughts were a confusion of reality and fantasy.

To get back into station *Vengeful* had to steam into the

[1] King's Regulations and Admiralty Instructions.

gale. Solid seas came over her bows and broke against the fo'c'sle breakwater and 'hedgehog', clouds of spray sweeping the bridge, the heavy elements sluicing away the snow which lay everywhere, the lighter freezing where they fell.

Redman stood with legs straddled, mittened hands on the bridge rail, steadying himself against the movement of the ship. He scarcely noticed the scream of the wind, the slap and roar of the sea, but his subconscious registered each *ping* of the asdic, every word relayed by the TBS bridge-speaker as escorts spoke to each other. It did so while odd unrelated thoughts drifted through his mind – like the fact that he'd not changed his clothes for eight days, that he was acutely conscious of the odour of his body, that a rash had developed inside his thighs – 'Captain's Crutch' they called it – that JW 137 was due at the Kola Inlet at 1000 the next morning: time now close to 1300: twenty-one hours to go. What would they bring?

Ahead of the convoy lay the Skolpen Bank and the minefield. With heavy-lidded eyes he peered into the darkness and on the screen of his mind saw fourteen U-boats driving through the gale towards the Bank. Conditions on the small bridges above their conning-towers would be appalling – worse than on *Vengeful*'s – but that would not deter them.

His thoughts switched to the enemy's signals. The German High Command in ordering U-boats to concentrate for an attack on a convoy invariably used the name of the U-boat captain who was shadowing it as a reference. Yet there had been no B-Bar signals other than the *KLEBER* weather reports. Was the weather reporter the shadower? The latest High Command signals had referred the *Gruppe Osten,* and HF/DF bearings of the fourteen U-boats acknowledging indicated that they were making for a position to the northwest of the Skolpen Bank. It was all too much for his tired mind, but he decided the weather reporter must be the shadower. Somewhere to windward, then, within ten or twelve miles, in steep seas and howling wind, hidden by darkness and blizzard, a surfaced U-boat was shadowing them. On the bridge there would be men, among them Kleber, the captain. He, too, would be peering into the darkness, but down-wind, towards the convoy, knowing that he would see nothing but impelled always to look towards

116

the sector from which the radar impulses came.

Redman moved across to the PPI and 'watched the sweep of its arm as if, among all those pips of light, he might see the shadower far to the south-west. But he knew it was not possible in that weather. Conditions for both radar and asdics, were bad, and with so much wave-clutter on the screen there would be no hope of isolating the momentary blip of a distant trimmed-down U-boat. While he watched the PPI he tussled with the insistent question . . . which Kleber? Could it be Hans? No, it couldn't, he would reassure himself. The coincidence was too remote. Then doubt would return, and with it misery.

Pownall's voice broke into his thoughts. 'We're back in station, sir.' Redman checked the display on the PPI. 'Good,' he said. 'I'm going below.'

In the sea-cabin he took off his mittens and gloves and hung them up with the night glasses, dusted frost and snow from his anorak, turned back its fur-lined hood, and lay on his bunk. His eyes focused on the lump of red ice. It was so close to his face that each time he breathed a cloud of condensation formed and drifted across it.

An old problem worried him. When should he take them?, He loathed the whole idea of using drugs to keep awake, and though the doctor recommended Benzedrine under certain conditions, Redman rarely resorted to it and then only towards the end of a journey. If one started too soon they caught up with you. Sleep couldn't be bought off indefinitely. In the end it was an account which had to be settled.

But there were fourteen U-boats ahead and there was going to be an attack on the convoy. For that he must be alert, on the top line. He made his decision. He'd take two tablets the next time he was called. He turned on his side, pulled up the damp, body odorous blankets and closed his eyes, trying to blot out the pictures which chased across his mind.

Over the years he'd found that if he was very tired it helped to shut and secure an imaginary steel screen between his eyes and his brain. The screen was a sliding one, very solid like the door of a vault. He always moved it from left to right, slowly, steadily, shutting out the images bit by bit until there was nothing but the door – then, when it was shut right across, he would screw down the cleats which secured it.

At 1300 Kleber made his second shadowing report. Like its predecessors it appeared to be a weather report. Again it included position co-ordinates in the new code. It was followed at 1315 by a conventional operational signal from High Command ordering all U-boats of *Gruppe Osten* to report their positions.

In accordance with *Plan X,* each of the seven U-boats responded by reporting its position twice, once on receipt of the High Command signal and again within the half-hour. The eight U-boats of *Gruppe Kleber* making for U-0117's position and maintaining radio silence made no report.

Once again the position of all reporting U-boats was plotted in the U-boat tracking-room at the Admiralty, in *Fidelix,* and in the HF/DF equipped escorts. The plots revealed that during the two hours which had lapsed since they'd last reported, six of the 'fourteen' U-boats making for the Skolpen Bank had already reached its north-western extremity, while eight had varying distances to go, the furthest being twenty-five miles. In those two hours the U-boats had made good an average distance of about twenty-five miles. Rather more than the Vice-Admiral had predicted, whereas the convoy's speed of advance had dropped to six knots. In *Fidelix's* operations-room this was attributed to the current in the Barents Sea setting more strongly to the west than usual.

In the U-boat tracking-room at the Admiralty there was some surprise at the time lag between some of the U-boats' responses to the High Command's request for positions since this was not normal practice. But nor was the use of weather reports for sighting and shadowing signals and both were presumed to be new procedures. The latest developments, however, confirmed the conclusion reached in *Fidelix* and at the Admiralty that *KLEBER* the weather reporter was in fact a shadower. The Vice-Admiral promptly dispatched two Home Fleet destroyers from the close screen to put *KLEBER* down for the third time that day.

The latest positions of the 'fourteen' reporting U-boats

118

caused the Vice-Admiral and his staff to revise their earlier predictions. They now estimated that by 1530 the convoy would be twenty miles from the Skolpen U-boats . . . the outer screen would then be only twelve miles from them. On the basis of these estimates the Vice-Admiral decided to order a major alteration of course to the southward at 1500 – away from the Skolpen Bank and towards the Murman coast west of the Kola Inlet – at which time he would detach the outer screen to deal with the Skolpen U-boats. This would put the enemy astern of the convoy and he had every confidence in the Fifty-Seventh Escort Group's ability to keep them down while the convoy made off to the southward. He would at the same time move the close screen of Home Fleet destroyers six miles ahead of JW 137 on its new course, to form a temporary outer screen, and re-dispose the close screen – the corvettes and frigates of the Eighty-Third Escort Group – so that most of them would be on the convoy's eastern flank, the side on which the Skolpen concentration lay.

The Vice-Admiral conveyed these intentions by TBS to the commodore of the convoy and the escort commanders. Kleber's shadowing report at 1300 – transmitted as a weather report – and the High Command's signal at 1315 were, of course, read by the U-boats of *Gruppe Kleber*, though they maintained radio silence.

The position co-ordinates in Kleber's signal, deciphered from the special code attached to *Plan X*, enabled them to determine the courses to steer and distances to go to reach him, since each knew its own position by means of cross-bearings of the German beacon stations on the Norwegian coast.

For the third time that day U-0117 had to dive under a temperature layer. This time to avoid the two Home Fleet destroyers detached to put the U-boat down. Again the area was subject to random depth-charging while U-0117 maintained the last-known course of the convoy at high submerged speed. Kleber knew that any U-boats of *Gruppe Kleber* close to him would be doing the same thing.

He surfaced again at 1415 and made off in pursuit of the convoy. Soon after 1430 Ausfeld reported contact. Kleber made a course correction to put the convoy on U-0117's port bow and reduced speed.

By 1430 three U-boats of *Gruppe Kleber* were within a mile or so of U-0117 and were themselves receiving radar impulses from the convoy's escorts. They, too, had turned on to parallel courses, keeping station abaft the beam of the convoy. Since radio silence had to be maintained, these boats were not in direct communication with each other, nor was there much likelihood of U-boat sighting U-boat in the darkness and bad weather prevailing.

By 1500 concentration was virtually complete, all but one of the boats of *Gruppe Kleber* being in touch with the convoy. The exception was U-0153, Willi Schluss's boat. Still two miles to the south of Kleber, it would have been a great deal farther but for Kolb, Meyer and Brückner who had fought, cajoled, threatened and cheated to such an extent that Schluss's efforts to delay the approach had been of little avail.

Kleber had no means of knowing if the concentration was complete, though one U-boat had been sighted close astern and visual signals had been exchanged by shaded lamp. Kleber found this comforting. He was pretty confident that other U-boats of the *Gruppe*, though hidden by darkness, were not far away.

He knew that the convoy commander would soon have to decide whether to pass north or south of the Skólpen minefield. Both contingencies had been provided for. The U-boats in *Gruppe Kleber* would remain in their present position relative to the convoy if it went north of the minefield, and they would in that event be reinforced by *Gruppe Osten*.

If the convoy went south it would be turning towards Kleber, and his *Gruppe,* up-wind of the convoy and on its starboard bow, would be in an ideal attacking position. *Plan X* was based on the probability that the convoy *would* go south of the minefield to avoid *Gruppe Osten* whose boats had been making their presence known to the enemy by reporting their 'fourteen' positions to High Command and by direct radio chatter to each other since 1430.

Soon after 1510 the voice-pipe buzzer sounded on U-0117's bridge. It was Ausfeld. 'Radar impulses increasing in strength, bearing changing from left to right. Already we hear language messages in English between the convoy and the escort force.'

'Good, Ausfeld. Can you make anything of them?'

'They use many code words but it seems they make a major alteration of course towards us.' Ausfeld spoke good English.

'*Ausgezeichnet. Sie gingen in die Falle* . . . splendid. They walk into the trap.' Kleber slapped his thigh and excitement showed through his normal composure. 'Let me have frequent reports.'

'I will, *Herr Kapitän*.'

A few minutes later Ausfeld reported, 'Signals still gaining in strength. The convoy has evidently altered to the south. The bearing moves steadily from left to right. Estimated range eighteen thousand metres. Closing fast.'

Kleber immediately altered U-0117's course to intercept. He would approach the convoy on its up-wind flank. The starboard columns would come under attack first and because of the diversion caused by the Skolpen concentration he expected to find few escorts to starboard. The remainder of his *Gruppe*, familiar with *Plan X*, would, he knew, be reacting in the same way to the radar signals coming into their search-receivers. Telling Rathfelder that he would be back soon, Kleber handed over the bridge watch and went down to the control-room.

Dieter Leuner, the navigating officer, had plotted the estimated position of JW 137 on its new southerly course. Kleber looked at the chart. 'So the convoy has altered course perhaps ninety degrees or more to starboard.'

'Yes, *Herr Kapitän*. If we maintain our present course we pass ahead of it.'

'Give me a course for interception. Assume the convoy to be steering south. Speed seven knots. We make twelve knots.'

Leuner set the factors on an inclination diagram and read off the answer. 'We should steer zero-nine-five degrees, *Herr Kapitän*.' He paused, measured, made a rapid calculation on a note-pad. 'We should meet the advance escorts in approximately twenty minutes. The convoy itself about twenty to twenty-five minutes later.'

Kleber's eyes were bright with the excitement of danger. 'Good,' he said. 'Alter course now to zero-nine-five.' The navigating officer gave the order to the helmsman. Kleber called Ausfeld on the voice-pipe. 'What is the range and bearing?'

'Fifteen thousand five hundred, *Herr Kapitän*. But . . .' Ausfeld hesitated.

'But what?' urged Kleber.

'The signals are confused. Those that were nearest before the alteration of course are receding. Others which were farthest gain in strength. They cover a wide sector.'

Kleber said, 'They must be redeploying the escorts. Detaching the outer screen to attack *Gruppe Osten.*' He laughed gaily. 'That is *Plan X*, Ausfeld.' He quoted in scholarly overtones: *'It will be the duty of Gruppe Osten to create a diversion with the object of diluting the escort force prior to the main attack down-wind* . . . I go now to the bridge. Let me know when the range is twelve thousand metres. Then we make the attack signal.'

Back on the bridge Kleber concentrated his faculties on a mental picture of the convoy ahead shrouded in darkness. He was barely conscious of the steep seas before which U-0117 ran, slithering and surging like a surf-rider; of the sting of sleet and snow driven by the wind; of the frost which numbed the flesh of his face outside its mask; of the buffeting of icy seas which flooded the small bridge, at times forcing its occupants to grip the rail and hold on for dear life or, losing their foothold, to rely on the steel belts which secured them to the superstructure.

The buzzer sounded again. 'Estimated range of nearest signals twelve thousand metres, *Herr Kapitän,*' reported Ausfeld.

'Right. Transmit at once the shadowing report. Leuner has it ready. Conclude the message with "*KLEBER* closing down. Repeat *KLEBER* closing down – 12,000. Time of origin 1527".'

On receipt of this signal the U-boats of *Gruppe Kleber* knew that Kleber had dived and within minutes of its transmission they, too, had done so.

# CHAPTER SIXTEEN

At a depth of one hundred and fifty metres, electric motors, ventilating fans and other auxiliary machinery humming in mechanical harmony, U-0117 moved along the course given by Dieter Leuner for interception of the convoy.

Immediately after the dive Kleber ordered the crew to action stations. Rathfelder reported bow and stern tubes ready for firing. Leuner went to the attack-computer in the conning-tower where the submarine's course and speed, the convoy's estimated course and speed and other data were fed in and the torpedo-firing angles computed.

There was an atmosphere of hushed expectancy in U-0117. The imminence of action, the knowledge that British escorts were notoriously efficient in dealing with U-boats, contributed to the fear and apprehension of the submarine's crew. With taut faces the men in the control-room watched their instruments under the keen eyes of Rathfelder and Heuser the engineer-officer.

Faces dark with anti-frost grease, eye-masks pushed up on foreheads, rubber diving suits still wet and glistening, Kleber, Rathfelder and the bridge dutymen were ready for their return to the bridge when the submarine surfaced. All knew that this was the crucial phase of the attack. Would U-0117 pass under the outer screen of destroyers undetected? Was the thermal layer beneath which the boat was moving sufficiently dense to deflect the asdic beams of the escorts? Were the other eight U-boats of *Gruppe Osten* in position?

The control-room's muted lighting ensured that the vision of those who went to the bridge would not be impaired on surfacing. Now it dissembled into Dantesque patterns of light and shade the faces of the men and the complex of instruments and controls which they watched.

The atmosphere was fetid with odours of diesel oil, decaying food, sodden clothing, human bodies, and a faint trace of chlorine gas from the battery compartments below the control-room. Gas leaks caused by depth-charge damage on her last patrols were supposed to have been made good during U-0117's last refit in Trondheim, but the turn round had been a quick one and the workmanship less than thorough.

Ausfeld's voice broke the silence in the control-room. 'Destroyer propeller noises ahead, red zero-two-zero to green zero-four-five. Low volume. Estimated range three thousand metres, closing steadily. No sound of asdic transmissions.'

Kleber replied, 'Good. The thermal does its duty.' He turned to smile at Rathfelder and Heuser. The men in the control-room must see that he was not worried though he shared the fears which assailed them. Perhaps in greater degree. While the men had infinite faith in his skill and judgment, he knew better than anyone else the chances U-0117 was taking – and his own limitations.

'Not long now,' he said in a low voice . . . '*Dann begint der Spass* . . . then the fun starts.'

Reports from the sound-room told of the shrinking distance between the submarine and the destroyer screen. The approach of danger made mouths dry, muscles taut, eyes blink. Some men coughed, others clenched their teeth, bit on their lips or tapped with nervous fingers. Voices were lowered when reporting and men held their breath as if to aid the submarine's concealment.

At most there were now eight minutes before the destroyers reached U-0117.

Three questions nagged at Kleber. Would the temperature layer sufficiently mask them? Would the convoy alter course at the last moment and so confound the attack? How many of the *Gruppe* were ready and in position? At least, he consoled himself, I shall soon know.

When Ausfeld reported the range down to 2000 metres, Kleber turned to Heuser. 'Rig for silent running. Fifty revolutions port and starboard engines. Strict silence throughout the boat.'

All ventilating fans, pump motors and other auxiliary machinery were stopped, and instruments not immediately needed were switched off. While thermal layers could deflect asdic beams they could not mask every sound in a U-boat. Now all that could be heard in U-0117 was the almost inaudible hum of the electric motors turning at slow speed, and Heuser's low key orders to the planesmen as he watched the depth gauges.

The absence of asdic *pings* indicated that the sonic beams

124

were bouncing off the temperature layer but, despite the thermal, Ausfeld's hushed report, 'Range five hundred metres,' was followed not long afterwards by the faint *shush-shush-shush* of churning propellers.

'Destroyer propeller noises passing overhead. Close to port.' Ausfeld's deep voice was muted. 'Bearing moving ahead. Range opening.'

Men bent their heads as if to avoid the destroyer above, prayed or swore under their breath and later sighed with relief as the muffled thrashing grew fainter.

'We're through the outer screen,' said Kleber. 'Another five or six miles to the close escorts and the convoy.'

Rathfelder said, 'I hope the other boats of the *Gruppe* are as lucky as U-0117, *Herr Kapitän.*'

'Not luck, Rathfelder.' Kleber's retort was sharp. 'Skill and guts.' He paused. 'But I'll grant you the weather is on our side.' Then he laughed to show the incident was forgotten. The men in the control-room silently thanked God for Kleber.

The ventilating fans were switched on and the hum of the electric motors reached a higher pitch as speed was increased. Twenty long drawn-out minutes – seeming to some like twenty hours – ticked away on the control-room clock before Ausfeld made the report Kleber had long awaited. 'Numerous propeller noises ahead and to starboard. Reciprocating engines. Spread over a wide sector. Estimated range three thousand metres.'

'The convoy,' said Kleber without emotion. 'It has not altered course. We come in on its starboard flank.' He added, 'In about seven minutes we go under the close escorts.' He turned to Rathfelder. 'Pass that message to all compartments and stand by for surfacing.'

'Jahwol, *Herr Kapitän.*'

As the minutes drifted away, Kleber focused his thoughts on the coming attack. Somewhere, not far away, were the other eight U-boats of *Gruppe Kleber*. The absence of reports of depth-charge explosions from the sound-room – they could be heard at considerable distances – was an assurance that no U-boat had yet been attacked. He prayed that meant all had safely penetrated the outer screen.

'Range one thousand metres, *Herr Kapitän.*'

Again all ventilating fans, ballast and bilge pumps were

shut off, speed was reduced to a bare minimum, and silent running was ordered. Once more the *shush-shush-shush* of propeller noises could be heard, this time against the faint but insistent background of a host of others. Kleber took a last look at the clock over the chart-table before moving to the periscope well. With steep seas and a blizzard superimposed on Arctic darkness he did not expect to see anything, but the superb Zeiss lenses would pick up the bow-wave of a ship nearby, and any illumination, however slight, from the convoy. A quick sweep round with the periscope was a precaution he could not omit.

'Bring her to periscope depth, chief,' he ordered. 'I know it will be difficult to hold her there in this weather but do your best. And raise the *schnorchel* mast. I want to surface at maximum speed.' To Rathfelder he said, 'Stand by all tubes.'

Orders were passed to the engine-room, to the men manning the hydrophones and valve controls. There was the hiss of escaping air as tanks were blown, the submarine took on a pronounced bows-up angle, and the readings on the depth-gauges dropped steadily as she made for the surface.

'All tubes ready for firing, *Herr Kapitän*,' reported Rathfelder.

The men in the control-room waited for the crucial report, each busy with his own thoughts and fears. Soon Heuser reported. 'Periscope depth, *Herr Kapitän*. Schnorchel mast hoisted.' The submarine began to pitch and roll as she neared the turbulent surface water.

Kleber ordered, 'Up periscope.'

An electric motor purred, the periscope came up from its well, Kleber knelt to meet it, snapping down the handles and rising with the instrument, his eyes pressed to the lens apertures. The deep roar of the diesels starting filled the boat, and welcome gusts of fresh air blew into the control-room through the *Schnorchel* vents.

There was a radar antenna on the *Schnorchel* and Ausfeld's report 'Radar impulses on all sectors – maximum strength,' was no surprise to Kleber. U-0117 had got through the escort cordon. Heuser was having difficulty in holding trim as the submarine felt the effects of the steep seas above her. Bracing himself against the boat's sudden gyrations, Kleber swung the periscope through three hundred and sixty degrees. There was nothing to see but the white blur of wave crests sweeping out of the darkness astern. The waves masked the periscope at times, shutting the float on the *Schnorchel* and creating a sudden vacuum which made men gasp for breath until the sea had passed and the float lifted to open the air intakes once more.

'Stand by to surface,' Kleber's barked command concealed much tension. 'Blow main ballast tanks. Stand by all tubes for firing.'

Ulrich Heuser repeated the orders. Once more there came the high pitched hiss of air forcing its way into flooded tanks. Soon afterwards Heuser reported, 'Bridge clear, *Herr Kapitän.*'

Kleber said, 'Both engines full ahead together. Give us everything she's got.'

Rathfelder released the clips on the conning-tower hatch as Kleber slipped on goggles, face mask and mittens and hurried up the steel ladder. Rathfelder and the bridge duty-men followed close behind.

The icy blast of the wind, the sting of sleet and snow struck them as they reached the bridge and clipped on their safety belts. The thunder of the diesels was challenged now by the roar of the wind and the seas surging past the conning-tower, their crests flooding the small bridge from time to time. U-0117 was driving down-wind, slicing through steep seas, the now moderate south-westerly gale astern.

From the sound-room came Ausfeld's urgent report. 'Numerous radar transmissions to port and starboard. Maximum strength.'

Kleber raised the Zeiss night glasses and swung them in a wide arc looking for a break in the wall of darkness. He picked up a white bow-wave as an excited shout came from a lookout. 'Ship close ahead to starboard.' It was less than three hundred metres away. In the submarine the crew could hear the drumming of countless propellers. It was an ominous sound, increasing steadily in volume.

Redman was on *Vengeful*'s bridge at 1440 when the bridge-speaker relayed the Vice-Admiral's signal ordering the convoy to prepare for a ninety-degree wheel to starboard to a course of 210 degrees, the Fifty-Seventh Escort Group to proceed with dispatch to the eastward to attack the concentration of U-boats on the north-western rim of the Skolpen Bank, while the Home Fleet destroyers moved up from their fighting stations to form the new outer screen. The signal concluded with an order to the close escort, the Eighty-Third Group, to place six of its eight ships on the port flank of JW 137 on which side the attack was expected.

At 1500 the flagship ordered execution of the signal. The convoy immediately commenced its wheel to starboard, the corvettes and frigates of the close screen proceeded to their new stations, while the Home Fleet destroyers moved up at speed through rough seas to form the outer screen in place of the Fifty-Seventh Escort Group now making for the U-boats off the Skolpen Bank. The nearest of these was estimated to be within twenty to twenty-five miles.

By 1530 the Twenty-Seventh Escort Group was in radar contact with U-boats at an initial range of eight thousand yards which, under the weather conditions prevailing, was no worse than expected.

At from four to five thousand yards, the targets disappeared from radar screens and it was evident they had dived. The escorts then carried out an A/S search in the course of which *Vectis* and *Bluebird* obtained firm asdic contact with a U-boat close to the Bank where shoaling water had failed to provide a temperature layer. After a short sharp hunt with intensive depth-charging the U-boat was blown to the surface. It dived again almost immediately, only to be caught squarely in the centre of a shallow pattern dropped by *Vectis*. The U-boat's bows lifted high above the surface before it sank stern first. There were no survivors.

Soon afterwards the destroyer *Whippet* reported an asdic contact and was joined by the sloop *Chaffinch*. While making her run-in to depth-charge the U-boat, *Chaffinch*'s stern was blown off by a *gnat* torpedo. The sloop sank rapidly and with heavy loss of life. *Vengeful* – contrary to standing orders, and explicit instructions at the convoy conference in Loch Ewe – stopped to pick up survivors.

*Whippet* held on to the asdic contact, and *Vallance* was ordered to join her. The captain of *Vallance* decided on his own initiative to cease asdic and radar transmissions and close *Whippet* at comparatively low speed. This sneak tactic soon paid a dividend. *Vallance*, keeping an asdic listening watch, picked up strong HE,[1] classified it as U-boat propeller noises, and steamed up the bearing until she almost stumbled over the submarine which, aware that her *gnat* had sunk an attacking ship, was surfacing to make up-wind in pursuit of the convoy. The U-boat surfaced two cables ahead of *Vallance,* fine on her starboard bow, and was caught and held in the destroyer's searchlight.

The submarine crash-dived, turning sharply to port, but *Vallance* was on to her like a terrier after a rat. Swinging to port the destroyer fired her 'hedgehog' before the U-boat had time to go deep. The pattern of mortar charges plummeted into the water into which the submarine's bows were turning.

Seconds later three detonations in quick succession left little doubt that mortal damage had been inflicted. This was confirmed not long afterwards by sounds on *Vallance*'s bridge-speaker of the U-boat breaking up.

At 1615 an urgent signal from *Fidelix* ordered all but two ships of the Fifty-Seventh Escort Group to rejoin at once as the convoy was under attack from surfaced U-boats which had come in down-wind on its lightly defended starboard flank.

Two ships of the Group were left to deal with any U-boats of the Skolpen concentration which might attempt to surface. On Ginger Mountsey's orders both streamed '*foxers*' as a protection against *gnats*.

The remainder of the Group made off to the south-west, steaming into wind and sea at fourteen knots which was all they could manage without incurring weather damage.

*Vengeful,* delayed by her attempts to rescue survivors from *Chaffinch,* brought up the rear. She had picked up fifteen men, but of these a number had died soon after being taken from the water.

[1] HE – Hydrophone effect. The sound of propellers as heard on hydrophones.

# CHAPTER SEVENTEEN

The bow-wave sighted by U-0117 less than three hundred metres from the submarine turned out to be that of a Liberty ship, thus confirming Ausfeld's report that the nearest propeller noises were slow revving piston engines.

Kleber swung hard to port to avoid the oncoming ship. The suddenness of the confrontation, the scuffle to avoid it, ruled out a torpedo shot. Running on opposite courses, the freighter and the U-boat quickly passed each other at a range of less than two hundred metres. There was no indication that the U-boat, trimmed down in the darkness and travelling at high speed, had been sighted.

Kleber shouted to Rathfelder, 'Too late. We'll run down between the columns. Fire one torpedo at each ship, port and starboard alternately. Then we'll dive and re-load.'

Slithering and plunging through watery hills and valleys, driving down-wind, the crests of seas washing the bridge, Kleber felt a strange exultation as flurries of sleet and snow masked the scene, clearing at times like a curtain drawn back across a darkened stage, replacing the anonymity of darkness with the shadowy outlines of ships.

With his night glasses Kleber saw to port the white flash of a sea breaking, behind it the dim outline of a ship. He shouted urgently, 'Target red, zero-two-zero.' Rathfelder swung the TBT[1] on to the bearing. 'I have it,' he answered as the dark shadow plunged steadily forward, its bows throwing up sheets of spray.

Events moved fast after that, Rathfelder passing the TBT bearings to Dieter Leuner in the conning-tower, getting back the target's course and speed and other vital information. Watching the angle on the bow open steadily, Kleber called, 'Stand by to fire.' The seconds went by. 'Shoot now,' he commanded.

[1]TBT – Target Bearing Transmitter. An instrument on the bridge of a U-boat used during surface attacks. It transmitted the bearing of the target to the attack-computer in the conning-tower, a device into which data was fed to enable automatic solution of the torpedo firing problem.

Rathfelder pulled the TBT safety lever to 'on'. 'Tube one, fire!' he shouted down the voice-pipe.

Time seemed to stand still as they watched the amorphous shadow of the target pass up the port side. There was a blinding flash, terrifying in its scale and suddenness, and a column of flame and smoke mushroomed into the sky. The shock wave struck Kleber in the face as the roar of the explosion rolled across the water. Falling snowflakes, hanging like curtains of coarse muslin, made the scene strangely unreal.

'Ammunition ship,' he said, ordering a correction of course to bring the submarine over to starboard.

Rathfelder swung the TBT to starboard, ready for a new target. They heard the rumble of what sounded like distant thunder and far away to port flames licked into the sky, the gale sweeping them down-wind. Another U-boat in *Gruppe Kleber* had found a target.

Suddenly, from every quarter, *Snowflake* rockets soared skywards, bursting at their zenith, scattering brilliant showers of light. Above the noise of wind and sea the men on U-0117's bridge heard the explosive thunder of gunfire. Flares filled the sky over the convoy and drifted down-wind, slowly losing height, conspiring with the rockets to turn night into day.

'*Herrgott! Lösden sie die verfluchten Lichter aus* . . . Christ! Turn off the bloody lights,' mocked Kleber. But he felt naked and afraid, and the men on the submarine's bridge bent lower as if hiding from a celestial observer.

Busy conning the boat into position for its next target, Kleber had a fleeting impression of long, widespread convoy columns; of the silhouette of a frigate astern of U-0117 turning towards them, a sea breaking over her as she came beam on to the weather; of brightly coloured balls of tracer approaching from many directions; of the rumble of gunfire and fountains of water leaping unaccountably from the sea around the U-boat. But trimmed well down, fast moving, hidden by steep seas and flying spray, U-0117 was a difficult target, particularly for guns on the pitching sterns of merchant ships.

To Kleber it was a wild scene, a sort of maritime ride of the Valkyries. Though his faculties were concentrated on the attack, he was aware of a strange euphoria, of man control-

131

ling the elements, of fighting in a hopeless cause yet fulfilling some strange Wagnerian destiny. He was too intelligent not to realise that Germany had already lost the war, but there was in him a curious mixture of resolution and romanticism, a liking for the knife-edge of danger, and he would not have chosen to be elsewhere. These emotive thoughts were soon swept aside by the urgencies of battle as a Liberty ship, ghost-like in the flares, showed up on the starboard bow and Rathfelder refocused the TBT. A rapid exchange of information between bridge and attack-computer was followed by Kleber's. 'Shoot as soon as you're ready.'

The Liberty ship and U-0117 were approaching each other on parallel courses at a combined speed of twenty knots, the bearing changing rapidly.

'Tube two – fire!' shouted Rathfelder. The submarine shuddered as the torpedo left its tube. The men on the bridge counted away the seconds, watching the plunging ship, waiting for the explosion. But none came. The magnetic pistol had failed or the wallowing of the submarine through rolling seas had upset Rathfelder's aim.

Kleber swore under his breath as more *Snowflake* rockets and starshell relit the waning sky. A lookout shouted, 'Warship bearing red, one-five-zero. Approaching.'

Kleber swung round to see a corvette outside the port wing column heading towards them. Bright flashes leapt from her forward gun. The shell splashes came suddenly closer. He said, 'She can't overtake us in this weather, Rathfelder. *Wahlen sie das nächste Ziel* . . . Select next target.'

There was no trace in his voice of the excitement he felt and this apparent nonchalance reassured the executive officer who'd decided that things were getting a bit too hot. He swung the TBT to port as the submarine's bow went that way and soon found a ship, darkly silhouetted against a low flare, smoke billowing from her funnel as she worked up the pressure in her boilers. The submarine rose on the crest of a following sea and Kleber took a precautionary look astern. The corvette was belting down-wind in pursuit, firing as she came. He was aware that a trim-downed submarine was a difficult target in heavy weather, but nevertheless disliked being the target. 'Hold everything, Rathfelder,' he called. 'We'll cut through the starboard column. Plenty of targets on the other side. And we'll be shielded from that damned corvette for a while.' The whine of a shell broke into his sentence. There was a sharp explosion close astern followed by the smell of cordite. Water cascaded on to the bridge. 'The escorts are beginning to wake up.' The note of gaiety in Kleber's voice masked his concern. 'We haven't much time.'

U-0117 swung across to starboard, passing close ahead of a merchant ship in the second column. Kleber altered course again to drive down between the second and third columns.

Ausfeld reported, 'Heavy depth-charging, starboard sector. Distant.' So one of the *Gruppe* at least had been forced to submerge, reflected Kleber. There wasn't time to speculate which it might be. He just hoped that whoever it was had gone deep enough in time, and found a good thermal. From far away came the sound of another explosion followed by a bright flash of light. Rolling billows of smoke and flame came from somewhere near the centre of the convoy. One of the *Gruppe* must have torpedoed a tanker.

A shell from a merchant ship's stern gun burst uncomfortably close to U-0117.

'*Verdammt!*' shouted Kleber above the hubbub of wind, sea and gunfire. He turned to see Rathfelder focusing the TBT on a ship in the starboard column. 'Shoot, Rathfelder,' he commanded. 'For Christ's sake, man, shoot. We can't hold this course much longer . . .' The end of his sentence was drowned by the executive officer's. 'Tube three, fire!'

Kleber looked astern and against the backdrop of starshell and *Snowflake* saw the bows of the pursuing corvette emerge from the port column. He knew that under those weather conditions the corvette would be hard put to it to gain on U-0117 which was travelling at fourteen knots, but he didn't like to be the target for her gunfire. The night was too brilliantly lit.

He altered course to starboard to pass astern of the ship at which they had just fired. Soon afterwards there was a rumbling explosion and a flash of light leapt from the freighter which had now drawn abeam. Kleber had no time to speculate on its cargo but he patted the executive officer's shoulder. 'Fine work, Rathfelder. Stand by for a target to port as soon as we've got through this column.' Another shell whined overhead and burst fifty metres or so from the submarine, while lines of oerlikon tracer converged on the conning-tower splattering the sea around it. But U-0117 was a fast-moving target, sheltered by the crests and valleys of seas through which she lurched and slithered, hidden from time to time by sheets of spray. To Kleber, keyed to the exigencies of the moment, revelling in the fast-moving action, it seemed as if his boat bore a charmed life.

As they passed ahead of the Liberty ship next in line, Rathfelder trained the TBT on to its bows now barely two hundred metres away. At that moment a lookout shouted, 'Warship on the starboard bow. Approaching fast.' Kleber, who'd been watching the Liberty ship as the submarine crossed its bows and turned to port, swung round to see a frigate coming up from astern of the convoy, heading for them and firing as it came. Its unpleasantly accurate gunfire caused fountains of water to erupt close astern of U-0117, the wind sweeping their spray across the bridge.

He steadied the submarine on a course to take it down close to the remaining merchant ships in the port column. Not only would this inhibit the frigate's gunnery but it would give Rathfelder a point blank shot for his next torpedo. But time was the critical factor. With the U-boat and merchant ship steaming on opposing courses, the bearing was changing so fast that only seconds were left.

'Shoot, Rathfelder, shoot,' yelled Kleber. 'We must dive now.'

The executive officer had never moved his head from the eye-pieces of the TBT which, notwithstanding the violent motion, he'd kept on the target ship throughout the submarine's ninety-degree turn to port. During this time he was passing rapidly changing ranges and bearings to Dieter Leuner in the conning-tower.

'Jahwol, Herr Kapitän,' he gasped, through a mouthful of spray as he pulled the TBT's safety lever to 'on'. To Kleber's relief there followed immediately the sharp order, 'Tube four, fire!'

Kleber felt the submarine jar and tremble as the torpedo left its tube. He decided the frigate was too far for a *gnat* which would have homed on to the propeller of the nearest merchant ship – the one they'd just attacked – so resisted the temptation.

Pressing the diving klaxon he shouted into the voice-pipe,

134

'Emergency dive. *Auf tiefe gehen* ﹒ ﹒ ﹒ take her down fast, chief.'

The alarm was still sounding when Kleber followed Rathfelder and the lookouts through the upper hatch. He slammed it shut behind him and secured the clips, then raced down the ladder into the control-room, shutting and securing the lower hatch. As he did so U-0117 was shaken by an explosion, its reverberations audiblè in the control-room. Ausfeld, imperturbable as ever, reported, 'Heavy explosion to port. Our last target. Probably an ammunition ship.'

'*Ausgezeichnet* . . . splendid!' Kleber had removed his mask and the blue eyes in the heavily greased face shone with exultation. He turned to the executive officer, slapping him on the back of his dripping diving suit, 'Well done, Rathfelder.' The young man began to say something but Kleber interrupted. 'Port twenty. We'll get under the convoy column. Disturbed water there will hide us until we find a thermal.'

U-0117 was held in a steep dive until Ausfeld reported that *pings* could no longer be heard. Kleber knew then that the submarine was under a temperature layer and he told Heuser to level off. Thereafter U-0117 turned back on to the convoy's course, following at four knots while fresh torpedoes were loaded into the tubes.

Later, when that task was completed, they would surface and attempt once more to regain the up-wind position. Kleber realised that everything would be more difficult next time. The element of surprise had gone, the escorts knew now where the attack had come from. They would be redeploying, the area would be combed, and it would not be easy for a U-boat to surface anywhere near the convoy.

U-0117's attack, from the moment of surfacing to that of diving, had occupied less than seven minutes. Kleber was well satisfied with what his boat had achieved in that time. He wondered what success the other boats of *Gruppe Kleber* had had, and how those of *Gruppe Osten* had fared on the Skolpen Bank.

Receipt of Kleber's 1527 shadowing report with its *KLEBER CLOSING DOWN* repeated twice, followed by 12,000, was for Willi Schluss traumatic. It meant that Kleber had dived, the attack had begun.

Schluss and his officers knew that *Plan X* required them to dive at approximately the distance from the convoy's outer screen ordered by Kleber and the 1527 signal had set that at 12,000 metres. To dive earlier would delay the attack, to do so later invited the risk of discovery by radar.

Schluss and his officers were also aware that U-0153 was two miles astern of Kleber, making good fourteen knots with a following wind and sea. Allowing the escorts six to seven knots, the combined speed of approach was twenty to twenty-one knots. U-0153 would be within 12,000 metres of the outer screen in about six minutes. With this knowledge Willi Schluss's bowels contracted into a cold and painful knot. He pressed the diving alarm, his lips trembled and he shivered. 'Take her down, Kolb. One-fifty metres. Make it a fast dive.' The alarm bell's urgent clamour sounded throughout the boat.

'Sound-room reports escorts' range sixteen thousand metres.' Kolb's voice was surly, obdurate. 'Our orders are to dive at twelve thousand metres.'

'How dare you argue with me, *Herr Ingenieur*! Carry out my orders at once.' The tremor in Willi Schluss's voice undid his attempt to assert authority.

Kolb was not impressed. 'It is our duty to obey Kapitän-leutnant Kleber's orders. He leads the attack.'

'Kolb is right, *Herr Kapitän*.' Gerhardt Meyer shouted into Schluss's ear, determined to make himself heard above the noise of wind and sea. 'If we dive now we destroy the co-ordination of the attack.'

Next it was Adolf Brückner at the attack-computer. 'We dive two miles too soon, *Herr Kapitän*? Is it your intention not to attack?' The voice-pipe amplified the sarcasm.

Confused, indignant, afraid, Willi Schluss realised that he was confronted with a sort of mutiny. What could he do about it? What sympathy could he expect from a court-martial? His officers would testify – correctly, he was bound to admit – that he had been reluctant to close the enemy; that he had disregarded Kleber's orders to commence the attack. What defence could he offer? The truth? That he *was* afraid. That he wanted to get U-0153 back to Trondheim in one piece. Not only for himself but for the fifty officers and men under his command. That he did not want them, or himself, to die for a mythical cause devised by a mad fuehrer who'd already lost the war and brought misery, death and

136

destruction to millions of people. What German court-martial would swallow that?

While these muddled, slightly hysterical thoughts occupied his mind he did nothing. He was too shocked. His diving order had been disregarded. Neither Gerhardt Meyer nor the other men on the bridge had moved in response to the diving alarm. U-0153 was still on the surface, plunging through the seas, the bridge flooded, the cold cutting into his bones despite the woollens beneath the diving suit.

It *is* mutiny, he kept repeating to himself. They are refusing to dive. They must be mad. Do they want to die? For what? In Christ's name, for what?

Furious, perplexed, above all terrified, Schluss looked into the gloomy darkness, biting his lips, holding back welling tears, the wind driving snow and sleet into his back, building it into frosted lumps which fell off as he moved.

The minutes passed and his thoughts became more confused. He felt an almost overwhelming desire to scream. He was about to indulge it when there was another call on the voice-pipe. It was Adolf Brückner. 'Sound-room reports distant propeller and radar impulses ahead and to starboard. Estimated range twelve thousand metres.'

Next it was Kolb on the voice-pipe. 'We are ready to dive, *Herr Kapitän.*'

Humiliated, emotionally exhausted, Willi Schluss again pressed the diving-alarm.

Long before Kleber's signal ordering the attack to begin, Schluss had given orders that the tubes of U-0153 were to be loaded with LUT torpedoes. These were designed to run in loops threading the convoy columns and thus giving a U-boat a chance to secure a hit without aiming at a specific ship. They had the advantage that they could be fired at a convoy from a distance and since selection of individual ships as targets was unnecessary they could be fired quickly. They were, however, unsuitable for use in a 'wolf-pack' attack where submarines penetrated the escort screen and ran between the convoy columns. There was always the danger that a LUT might torpedo another U-boat.

Meyer, Kolb and Brückner had so strenuously objected to the use of LUT torpedoes – emphasising their limitations and dangers and pointing out that *Plan X* did not envisage their use – that Willi Schluss had reluctantly given in. The tubes had been loaded with conventional torpedoes, but for the *gnats* in the stern tube.

Apart from fear, which was his overriding emotion, Schluss's mind, as U-0153 made her submerged approach, was occupied with the problem of how to get rid of those torpedoes quickly, so that the critically dangerous time on the surface between convoy columns could be reduced to a minimum.

One thing was certain. He would have to man the TBT himself. Not leave it to Gerhardt Meyer the executive officer. Fortunately it was by custom a U-boat captain's prerogative to do this if he chose. It was fortunate, too, that on surfacing the captain had to be the first man on the bridge.

As the escorts of the outer screen were heard to pass over, and those in U-0153 settled down to the unnerving wait for the convoy itself, Willi Schluss died many deaths, and these were multiplied many times as the *shush-shush-shush* of approaching propellers could be heard with the naked ear. At last the awful moment came. There was no avoiding it. Schluss gave the order to surface. When Kolb reported, 'Bridge clear,' Schluss clawed his way up the ladders through the conning-tower hatches and made for the TBT. But having reached it he hesitated, numbed by what he saw. U-0153 had surfaced between two columns of the convoy. The attack was at its height. Night had become day. Starshell flares hung everywhere in the sky. *Snowflake* rockets burst in all directions scattering their illuminants, brightly coloured lines of tracer drew criss-cross patterns over the sea. Two ships were burning fiercely, their flames licking into rolling billows of black smoke. Above the wind he could hear the sound of gunfire. Shell spashes leapt from the water around the bridge. With sudden terror he saw a destroyer making for U-0153. It was about 3000 metres astern. The orange flashes from its forward guns left him in no doubt as to its target.

Schluss abandoned any idea of using the TBT. 'Tubes one to four stand by for fan shots on both bows – spread ten degrees,' he shrieked into the voice-pipe. He paused, breathing heavily, letting the minimum of time pass, then shouted, 'Fire one – fire four – fire two – fire three.'

He looked up, holding on to the TBT, twisting his head to see astern. The destroyer seemed closer, the orange gun flashes larger, more menacing. Fountains of water cascaded on to the bridge. He felt the shock and heat of shell explosions. 'Fire five!' he screamed. This was the stern-tube loaded with a *gnat,* the acoustic torpedo designed to home on a pursuer's propellers. He intended it for the destroyer.

U-0153 shook as the torpedoes left her tubes. When the last had gone Willi Schluss pressed the diving-alarm. '*Auf tiefe gehen* . . . take her down fast, Kolb. We've fired the *gnat* and there's a destroyer astern.' It was more a cry for help than a command.

This time there was no argument. Gerhardt Meyer could see the destroyer astern. It wasn't quite as close as the captain had made out, but the *gnat* already fired from the stern-tube would home on U-0153's propellers if she didn't dive immediately. Meyer and the lookouts went quickly down the steel ladders which led through the conning-tower to the control-room, Willi Schluss close on their heels.

## CHAPTER EIGHTEEN

After the hurried firing of her torpedoes, U-0153 dived to one hundred and fifty metres, Schluss altering course to starboard. He did this to get away from the diving position which the pursuing destroyer would depth-charge, and to get under a convoy column where the propeller noises of merchant ships and their turbulent wakes would protect the submarine.

At one hundred and fifty metres U-0153 levelled off and Schluss ordered 'silent running'. Soon afterwards the U-boat was shaken by a series of depth-charge explosions to port. The hammer effect of a twenty-six-charge pattern made her reel and pitch, the hull whipping and straining, the glass on gauges breaking and the lights in the control-room failing. The emergency lighting came on. The faces of the men were strained as they stared bright-eyed at their instruments. When they looked up it was not at Willi Schluss but at Meyer, Kolb and Brückner, the officers in whom they pinned their shaken faith.

There came a cry from the after-end of the control-room,

'Fire in the sound-room.' Hahn came in at a run, snatched a fire extinguisher from its rack and ran back. Acrid smoke fumes drifted into the control-room. There was the smell of burning rubber. Willi Schluss shouted, 'For God's sake, Meyer, go and help Hahn. *Schnell, Mann, schnell.*' By the end of the sentence his voice had broken. Meyer looked at him with contempt, took an extinguisher from the rack, and made for the sound-room.

Before long Hahn and Meyer were back, Hahn's eyes red and streaming, his hair dishevelled. Meyer returned the unused fire-extinguisher to the rack.

'The fire is out, *Herr Kapitän.*' Hahn's breathing was distressed.

'Thank God. What is the damage?'

'Burnt out armature on the motor which drives the hydrophones training gear.' He paused, panting. 'Also, in consequence, an electric fire has damaged some of the leads.'

'The depth-charging?' said Schluss.

'No, *Herr Kapitän.* Bad workmanship in Trondheim. Possibly sabotage. A new armature was fitted there.'

'Can you repair the damage?'

The underlying note of optimism in Schluss's voice arose from his hope that the answer might be 'no'. It would provide a splendid excuse for withdrawing from the attack.

Kolb, standing behind Schluss, answered the question. 'It *can* be repaired. We will take an armature from a fan motor to replace the damaged one.'

Schluss's heart sank. 'Will that take long?' He would like to have added, 'Don't hurry. Take your time. The longer the better.'

Hahn said, 'Not too long.'

Schluss looked uncertainly from Hahn to Kolb. 'Bad business that.' He coughed. 'But you made a fine crash-dive, Kolb. The damage would have been more serious but for that.'

Kolb stared at him in silence.

'I mean you took her down fast,' Schluss explained.

'Not as fast as you got rid of our torpedoes, *Herr Kapitän.*' Kolb's studied insolence was like a kick in the stomach, but Schluss ignored it. After all it was more important to be alive, to have saved the submarine and her crew, than to argue with a mutinous pig like Kolb.

Meyer said, 'We started the stop-watches on each torpedo firing,. *Herr Kapitän*. There were no hits. Only terminal explosions.'

Schluss spread his hands in a gesture of despair. 'We did our best. In the face of great danger.'

A derisory sound came from Kolb.

This was too much for Schluss. 'I've been watching you, Kolb. You are insolent. You have disobeyed orders. You will be required to account for your actions on return to Trondheim. In the meantime get that main lighting going again.' Schluss turned away as if that was the end of the matter.

'I won't be the only one,' muttered Kolb under his breath. Schluss heard though he pretended not to. He had other things to worry about. U-0153 was still in danger, submerged somewhere under a large convoy, escorts all over the place dropping depth-charges and steering unpredictable courses. From many directions, mostly distant, came the thunder and tremors of explosions. Of these some might have been torpedo explosions, but Schluss was in no mood to differentiate. All explosions spelt danger. The thing was to get away from where they were happening. The convoy would get through to the Kola Inlet. There was no hope of stopping it. Of that he was certain. It was too heavily defended and the British had fanatical determination. In that they were as bad as the Germans.

Schluss assumed from the absence of *pings* and the muffled propeller noises of the convoy that the submarine must be under a thermal, reasonably safe from direct attack. But he was appalled at the possibility that they might be on the receiving end of some of the indiscriminate depth-charging which was taking place. It was but one of the many problems he saw in getting U-0153 away safely.

They would soon come clear of the convoy column under which they were sheltering, since the submarine and the merchant ships were on opposite courses. There were certain to be escorts astern of the convoy. Schluss went to the chart-table, noted the time and worked on the chart, making hurried calculations in its margin. He quickly made his decision. At 1645 he would consider surfacing. By then the submarine would be seven or eight miles astern of the convoy. Reloading of the torpedo tubes would not have been completed but that might later be turned to advantage. A further attack on the convoy was not envisaged in the plans he had in mind.

Yes. Provided there were no asdic *pings* or propeller noises within close range he would go to periscope depth at 1645 and take a look round. If visibility was still bad he'd surface and make off down-wind at high speed – *away* from the convoy. Any objections from his officers would be met with the reasonable explanation that he was not prepared to renew the attack until the training gear was serviceable. Once repairs were completed he would turn towards the convoy. U-0153 would then be some distance from it. He would submerge and complete reloading. He couldn't see further ahead than that, but it was a workable programme for the next few hours.

At that moment he was obsessed with the need to return to the surface – to get away from the battle area as quickly as possible. There might well be, probably would be, arguments with his officers, recriminations, and more serious trouble when U-0153 got back to Trondheim. But Willi Schluss was close to breaking-point and no longer cared. They could do what they liked with him as long as he got out of submarines. Unless that happened he would end his life trapped in a filthy, lethal, odorous steel tube, the water rushing in, the pressure bursting his lungs. He brushed away the tears which filled his eyes.

When the clock above the chart-table showed 1645 Brückner estimated the convoy to be 16,000 metres astern. Willi Schluss – clutching at a last minute safety margin to assuage his gnawing fear – allowed five minutes to pass before coming to periscope depth.

The *schnorkel* mast had been hoisted and the sound-room was able to listen for radar transmissions on the search-receiver. Hahn reported that there were none within six miles of the U-boat. The repairs to the training gear had not been completed but since *pings* and propeller noises within medium range could be heard in a U-boat with the human ear, the absence of either had emboldened Schluss to come to periscope depth. When the powerful Zeiss lenses revealed a curtain of snow to compound the darkness, his spirits rose and U-0153 surfaced. The diesels were started, clutched in,

142

and the submarine headed to the north-east, away from the convoy, making fourteen knots with following wind and sea. Though the weather had moderated, seas still flooded the bridge at times, and flurries of snow and sleet which swept it in dreary succession completed the misery of an Arctic winter.

Looking into the darkness through a curtain of snow, the high tide of Schloss's fears receded. For the first time that day he felt moderately secure. The convoy and escorts were miles astern, steaming away from the U-boat, so that allowing for their combined speed, U-0153 was withdrawing from the danger zone at about twenty knots. Through frozen lips he hummed *Der Stille, Nacht*. Emil Meyer coughed deliberately, offensively. Schluss took the hint and stopped.

## CHAPTER NINETEEN

The buzzer from the radar office sounded on *Vengeful's* bridge. Redman went to the voice-pipe. 'Forebridge-radar. Captain here.'

'We've picked up the convoy, sir. Bearing two-four-eight, eighteen thousand yards.'

'Well done, Blandy. Watch for small blips below that range. There may be U-boats trying to get away on the surface astern of the convoy.'

'Aye, aye, sir. Lot of wave clutter, sir.'

'Yes. I know it'll be difficult, Blandy. But if anybody can do it, you can.' He moved back to the bridge-screen. 'Put her on two-four-eight, pilot,' he said.

Pownall repeated, 'Two-four-eight, sir,' and passed the new course to the wheelhouse.

Redman said, 'The convoy must have altered to port.'

'Yes, sir. We should be up with it in thirty minutes.'

*Vengeful*, coming back from the skirmish with *Gruppe Osten* off the Skolpen Bank, was steaming into wind at fifteen knots, clouds of spray sweeping the bridge as she dug her bows into head seas. The asdic dome had been raised. At that speed in bad weather A/S conditions were hopeless and the dome which projected from the bottom of the ship's hull might be damaged.

Every ten minutes Redman stopped engines, the dome was lowered and A/S operators listened for HE, hoping to hear the propellers of a submerged U-boat. Redman knew that those which had taken part in the surface attack were likely to have submerged astern of the convoy to reload tubes before surfacing to get up-wind for a further attack. But he did not expect to find a U-boat until *Vengeful* was a good deal closer to the convoy.

On the PPI Redman could see four tiny but distinct pips of light ahead of *Vengeful*. They were ships of the Fifty-Seventh Escort Group, strung out in ragged quarter-line, making for the convoy as fast as they could in response to the Vice-Admiral's recall. *Vigorous* was nearest the convoy, *Vengeful* brought up the rear, with *Violent* a good two miles ahead of her.

Somebody arrived on the bridge. 'Captain, sir,' came from the darkness.

'Who's that?' asked Redman.

'The doctor, sir.'

'Yes, Elliot. What is it?' Captains of destroyers usually called their doctors 'Doc'. Redman studiously avoided this. It was always 'Elliot'. The doctor wondered about this. Was it an expression of contempt?

'*Chaffinch*'s survivors, sir. We've lost five. Two others are unlikely to make it. The remaining eight should be all right.'

Redman shivered. It was as if death had touched him with a cold hand. There had been close on two hundred men in *Chaffinch*. Now only ten were alive. Her captain had gone down with his ship. He was an old friend. Redman said, 'Anything you want?'

'No, sir. I thought I should let you know.'

'Thank you, Elliot. I'm sure you're doing everything possible.'

The doctor made no move to go. He'd heard Redman's laboured breathing, knew the captain must be close to exhaustion. But he didn't know what to do. How to get across the message that maybe he could help. 'Yes, sir.' The doctor gulped. 'Is there anything I can do for you?'

'No,' Redman said sharply. 'Why?'

'You've had very little sleep, sir.' The doctor lowered his voice so that others on the bridge might not hear.

144

'So have a lot of other people,' said Redman. 'I'm quite fit. Better get back to the sick-bay. You're needed there.'

The doctor took the hint and left the bridge. He knew that tone only too well.

Redman spoke to the asdic cabinet. 'Stopping now, Groves. Get the dome down as soon as you can and listen for HE. Make it snappy. We don't want to remain stopped for long.'

To Pownall he called, 'Stop engines.'

Pownall repeated the order to the quartermaster. The telegraph bells tinkled and the destroyer's hull ceased to vibrate.

Redman was irritated by the doctor's remark. Of course he hadn't had much sleep. Of course he was tired. But no more than any of the others who were in command. Did the doctor imagine there was some idyllic system under which escort captains could get a good night's sleep? Actually he didn't feel too bad. He'd taken the Benzedrine tablets earlier in the afternoon and much of the tiredness seemed to have worn off. A bad headache worried him but as he hadn't emptied his bowels for six days that wasn't surprising.

Bowrie the midshipman answered the buzzer from the radar office, and passed on Blandy's report. 'R-range of convoy f-fifteen thousand yards, sir.'

'Very good,' said Redman. He wiped the snow from his eyebrows with a gloved hand. 'Ugh! Bloody cold. This damned snow never lets up.'

'I think the weather's moderating, sir,' said the first-lieutenant with almost offensive cheerfulness.

'Yes. We're closing the Murman coast. Beginning to feel its lee. But I'd like to see less snow. The wind's bringing it off the land.'

*Vengeful* lost way quickly and her bows began to fall off in the wind. A faint rhythmic sound obtruded suddenly on the medley of water noises coming from the asdic-speaker. The buzzer from the asdic cabinet sounded. Lofty Groves's calm voice reported. 'Faint HE on oh-four-eight, estimated range six thousand yards. Radar reports no surface vessel on that bearing, sir.'

'Well done, Groves. I think we can just hear it on the bridge-speaker.' In the darkness he called, 'A/S action stations. Start the plot, pilot.'

Pownall said, 'Aye, aye, sir.' He didn't add that he'd given the order while the captain was speaking to Groves.

The first-lieutenant had sounded the alarm for anti-submarine action stations before the captain finished speaking.

'Slow ahead together, starboard ten,' Redman ordered. He was determined to go about this business slowly, methodically and above all quietly. If he rushed it the U-boat would hear the destroyer's propellers and dive deep. The chart showed average depths of one hundred and forty fathoms.

'Shall I signal the general alarm, sir?' It was Burrows the yeoman.

'Not yet, yeoman. We don't want other escorts bounding to our help, frightening this U-boat into going deep. We'll tail him for a bit.'

Redman spoke to Groves. 'I'll try and get dead astern of him. But we'll do it slowly. Give you a sporting chance of picking up HE while we're under way. Let me know if our speed's too much. Once we're headed on the bearing we'll do revolutions for eight knots. The U-boat can't be doing more than six.'

'Aye, aye, sir. Bearing oh-five-oh, moving right. HE very faint. Lot of interference from water noises.'

Slowing, taking a buffeting from the seas now on her beam, *Vengeful* came round on to the new course. As the HE bearing moved to starboard, Redman conned the ship round until she was steady on 058 degrees, almost directly down-wind. The submarine was running submerged on electric motors, presumably reloading tubes. But he would have expected it to have turned by now to follow the convoy. He would also have expected it to have gone deep to get under a thermal. The operation of reloading would take about an hour and a half. The first surface attack on the convoy had been broken off thirty minutes earlier, so the U-boat was unlikely to surface for another hour. Why was she steering away from the enemy . . .?

His thoughts were interrupted by Groves's report. 'Submarine blowing tanks, sir. Engine revolutions increasing. She's about to surface.' His voice was as near to excitement as the captain had heard it.

Redman at once said, 'Cease radar transmissions.' Bowrie passed the order to the radar office. Once surfaced, the U-boat would pick up radar transmissions on its search-receiver and almost certainly dive again.

As if nature felt it owed a special duty to U-boats what

had been a steady but moderate snowfall intensified, the wind driving blankets of snow before it, swirling and sweeping over the destroyer, reducing visibility to zero.

Redman realised that the U-boat, up-wind of *Vengeful* when first heard, would have experienced the snowstorm first. Presumably her captain had come to periscope depth prior to surfacing, or simply to test weather conditions, and had decided the moment was opportune for surfacing and making off down-wind. Maybe he'd only had two or three tubes to reload and having done that he'd surfaced to work round to the westward ahead of the convoy.

With these thoughts in mind, Redman formulated his plan of attack. It would be based on the tactics used so successfully by the captain of *Wolverine,* the destroyer which had sunk Guenther Prien, captain of U-47, top German U-boat ace, early in the war.

From the asdic cabinet Groves interrupted. 'Submarine running on diesels, sir. Revolutions for high speed. Bearing oh-five-four. Range opening.'

'Good. Now listen, Groves. We'll hunt this chap on HE. In this sea he'll work up to fourteen maybe fifteen knots as long as he keeps running down-wind. We'll have to try and improve on that if we're to overhaul him.'

'Be difficult to hold his HE at that speed in this weather, sir.'

'I know. But I'll stop at five-minute intervals and on each occasion I want you to give me a fresh bearing. Then we'll steam as hard as we can on that bearing for another five minutes before we stop and listen again. We've ceased radar and asdic transmissions and since we're dead astern of him his own propeller noises should mask ours. There'll be nothing to tell him he's being followed.'

Lofty Groves's hoarse chuckle was followed by, 'Aye, aye, sir. We'll do our best.'

'I'm sure you will,' said Redman. 'What's so bloody funny?'

'Nothing, sir. Just reminded me of something.'

Redman managed a frost-cracking smile in the darkness. 'Steer oh-five-four, pilot. Work up the revolutions to whatever she'll take. I'll let you know when it's enough.' He looked at the luminous dial of his watch. It was 1650.

With wind and sea astern, *Vengeful* was able to make eighteen knots without risk of weather damage, but storms of snow and sleet followed each other in monotonous succession. Visibility was seldom over a thousand yards.

'Five minutes up, sir,' called Pownall.

Redman ordered, 'Stop engines.'

The hull vibrations ceased and the destroyer drifted.

'Quick as you can, Groves,' Redman was urgent. 'We don't want to lose steerage way.'

'Aye, aye, sir.'

Time passed. The men on the bridge listened compulsively to the sounds from the asdic-speaker.

Beneath the confusion of water noises the HSD,[1] Callan, leader of Groves's A/S team, heard a faint pattern of sound. He turned the training wheel to port, watching the bearing indicator, and then, as the HE faded, he turned it back to starboard stopping when the volume of sound was greatest. He was a singular man, Callan, with an ability to hear sounds so low in volume that they were inaudible to most people.

'Bearing oh-four-one, sir,' he said. 'Range has opened.'

Groves repeated the information to the bridge.

'I can give you another minute,' said Redman. 'See if the bearing changes.'

The minute passed. 'Might be a slight movement to port, sir. Very difficult to check under these conditions.'

'Steer oh-four-oh, pilot. Revolutions for eighteen knots.'

The navigating officer relayed the orders to the wheelhouse. *Vengeful* came alive, her turbines whirred, the propellers began to churn, the bow moved to starboard and she steadied on the new course.


The first-lieutenant came on to the bridge. 'I've been round the ship, sir. The coxswain's getting cooks of messes to organise hot food and cocoa for the men at action stations.'

'Good. Hope they're better at hot meals than Cupido. I suppose the bridge won't be forgotten?'

The first-lieutenant chuckled. 'It's on its way, sir. May even get here before Topcutt. I think he's . . .'

A voice from the darkness interrupted. 'Captain, sir. Hot cocoa and a sandwich, sir. '

'My God,' said the first-lieutenant. 'He's beaten the bridge messenger to it.'

[1] HSD – Higher Submarine Detector. The rate given to a leading-seaman who specialised in operating asdic equipment.

148

'Bless you, Topcutt. You're psychic.'

'Pardon, sir?'

'My mind,' explained Redman. 'You read it.'

'Bit nippy up here, sir,' said Topcutt. Redman could hear the able-seaman's teeth chattering.

On the after side of the bridge the yeoman-of-signals moved aside the canvas screen of the signal desk and switched on the shaded light. 'Got the tally so far, Willy?' Williams, signalman-of-the-watch, said, 'Here it is, Yeo. All that we've received up here. Plus what the W/T office's given us.'

'Let's see it then.' The yeoman took the list and held it under the light. He began reading aloud, slowly, authoritatively, as if checking an inventory. 'Our losses. One AA sloop. *Chaffinch* – Christ, poor old Ridley's copped it.' – Ridley was *Chaffinch*'s yeoman-of-signals. – 'One fleet oiler, *Surfol*. Three Liberty ships.' He read out their names. Two US, one British. He coughed, cleared his throat importantly. 'Enemy losses. Two U-boats sunk by Fifty-Seventh Escort Group vicinity Skolpen Bank. Further U-boat sunk by Eighty-Third Escort Group during surface attack on convoy.' The yeoman switched off the light and passed the list back to the signalman. 'Not too bad, Willy. And that's not to mention the one we got off Loch Ewe. Not bad at all.'

'Think they'll attack again, Yeo?'

'They likely will, lad. Reloading now. Then they'll work into the ahead position. We've another seventeen hours to Kola. And don't forget that Skolpen lot. Maybe we'll be hearing from them later.'

Williams sucked his teeth loudly. 'Heard SO Escorts report no sign of any surfaced U-boats. Few minutes back that was. Escorts still hunting two submerged. Finding difficulty holding A/S contact.'

'Yes. Heard that lot meself. Not surprising in this weather. Freeze the balls off a brass bound monkey, it would.'

'Funny the Old Man not letting you give the general alarm for this flipping U-boat, Yeo. And not answering those recalls and all.'

'He's doing the right thing, Willy. We reported we were investigating an A/S contact at the start. Before it surfaced. If we make a signal now Jerry'll pick it up right away on his GSR and dive deep. We'd never get him after that.'

149

# CHAPTER TWENTY

During the first fifty-five minutes after the U-boat surfaced, *Vengeful* stopped engines on nine occasions. After each Callan, the HSD, was able to pick up HE. Not always immediately. Three times contact was lost and *Vengeful* set off on a square search at slow speed and somehow Callan picked up the HE again. Each time contact was regained and an approximate bearing established, the destroyer set off along it, quickly working up speed to eighteen knots.

During those forty minutes *Bluebird* had recalled *Vengeful* several times. First on TBS, then on W/T which could now be used since the enemy was in contact with the convoy. But Redman made no reply. *Bluebird* had his signal made at 1640, *Am investigating A/S contact,* and would have seen from her PPI that the destroyer had turned back astern of the convoy. If *Vengeful* was to get this U-boat, silence was imperative.

He went to a voice-pipe. 'Forebridge – Plot. Captain here. What's our estimated distance from the convoy?'

'Just on twenty-three miles, sir.'

'And from the nearest escort?'

'Twenty-one miles, sir. None in radar range now.'

'Good.' Redman moved back to the forepart of the bridge. The hunt had taken *Vengeful* further from the convoy than he'd realised. It explained why TBS signals had faded and could no longer be heard. He felt suddenly uneasy about his failure to answer the recall signals. On the other hand, he argued, he was in contact with a surfaced U-boat and had a reasonable chance of sinking it . . . or at least a chance.

U-0153 had been running on the surface for close on an hour when Gerhardt Meyer answered the call from the control-room.

It was Kolb. 'The armature has been replaced. Training gear operating normally.'

Meyer repeated Kolb's report to Schluss who said, *'Das ist gut . . .* that is good.' It wasn't what he felt. He'd liked to have run on the surface for hours yet. Now he knew he must turn towards the convoy and give the order to dive to complete reloading. After that his officers would expect him to renew the attack. Well, he thought, we shall see. We'll not attempt to cross that bridge just yet.

Meyer seemed to read the captain's mind. 'We still have two bow-tubes and a stern-tube to reload, *Herr Kapitän.*'

'I know, I know,' said Schluss testily. 'You don't have to tell me the obvious.' Through the voice-pipe he asked, 'What is the bearing and distance of the convoy now, Brückner?'

'We are about twenty-five miles astern of it, *Herr Kapitän*, unless it has altered course.' Brückner emphasised the *we*. 'Convoy's estimated bearing two-one-eight.'

'We'll alter course to port, Brückner. I'll bring her round into wind and sea. When she's headed on two-one-eight we'll dive and complete reloading.'

Schluss gave the order to clear the bridge and U-0153 dived, catching a trim at one hundred metres. Schluss ordered a course of 218 degrees, revolutions for four and a half knots. The convoy would be doing six or seven. As long as the submarine remained submerged it would be falling astern. That pleased Schluss. It was a contribution, however small, towards delaying U-0153's approach. The time was 1753.

For the tenth time since the submarine had surfaced Pownall said, 'Five minutes up, sir.'

'Stop engines.'

*Vengeful's* engines ceased to turn and she pitched and wallowed in the seaway. There were the usual sounds: the noise of seas surging down her sides; the slap of water against the hull; the wind screeching and shrilling in the rigging; the muffled voices of unseen men; the hum of the motors spinning the clear view screens; the dull blows and metallic scrapes of ice clearing operations on the upper-deck.

It was bitterly cold. Snow, sleet and frozen spray had collected everywhere. On the bridge two seamen were breaking it up, shovelling it over the side from the signal platforms. Guns' crews, depth-charge and hedgehog parties, searchlight crews and others in exposed positions were doing the same thing. It was a miserable task but it was better than doing nothing. It helped to keep a man's circulation going.

The ship lay in a black limbo, alone, unrelated, a universe in itself, the only substance in a vast nothingness. Men spoke in low voices as if they might scare away the quarry they were hunting. Redman peered into the blanket of darkness, waiting for Groves's next report. He felt suddenly alone, tired and despondent. The effects of the Benzedrine wearing off, the lack of sleep, the long nervous strain, engendered a sense of futility. In the course of forty-five minutes *Vengeful* had succeeded in keeping in touch with the U-boat, but the range remained at about 6000 yards. The destroyer wasn't able to steam fast enough in that weather to gain on the submarine. Somewhere out there, hidden in the snow and darkness, the U-boat was driving down-wind at a speed the plot estimated to be fourteen knots, *Vengeful*'s stops and starts were giving her an average speed no greater than that.

Redman thought of the German captain. What was going on in his mind? He couldn't know he was being followed or he'd have long since taken evasive action. His behaviour was puzzling. He should have turned to follow the convoy long ago. Where was he making for? Not for the Skolpen concentration. The course he was steering would take him north of that. Under what special orders was he operating? Redman sighed wearily. There were too many imponderables and he was too tired to sort them out. He shook himself like a dog and lumps of snow fell from his duffel coat.

Thinking of the strange conduct of the U-boat captain, he remembered something he'd forgotten in the excitement of the hunt – Kleber, the weather reporter. The U-boat they'd all thought was a loner until the attack on the blind side of the convoy developed. The moment when the German tactical plan became clear.

This U-boat *Vengeful* was hunting was behaving like a loner. Could it be Kleber again, engaged in some unpredictable tactic which might later reveal itself? And was this Kleber *his* Kleber?

In Redman's tired mind the conviction grew that it was, and his mental picture of the man on the U-boat's bridge changed from archetype Teuton to a tall fair man, square jaw and beaky nose prominent, smiling crowsfeet at the corners of ice-blue eyes. Redman's thoughts went back to the glacier above Crans-sur-Sierre. He remembered looking up at the stranger who smiled and said, 'Don't worry. It's all right. I'll get you out of here.'

Redman shook away the mental picture, spoke into a voice-pipe. 'Any luck, Groves?'

'No, sir, we've lost it. We're still trying.' Groves and his A/S team kept on trying but after fifteen minutes, during which *Vengeful* carried out a square search, they had to admit defeat. Groves reported, 'I'm afraid contact has definitely been lost, sir. I'm terribly sorry but . . .'

Redman said, 'Don't apologise. You and your team have done bloody well.' Beneath his professional disappointment there was a curious sense of relief. It was something deep down, secret, something of which he was ashamed. A sort of treachery, some would say. But it wasn't that really.

It was only that he was glad Hans Kleber had got away.

After contact with the U-boat had been lost, *Vengeful* set off on a southerly course to rejoin the convoy then estimated to be some twenty-five miles distant. The weather had continued to moderate and at 1800 wind and sea were logged as force 5.

Redman was in a subdued mood. He realised he'd stayed away too long, strayed too far from JW 137. The prime duty of an escort was to remain with the convoy it was protecting. He'd allowed obsession with the hunt to upset his judgment. Had he sunk the U-boat he might have got away with it. Nothing succeeded like success. But he hadn't.

As it was Ginger Mountsey would have a good deal to say, not only about the length of *Vengeful's* absence but the failure to respond to signals. He would dish out a pretty sharp reprimand. But being Ginger Mountsey it would soon be forgotten. Back on the Clyde when Captain (D) read *Vengeful's* report of proceedings there'd be another rocket. Within a few days, however, Captain (D) would probably invite him to the pleasant afternoon teas for which he was noted and the matter would not be mentioned again. Captain (D) had spent much of the war at sea. He knew what went on on the bridge of a destroyer.

*Vengeful* had resumed radar transmissions and the bridge-speaker once again echoed the *pings* of the asdic with metronomic precision. The destroyer was still outside radar and TBS range of the convoy and its escorts. Redman, knowing that wireless silence could not be broken, had made a W/T signal reporting loss of contact with the U-boat. He had also given his estimated time of rejoining JW 137.

Terence O'Brien arrived on the bridge. 'Captain, sir. You sent for me?'

'Yes,' said Redman. 'Your guns' crews all right?'

'Yes, sir. They've had some food and mugs of hot cocoa. Bit cold but they've been clearing away snow and ice and that has helped.' O'Brien's duties included those of gunnery control officer.

'B gun loaded with starshell?'

'Yes, sir.'

'Long fused?'

'Yes, sir.'

'X gun?'

'High explosive with delayed action fuse, sir.'

'I think you'd better . . .' Redman broke off his sentence as the *ping* on the bridge-speaker was followed by an unmistakable *pong*. Twice more the *pings* were answered by *pongs*, then came Groves's incisive report, 'Contact, sir. Dead ahead . . . range nine hundred . . . closing . . . bearing drawing slowly left . . . strong HE.' With the calm of a judge pronouncing the accused 'guilty', he added, 'It's definitely a submarine, sir.'

'Sound the alarm. Start the plot. Steer five degrees to port. Revolutions for fifteen knots.' The orders came from Redman in a sharp staccato. 'Pounce attack. Heavy charges five hundred feet. Light charges two hundred. Stand by to illuminate with searchlights.'

From somewhere in the darkness Pownall announced the new course – 218 degrees, and the time – 1807.


CHAPTER TWENTY-ONE


Kolb's report, shortly before U-0153 dived, that the armature had been replaced and that the training gear was operating normally was correct. But soon after making it he and Hahn had found that though the hydrophones could be trained through their full travel of 360 degrees they were soundless. The amplifier circuit had been damaged by the electric fire. This was not discovered until the burnt-out leads were replaced and tested. By then the submarine had been submerged for some minutes. Believing that repairs to the circuit would not take long and conscious of their failure to test the hydrophones before making the report, Kolb and Hahn decided against informing Schluss. Apart from any other consideration, they knew that if he learnt that the hydrophones were not working he would seize the excuse to surface and move away from the convoy.

As it happened the hydrophones were unlikely to have made any difference to what was happening. At that moment unknown to Schluss, *Vengeful* was dead astern, steering the same course and overhauling U-0153 at ten knots. The sounds of the destroyer's *pings* and her propellers which would normally have been audible not only to the submarine's hydrophone operator but, at close range, to the naked ear of the men in the control-room, were effectively masked by the noise of U-0153's own propellers.

It was only at the last moment that those in the control-room heard the chilling roar as the destroyer's propellers passed overhead. For a moment, numb with shock, Willi Schluss did nothing. Then he came to life and screamed, 'Hard-a-port, emergency full ahead together!'

It was a desperate attempt to swing clear of the depth-charges which he knew would already be sinking towards the submarine in groups of two's and four's. But it was too late.

The turn to port took U-0153 directly into the path of one side of the pattern of twenty-six charges as the first pair exploded. They were followed at regular intervals by others. The explosions were not only to port and starboard but, set for depths of 200 and 500 feet, they rocked and hammered the submarine from above and below.

The effects of the first explosions were catastrophic. There was a muffled roar like a volcano erupting and U-0153 was flung to starboard, heeling over sharply, the hull whipping, expanding and contracting, as the pressure waves struck. Lights went out. Gauges blew, air, water and telemotor pipes

155

fractured and burst, men screamed as they were flung against the sides of the control-room. Limbs were broken, and wounds were inflicted by controls and other protuberances. Shortly afterwards there was another explosion. Enormous forces struck the stern, throwing it upwards so that the boat assumed a bow-down angle.

The emergency lighting came on, flickered and went off. Another thunderous explosion checked the fall of the bow and threw the boat once more into a stern-down position. By some strange quirk the explosion caused the emergency lighting to come on again.

The buzzer on the telephone from the engine-room beep-beeped. Gerhardt Meyer – white-faced, a bloody gash across his forehead – staggered across and put the phone to his ear. It was Obermaschinist Zeck, reporting that the steering-engine had been damaged. The rudder was jammed in the hard-a-port position. Worse still, he said, chlorine fumes from the battery-room were entering the motor and diesel-room in such quantities that masks were insufficient. Both compartments had to be evacuated. Before he'd finished speaking, hammering was heard on the watertight door at the after end of the control-room.

Meyer passed the news to Schluss who shook his head as if trying to rid it of a nightmare. 'Don't open that watertight door,' he shouted. 'We'll all die if you do.'

Kolb called out, '*Du feiges Schwein* . . . you cowardly pig,' and ran aft to release the holding cleats. The door opened and men streamed through, dragging and carrying their wounded.

'Shut it, you stupid fool,' shrilled Schluss. 'Do you want to die . . .' His sentence was broken by a further explosion which tilted the bow even higher so that the crew had difficulty in keeping their feet on the steep angle of the deck. 'Emergency surface,' yelled Schluss. 'Blow all tanks.'

High-pressure air forcing its way into the ballast tanks lifted the submarine rapidly and, as if that were not enough, yet another prodigious explosion beneath the hull blew the U-boat to the surface.

The emergency lighting flickered and failed once more. Above the noise and turmoil Meyer shouted, 'We've surfaced. Bridge is clear.' The submarine began to pitch and roll in the seaway.

156

In the darkness Schluss – training and tradition forgotten in his terror – led the rush up the ladder to the lower hatch. With desperate energy he released the clips and opened it, then clambered up the ladder through the conning-tower and opened the upper hatch. As he made his way on to the bridge he was swept to one side and drenched by a sea. He clawed in the darkness for the rail on the bridge-screen, found it and pulled himself to his feet. The night was ebony black. Snow still fell, though lightly now. The submarine lay beam on to wind and sea, wallowing helplessly, seas breaking over her, spray freezing on the upperworks.

Schluss scarcely noticed these things. He was alive, able to breathe fresh air, and the horror of the control-room, the screams of dying and wounded men, and the odour of chlorine gas were far below him.

Dark shapes emerged through the upper hatch and joined him on the bridge. One man was whimpering. '*Halt die Klappe* . . . shut up,' said a hoarse voice. Schluss recognised it as Kolb's. So he'd not stayed down there either.

Schluss was blinded by a searchlight beam. Beneath it orange flashes were followed by the sound of gunfire. Streams of tracer splattered against the conning-tower. Shells began to fall astern of U-0153. The error in range was corrected and the splashes drew closer. Moments later a shell burst on the anti-aircraft gun platform abaft the bridge, killing and wounding the men clustered there.

In the glare of the searchlight Schluss saw that the stern of the submarine was sinking, the bow thrusting steeply out of the water. Somewhat unnecessarily he cried, 'Abandon ship,' as he joined the leaping figures who'd anticipated his order. As soon as he'd recovered from the shock of immersion he struck out, swimming away from the fast disappearing hull of his first and last command.

Instinct backed by reason had decided Redman on a pounce attack. The reasons were sound . . . one, the U-boat was obviously unaware of *Vengeful*, nine hundred yards astern, for it had taken no evasive action. Two, it would certainly go deep if it detected the destroyer. This might happen at any moment, particularly after a material alteration of course. Three, Redman was in no mood for another prolonged hunt and further delay in returning to the convoy.

A pounce attack was often not successful, but at least it forced a submarine to go deep and delayed its attempt to catch up with the convoy. This suited Redman. Close to exhaustion, his nerves strained, he was obsessed by a vision of Kleber in the control-room of the U-boat 1000 yards ahead, groping its way through the gloomy depths of the Barents Sea.

The technical requirements of the attack dominated his thinking as *Vengeful* made her run in, but the human brain has a remarkable capacity for distributing its attention and a part of his mind had been busy with these thoughts from the moment Groves had reported. 'It's a submarine, sir.' There was no doubt in Redman's mind that this was the U-boat they'd been hunting on the surface before contact was lost.

The bridge-speaker relayed a series of range reports from Groves as the distance between *Vengeful* and the U-boat closed, but the bearing remained steady. Clearly the U-boat still did not know it was being hunted.

At last Groves made the report for which Redman had been waiting. 'Contact lost . . . range two hundred yards, sir.'

That gave Redman a fair idea of the depth at which the U-boat was running. He breathed a sigh of relief. *Vengeful*'s pattern settings were right.

All now depended upon what last minute alteration of course the U-boat might make. In the A/S cabinet Groves and his team focused their attention on the stop-watch which had been started the moment contact was lost. As the second-hand swept the dial they read off ranges from the time/speed/range table on the bulkhead above their instruments .

'One hundred yards,' reported Groves through the bridge-speaker. 'Fifty yards . . . twenty-five . . . over the target *now*, sir.'

Next Groves reported the ranges as they opened, for the pattern had to be dropped ahead of the submarine to allow time for the charges to sink to the depth at which they were set to explode. 'Fifty yards ahead . . .' Groves's steady voice proclaimed . . . 'Seventy-five yards . . .'

'Fire!' ordered Redman.

Groves's orders to the depth-charge parties on the quarter

158

deck came through the bridge-speaker – 'Fire one! . . . fire two! . . . fire three! . . .' – as he called the sequence at short intervals. In response to his orders depth-charges were rolled off the chutes astern and fired from throwers to port and starboard. Before he'd ordered the firing of the last of the twenty-six charge patterns the first were already exploding.

'Searchlight,' ordered Redman. The powerful beam poked tentatively into the darkness astern, revealing white fountains leaping skywards as the charge exploded. At their base the sea boiled and trembled.

*Vengeful* swung round to port, the searchlight holding the turbulent water in its beam, turning the falling snow into luminescent streamers joining sea and sky.

Soon after the fourteenth and fifteenth charges had exploded there was a shout from the yeoman-of-signals, 'Submarine surfacing, sir.' It was in a sense unnecessary for so many in *Vengeful* witnessed the extraordinary spectacle of a U-boat leaping from the sea as a double explosion blew it to the surface.

Redman at once stopped engines and put his ship head on to the submarine. This was the moment when the U-boat was most likely to fire a *gnat* and he was taking no chances. At the same time he gave the order to O'Brien to open fire. The range was about five hundred yards. Streams of tracer sped from the 20 mm oerlikon guns beneath the bridge, their repetitive bark drowned by the heavier reports of the forward 4-inch which was producing a commendable rate of fire. Fire-control in an old V and W class destroyer was fairly elementary. But to Redman's astonishment *Vengeful*'s seventh shell scored a direct hit abaft the conning-tower which was already raked with oerlikon fire. In the bright beam of the searchlight he saw men jumping over the side as the U-boat began to slide under stern-first, her bows inclining upwards at a steep angle until she disappeared finally in a cloud of spray.

A ragged cheer came from the guns' crews near the bridge as Redman ordered 'cease fire'. Next to him he heard the first-lieutenant's delighted 'Oh, good show, sir.' It sounded like Twickenham and Lords.

Redman said, 'Get a scrambling-net over the starboard side. Number One. Have men on life-lines standing by. We'll go round to windward of these poor devils. See if we can pick some up in our lee.'

'Aye, aye, sir. The first-lieutenant was already heading for the bridge ladder. 'I'll be difficult in this weather.'

'I know.' Redman's voice was flat. 'But I want some survivors.'

How badly the captain was going to congratulate the ship's company on sinking the U-boat. It had been a tremendous hunt – a splendid kill. Surely he was going to say something about it.

Redman had never questioned his duty. He had to sink the U-boat. Of that he had no doubt and his actions had been quick and decisive. But now, worn out, nerves frayed, his belief that he'd hunted down Hans Kleber acquired an absurd, almost nightmarish quality.

While he manoeuvred *Vengeful* to windward so that the ship would drift down on the survivors, the fantasy became a fixation. Hans, he was sure, was one of those black dots struggling in the glare of the searchlight. The struggle wouldn't last long. A matter of minutes. It wasn't so much the icy water as the thirty degrees of frost in the atmosphere that killed a man quickly in Arctic waters.

This was the compelling reason for the rescue attempt. If *Vengeful* didn't pick up the U-boat's captain, at least his name could be obtained from those she did.

One way or another, decided Redman, there had to be an end to the dreadful uncertainty.


# CHAPTER TWENTY-TWO


Redman heard the scrape and clatter of feet up the steel bridge-ladders. Only one man in the ship came up as fast as that. The first-lieutenant. He joined Redman at the bridge-screen.

'How many, Number One?'

'Three, sir. We had a fourth but couldn't hold him. A sea . . .''

Redman interrupted. 'Any officers?'

'Yes, sir. One.'

Redman drew a deep breath. 'Tall? Fair?'

160

'No, sir. Small and dark.'

So they hadn't got him. He was somewhere back there in the crushed hull of the U-boat. On the bottom under that cold black water. Redman had feared that. Fought against the probability. Tried to convince himself it wouldn't happen. But he'd known all along that Hans wouldn't be among the survivors. He would be the last man to dive over the side, leaving the crew below once he knew his boat was sinking. He'd have gone down to help them. Done all he could to get them up through the hatches. He'd have stayed with those who couldn't get away. It was wishful thinking to have supposed he'd been one of those black dots struggling in the water.

His mind numbed. At last he forced a question. 'How are they?'

'Pretty bad, sir. The doctor's in the sick-bay with them now.'

'Can they speak?'

'Not when I was there a moment ago. They're badly frozen.'

Redman was silent.

'Anything you want me to do, sir?' The first-lieutenant sensed that something was wrong. The captain hadn't spoken to the ship's company on the broadcast. No word of congratulations on sinking the U-boat. It was fantastic. *Vengeful's* second U-boat in eight days and not a peep from the captain. Just that odd inexplicable silence. Okay. This kill wasn't as exciting as the one outside Loch Ewe a week back. They hadn't expected that one. They were fit and fresh then. The ship's company was worn out now, short on sleep, nerves strained. But that was no excuse for failing to tell them that they'd put up a good show.

It seemed a long time before the first-lieutenant's question was answered. At last Redman said, 'No. Nothing at the moment. We'll get back on course for rejoining. I'll let *Bluebird* know what's happened.' The first-lieutenant thought he could hear the captain's laboured breathing above the sound of the wind.

*Vengeful* sank U-0153 at 1815. Twelve minutes later, having picked up three survivors, Redman put her on a south-westerly course and set off at sixteen knots to rejoin the convoy.

Pownall looked at the plot, did his chartwork, and reported the estimated time of rejoining as 2010. *Vengeful* should, he said, be within TBS range an hour before that.

Wind and sea had continued to moderate but not the storms of snow and sleet. The intervals between them were longer, but visibility remained bad. Conditions still did not permit the operation of aircraft.

A W/T signal was made to *Bluebird* repeated to *Fidelix,* reporting the sinking of U-0153, the picking up of three survivors, and the estimated time of rejoining.

These matters having been attended to, Redman handed over the bridge to the first-lieutenant and made for the sick-bay.

This was the moment he'd been waiting for. There was something he had to know.

The sick-bay was two decks below the bridge. In it four canvas cots were stacked in tiers of two. Men wrapped in blankets lay in them. The pervasive smell of iodoform and diesel oil, of steam from radiators, filled the stuffy compartment. At one cot, Jackson, the leading sick-berth attendant, was bathing a scalp wound. At another Elliot, the surgeon-lieutenant, was massaging a man's heart. The ERA who'd been struck by a fire extinguisher was in the fourth cot, his head swathed in bandages. He stared vacantly at the deckhead. Redman went over to him. 'How are you getting on, Rogers?'

The ERA blinked but didn't turn his head.

'He's still concussed, sir,' said Elliot. 'Can't understand what you say.'

Redman looked at the doctor without seeing him. 'How are the *Chaffinch* survivors?'

'Nine left of the fifteen we picked up, sir. Seven are all right. They're up in the forward messdecks. The other two are badly injured. Outlook for one's pretty hopeless.'

'Where are they?'

'In the midshipmen's cabin, sir. SBA Wyllie's with them.'

'Where are the midshipmen living?'

'In the wardroom, sir.'

'H'm.' Redman looked from Elliot to the three Germans. Now he could get on with what he'd come for. 'How are these people?'

Elliot gestured towards an upper cot. 'He's dead, sir. Moving him in a moment. These two are still unconscious. Badly frozen. We're doing what we can. Afraid they've been in the water too long.'

Redman shook his head, said nothing. He went to an upper bunk and turned back the blanket. The face was blue-white, the skin puckered, sightless grey eyes staring, lips drawn back in a macabre smile.

It wasn't Hans.

Redman went to the next cot. The man with the scalp wound. That wasn't Hans either.

'Which of them is the officer?'

'This chap, sir. I'm massaging his heart. Trying to get a kick out of it.'

Redman looked down on the dark skeletal face. There was no sign of life. 'Poor devil,' he said hoarsely.

The sound of the captain's breathing worried Elliot. He could help. Ephedrine would do it. But what was the point? He'd only invite a snub. There were more urgent priorities.

'Where's the clothing? The gear they were wearing?'

'Over there, sir.' Elliot pointed to a corner.

Redman saw the heap, a pool of water round it, damp streaks running across the corticene deck as the ship rolled. 'Been through it?'

'No, sir. Haven't had time.'

'Of course.' Redman knelt and sorted through the soggy mass. In the inner pocket of a leather jacket with rank badges he found a wallet. He held it under the light. One by one he took out its sodden contents. A paybook in the name of *Kapitänleutnant W. Schluss*; a letter addressed to Schluss; some German banknotes; a folded slip of paper, in it a lock of hair; two snapshots; a plain bespectacled young woman holding a child with curly hair. But it was the other snapshot which froze Redman. A group of three officers on the bridge of a U-boat. On the left, easily recognised, the small dark man with the skeletal face whose heart Elliot was massaging. Obviously Schluss, the owner of the wallet.

The man on the right of the group, broad faced and smiling, was not among the survivors. Nor was the man in the centre – the tall fair man with the beaky nose, strong chin and smiling eyes.

That was Hans Kleber.

With shaking hands Redman turned over the snapshot. The water-smudged inscription read, *U*-0153 . . . *Trondheim Fjord* . . . 18.10.44.

So Kleber *was* the captain of U-0153. He'd killed him after all. It had been a hunch – at first no more than a frightening possibility – for all those long hours. Now it was a fact. As if from far away he heard Elliot's voice. Redman said, 'What's that?'

'I'm afraid we've lost this one, sir. Can't get his heart going.'

Redman stared at the doctor in silent misery, shook his head and left the sick-bay. He went up the ladders to the wheelhouse, through it to his sea-cabin. 'Captain – forebridge,' he spoke into the voice-pipe.

'Forebridge – captain, sir.'

'Let Topcutt know I want him. Make it sharp.'

Pownall said, 'Aye, aye, sir.'

While he waited Redman stood wedged between the bunk and the wash-basin, staring at the ruby ice lump on the porthole. But all he saw was the ice in the glacier above Crans-sur-Sierre. The blood and the broken skis and the tall fair stranger smiling down at him. 'Don't worry. It's all right. I'll get you out of here.'

Redman's teeth were chattering. He couldn't stop shivering. Something inside him was near to breaking-point. A sense of desperation, of approaching calamity, overcame him. He'd read somewhere that hysteria was cured by slapping the victim's cheeks. He slapped his own, hard, and the noise was heard in the wheelhouse. Only once before in his life had he felt like this. When he'd seen the limp figure lying inside the knot of people on the Boulevard St Germain-des-Prés and known she was dead.

He was younger then. He'd broken down. But this was different. He was older, tougher. He'd seen a lot of death. He wasn't going to break down now. Not on his bloody life. Where the hell was Topcutt?

He went to the voice-pipe. 'Where the bloody hell is Topcutt?'

'Messenger's gone for him, sir.' Pownall's tone was chilly. He was administering a rebuke.

Redman stood glowering, shaking, wanting to tell Pownall what a supercilious little bastard he was. There was a knock and the curtain was pulled aside.

'You sent for me, sir?' Topcutt saw the dark shadows under the captain's red-rimmed eyes, the tired face. He grieved privately. The captain needed sleep. He was killing himself. But Topcutt couldn't tell him that. He was only his servant.

The captain stared at him. 'Topcutt?' he said, frowning as if in doubt. 'Topcutt?'

'Yes, sir. You sent for me.'

'Yes. Yes, I did. You've taken a long time.'

Topcutt knew that he hadn't, but he said, 'Sorry, sir.'

Redman opened the cupboard at the far end of the sea-cabin, took out a clean handkerchief. His back was to Topcutt. Why had he sent for him? Why? He remembered. 'Get me a bottle of whisky from the wardroom, Topcutt.'

'Whisky, sir?' Topcutt's eyes widened. The captain never drank at sea. Captains didn't in wartime.

'Yes. Whisky.' Redman turned and glared at him. 'And shake it up. I can't wait all night.'

Topcutt let out a startled, 'Very good, sir,' before disappearing at the double.


## CHAPTER TWENTY-THREE


Rathfelder came into the control-room. 'The reloading is complete, *Herr Kapitän*. All tubes are ready.'

'Good,' said Kleber. 'We shall need them.' He grinned. 'Don't expect round two to be as easy as round one.'

'I don't,' said Rathfelder.

The buzzer from the sound-room *beep-beeped*.

'Propeller noises fading. Difficult to hold,' reported Ausfeld. 'Bearing moving from right to left. Convoy has altered from a southerly to a south-easterly course.'

'Good. We'll alter to port. But not too much. I want to open the distance before surfacing.' Kleber went across to the chart-table, looked over the navigating officer's shoulder. 'How far do you put us now, Dieter?'

'About eleven thousand metres astern of the convoy, *Herr Kapitän*. I estimate its speed at six knots. We make four, submerged.'

'Right. Alter course to one-five-zero. When we've surfaced we'll work round the enemy's starboard flank. Get well up-wind and wait.'

Dieter Leuner passed the new course to the quartermaster. When he was satisfied that the submarine was steady on it, he went back to the chart-table. 'How long before we surface, *Herr Kapitän*?'

'About fifteen minutes, Dieter. Then we'll have a look round. See what Ausfeld can find.'

U-0117 surfaced at 1810.

Almost immediately Ausfeld reported low-volume radar transmissions from the port ahead sector. Distance estimated at 14,000 metres.

Kleber ordered speed to be increased to fourteen knots. With the submarine trimmed well down he drove to the south-east. Washed and doused by breaking seas and freezing spray, U-0117 overhauled the convoy steadily.

By 1900 the U-boat was drawing ahead, passing up JW 137's starboard flank. The distance of the nearest escorts was estimated to be 15,000 metres. The multiplicity of radar transmissions told of a substantial escort force concentrated on this the up-wind flank. The enemy was evidently not going to be taken by surprise again.

At 2000 speed was reduced, the submarine then being some seven miles ahead and to starboard of the convoy. Kleber knew it was there, though he could not see it. Vast and purposeful, plunging on through the south-westerly storm, sheltered by darkness, snow, sleet and its powerful escort, JW 137 was within 100 miles of its destination, the Kola Inlet. Time was running out.

Kleber said, 'When Ausfeld reports the advanced escorts to be twelve thousand metres distant, we'll dive. Find a thermal. Sit under it until they've passed over.'

'The mixture as before,' said Rathfelder.

'That's a Somerset Maugham title. Read him?'

'No, *Herr Kapitän*.'

'You should. He's good.'

'I haven't had much opportunity to read English novelists in the last five years.'

Kleber was silent, remembering where he'd read the book. In Surrey in the summer of 1938. He and Marianne had spent a week with Francis Redman in East Horsley. At the house of Jane Redman who seemed more like a mother than an aunt to the Englishman. Kleber thought of the walks in Ranmore Forest and along the downs above Dorking and Leatherhead. Beautiful country, marvellous June days, soft and warm. Wonderful afternoon teas on the lawn to the sounds of birds and bees and garden mowers. It had been a carefree happy time, dreamlike in retrospect.

But Marianne was dead, there'd been five years of war. It was no use living in the past. Francis Redman? for Kleber the name conjured up a picture of broken skis, blood-stained snow, a broken leg, absurdly unsymmetrical, and frightened brown eyes. He wondered where the Englishman was. Somewhere at sea? Or in a staff job ashore? How could one know? It had been a long and bloody war. Maybe he was dead.

Kleber shrugged his thoughts away. It was no good living in the past. It was the present that mattered. He pressed the buzzer to the sound-room. 'What is the range of the nearest escorts, Ausfeld?'

As *Vengeful* came within TBS range of the convoy the bridge-speaker relayed a steady flow of messages between escorts, their group commanders and the flagship. There was a lot going on. A further attack on the convoy had just broken off. Believed to be the work of two U-boats from the Skolpen Bank concentration, it had come from the down-wind side. One U-boat had been attacked by *Isis* and *Peaflower* of the Eighty-Third Escort Group soon after tor-pedoing a Liberty ship. The hunt was still on. The rescue ship was busy picking up survivors, a frigate standing by.

*Vengeful* reported her position to *Bluebird* and was ordered to take station five miles on the starboard bow of the leading ship of the starboard column, the billet presently occupied by *Mainwaring*, a fleet destroyer. It was on this flank that the next attack was expected to develop.

The first-lieutenant reported the signal by voice-pipe to Redman who was in his sea-cabin.

'Carry on, Number One.' Redman's voice was hoarse, subdued.

The first-lieutenant hesitated. It was unlike the captain not to come up for the execution of a stationing signal. But nothing more came from the voice-pipe so he said, 'Aye, aye, sir,' and turned to Pownall who was on the compass platform. 'Give me a course for that stationing signal, Geoffrey.'

Pownall spoke to the plot, then said, 'We'll have to cross from port to starboard astern of the convoy. Work up its starboard flank.'

'Thanks for the lesson,' said the first-lieutenant. 'Give me a course to steer.'

Pownall made a clicking noise. 'I was trying to be helpful.'

'Well. Let's have the course. That'll be helpful.' The first-lieutenant was a tired man. It had been a long journey and the strain was telling.

'Two-four-oh,' said Pownall. He, too, was a tired young man.

The first-lieutenant passed the course to the quartermaster and ordered revolutions for eighteen knots.

Pownall saw his chance. 'Pushing her a bit, aren't you? In this weather, I mean.'

'Wind and sea are easing off. Anyway, it's my decision.'

'Yes.' Pownall sounded doubtful. 'I know. I'm surprised the Old Man hasn't come up.'

'He'll be up soon.' The first-lieutenant's tone suggested that the subject was not one for discussion on the bridge. But he, too, was surprised. Perhaps the captain had succumbed to exhaustion. His responses to voice-pipe reports had been slow, his voice thick. Like a man woken from deep sleep.

The night was dark, wet and bitterly cold.

Nothing could be seen of the ships and escorts as *Vengeful* passed astern of the convoy, but the PPI continued to present its faithful display. Each sweep of the arm left a pattern of dots which glowed and faded, the eight columns of the convoy, around and ahead of them its escorts, the bulk of them on its starboard flank.

Reports from the asdic cabinet and radar office flowed continuously to the bridge, the *pings* on the loudspeaker evoking frequent response as the destroyer cut across the sterns of merchant ships and escorts, the disturbed water in their wakes reflecting woolly echoes which the asdic team sorted out and classified before reporting, 'Wake effect.'

As the destroyer moved up the convoy's starboard flank

Petty Officer Blandy kept up a running commentary on the many radar contacts to port. The first-lieutenant interrupted him. 'Don't worry too much about the port side, Blandy. It's thick with convoy and escorts. Any U-boats near us are likely to be to starboard. Either up-wind on the bow or working their way up our starboard beam into the ahead position.'

'We're watching for them, sir.' Blandy's voice was a mixture of irritation and respect. To the radar operator beside him he said, 'Christ! You'd think we'd never been on one of these.'

Petty Officer Blandy, too, was a tired man. Soon afterwards he reported a contact ahead, classified surface ship, closing the convoy at high speed.

'It's *Mainwaring*,' said the first-lieutenant. 'We heard her recall a few moments ago. She's to take up station inside the close-screen.'

At 2000 the watch changed. O'Brien came to the bridge with Rogers the midshipman. O'Brien announced his arrival with 'Holy mother o' Jesus, it's cold. Where's the Kai[1] boat?'

The first-lieutenant interpreted the PPI for O'Brien, showed him the convoy's position on the chart, reported the course and speed, weapons' state of readiness, gun loadings, depth-charge settings, challenge and reply for the night, the U-boat disposition and attack situation, and much else. 'We're just beginning to move ahead of the convoy,' he said. 'Drawing clear of the starboard column. Another three miles and we'll be in station. *Mainwaring's* closing us fast.' He pointed to a dot of light on the PPI. 'That's her. She's to take up station inside the close-screen.'

'Well now. For a tired Irishman that's a lot to remember.'

'Your midshipman will keep an eye on things. Consult him when in doubt.'

O'Brien yawned. 'Haven't had two hours of proper sleep in the last forty-eight. It's worse than a couple of St Patrick's nights strung together.

'Two hours! You *must* have been hogging it.'

'You know what, Number One?'

'What?'

[1] Kai boat – a particularly strong and greasy brew of Admiralty cocoa.

'I wish this shenanigan would stop. It's after the salmon I'd like to be. On the Boyne. With a fine Irish colleen waiting for me in the pub at the end of the day. A girl of great beauty, fine breasts and randy as hell.'

The first-lieutenant expressed his disapproval by becoming suddenly businesslike. 'I'm going down to see the Old Man.'

'Right, Number One. I've got her. The ship's in safe hands.'

'Your night vision okay?'

O'Brien searched the darkness with night glasses. 'It's fine.'

'What d'you see?'

'Bugger all, your honour. Just bloody black nothing.'

'You'll do. That's all there is. I'll be back as soon as I've seen the Old Man. Can't trust you to get her into station. You know. RNVR. *Really not very reliable.*'

O'Brien groaned. 'Oh, God! Not that again.'

The first-lieutenant went down to the chart-room and wrote up the log. That done he went through the wheelhouse to the captain's sea-cabin. The door was shut. That was unusual. It was normally latched to in the open position, the curtain drawn across for privacy. He knocked. There was no response, so he knocked again and heard a muffled reply. He opened the door and pulled the curtain aside.

The captain was lying on the bunk, blankets over him, back to the door. The stale smell of past meals, of body odour and steam from the radiator had been joined by another. The potent smell of whisky.

The first-lieutenant saw the part-empty bottle and the tumbler in the rack above the wash-basin. The captain breathed noisily. A wheezy, asthmatic rumble.

My God, thought the first-lieutenant. He's drunk. He said, 'Captain, sir.'

'Yes, Number One. What is it?' The recumbent figure didn't move.

'We should be in station in five minutes, sir.'

'What's the time?'

The first-lieutenant was surprised. In spite of his hoarseness the captain sounded remarkably sober. 'Just after twenty hundred, sir.'

'Shut the door.'

The first-lieutenant shut it, looked once again at the wash-basin and wondered if somehow he'd got things wrong. The captain had half raised himself in the bunk. 'Yes. It's whisky, Number Once. I've been drinking.' The red-rimmed eyes narrowed into a smile. 'Terribly tired. No excuse, but I am. Thought the whisky would wake me up. Stimulant, you know.' He began to move off the bunk. The first-lieutenant stood back to make room.

'Put me into a heavy sleep. Quarrelled with the Benzedrine, I dare say.'

'I expect so. I'm sorry, sir.' The first-lieutenant hesitated. 'I know you're terribly short of sleep.'

'Who isn't?' The captain slid off the bunk. He was a big man and moved cumbrously. 'Right, Number One. Carry on. I'm coming up.'

'There's a marvellous signal from the Vice-Admiral, sir.'

'About what?'

'Congratulating you on sinking U-0153, sir.'

The captain was holding on to the bunk-board, steadying himself against the roll, staring at the first-lieutenant in a strange way. 'Did it add, "and for killing her brother, thereby making a pigeon pair"?'

The first-lieutenant looked at him blankly, half-puzzled, half-embarrassed. 'I don't know what you mean, sir.'

Redman drew his hand across his face.

'No,' he said wearily. 'You never will. Now carry on, Number One.' He gestured towards the door.

The first-lieutenant didn't move. He was worried, uncertain. 'Sure you're all right, sir?'

'Get out.' The captain spoke with restrained but sudden fury. 'For Christ's sake, get out.'

The first-lieutenant gave him a startled look, opened the door, pulled the curtain across and shut the door behind him. When he'd gone Redman sighed deeply, pressed the palms of his hands into his eyes, then looked round the cabin seeing nothing but his own desolation. There was no escape. He took the bottle of whisky from the rack, examined the label, reached for a tumbler, changed his mind and, with savage violence, smashed the bottle against the ruby ice lump. Whisky, chips of ice and broken glass splattered the Admiralty blankets and soiled the pillow.

He fell forward on to the bunk burying his head in his arms. For a moment he gave way, his sobs muffled by the pillow. He soon pulled himself together, took the duffel coat from the hook, put it on, raised the hood of the anorak and reached for his night glasses.


# CHAPTER TWENTY-FOUR


The propeller noises of the destroyer passing overhead began to fade and from the bearings reported by Ausfeld it was evident she was making for the convoy. In the control-room of U-0117 men looked at each other with a mixture of fear and relief. Though they did not know it, the destroyer was *Mainwaring*. They had thought at first that she had detected them and was running in for an attack. Beads of perspiration stood out on wet foreheads, face muscles were taut, eyes bright with danger. The atmosphere in the control-room was hot and foetid. Water dripped everywhere, there was the green of verdigris on all the metal surfaces, the air was foul with diesel and chlorine fumes; and the smell of decaying food, of vomit and urine, sodden clothing and unwashed bodies hung in the air like an invisible pall.

Rigged for silent running, the only sounds in U-0117 now were the faint hum of electric motors at low speed, the subdued voices of men giving and acknowledging orders, and the click and whirr of instruments. The submarine had reversed her course and was steering for the convoy, approaching its starboard bow, making just enough headway for the planesmen to hold her trim.

As he moved to the periscope well Kleber nodded to Rathfelder. 'Soon now,' he said.

Ausfeld reported from the sound-room. 'Numerous propeller noises. Slow-running piston engines. Freighters. Range six thousand metres.'

Kleber consulted his watch. 'Bring her to periscope depth, chief.'

Heuser repeated the order.

'Stand by all tubes.' Kleber looked at Rathfelder as the conductor of an orchestra looks at his first violin. The executive officer repeated the order, passing it to the fore- and after-ends.

172

The bows of the submarine began to lift as she made for the surface, the needles in the gauges clicking off the depths ... 140 metres ... 120 ... 100 ... 80 ... compressed air hissing into the ballast tanks, forcing the water out through the open vents. Another sound intruded – familiar but chilling: the *pings* of asdic transmissions. U-0117 had come clear of the temperature layer.

'Asdic transmissions green zero-three-zero. High volume. Closing.' There was sudden urgency in Ausfeld's voice as he added, 'Destroyer propeller noises.'

Rathfelder reported, 'All tubes ready, *Herr Kapitän*.'

The submarine's movements became lively as she neared the surface, and to Heuser, trying to hold her trim, it was like controlling the antics of a giant cork.

Kleber ordered, 'Up periscope!' An electric motor hummed and the periscope came up from its well like a smoothly functioning lift. He knelt to meet it, snapped down the handles, rose with it, eyes pressed to the lens apertures, his body swivelling as he trained the instrument on to the bearing given by Ausfeld.

'*Unterwasserangriff* . . . submerged attack.' Kleber's orders were sharp, like the crack of a whip. '*Klar zum Gefecht* . . . stand by for immediate action.'

He settled the periscope on the bearing, searching along it with eyes not yet adjusted to night vision. The snow had stopped. That helped, but the sudden, unpredictable antics of U-0117 as Heuser tried to hold her trim didn't. At times the U-boat would lift suddenly, the conning-tower almost awash in the troughs of the seas. Kleber moved the periscope left and right of the bearing and with a sudden tightening of nerves focused on a white splash on the starboard bow; one which grew and faded but always returned. Realising that it was made by the plunging forefoot of a fast-moving ship, he probed the darkness until the Zeiss lenses revealed the shadowy outline behind the bow wave. The crests and troughs of passing seas masked the target at times, but Kleber decided it was a fast escort. Probably a destroyer. He wondered if it was the warship they'd heard speeding towards the convoy. Had she got a contact and turned? Her course was roughly parallel to the U-boat's, but in the reverse direction. The relative bearings were changing rapidly. Kleber judged there was just time for an attack. The destroyer was evidently unaware of the submarine's presence. The opportunity was unlikely to recur. His estimate of the range at six hundred metres, closing, was confirmed by Ausfeld's reports from the sound-room. In terse, incisive sentences Kleber passed the attack information to Dieter Leuner in the conning-tower: target's range and bearing, course and speed; submarine's course and speed. Leuner fed the data into the attack-computer where an electronic system computed instantly the gyro-firing angle, setting it automatically on the torpedoes in their tubes.

The destroyer's *pings* and propeller noises could now be heard clearly in the control-room, but they were strangely woolly. Once again U-0117's crew waited in a sweat of tension.

Kleber aimed the periscope cross-wires at a point abaft the destroyer's bow-wave which he judged to be under the bridge. When the target was almost abeam he called, 'Fire one!' then – after the briefest pause – 'Fire two!' The torpedoes left their tubes and the submarine shuddered.

Rathfelder started the stop-watch and called aloud the seconds lapsed as the red hand swept the dial. Twenty seconds should pass before they covered the four hundred metres to the target.

'. . . eight . . . nine . . . ten . . .' Rathfelder incanted.

Kleber saw the shape of the white bow-wave alter, the rate of change of bearing slacken. The destroyer was turning to starboard, towards U-0117. Her hydrophone operators must have picked up the sound of torpedoes. She was trying to turn bows on to them.

'Eleven . . . twelve . . .'

Kleber ordered, 'Fire five!' and then with sudden urgency, 'Down periscope . . . emergency dive . . . take her down fast, chief . . . destroyer's heading for us.' *Five* was the stern-tube loaded with *gnats*. Kleber was taking no chances with a destroyer.

Heuser barked his orders at the men on the hydrophones and flooding valves. The submarine took on a bow-down angle. There was the familiar hiss of air escaping as water flooded the ballast tanks.

'. . . fifteen . . . sixteen . . . seventeen . . .' called Rathfelder, eyes never moving from the stop-watch. His report was interrupted by the deep rumble of an explosion. It

174

shook the submarine. 'A hit,' shouted Rathfelder exultantly. 'On seventeen.'

'Luck,' said Kleber. 'She would soon have been bows on to us.'

The submarine took on a steeper diving angle. 'Destroyer's asdic and propeller noises have ceased,' reported Ausfeld. Kleber said, 'That's a *gnat* wasted.' He looked round the control-room, his glance embracing them all. 'Well done,' he said. 'Not many U-boat crews could have done better.' The silence was broken suddenly by laughter and excited chatter. The tension had gone.

'*Halt die Klappe* . . . shut up!' snapped Kleber. 'Keep calm. We've still got the convoy to attack. That's going to need all you can give. Listen!'

There was silence again, each man concentrating on his task, hearing the distant beat of many propellers, the volume of sound growing steadily.

'Hear them?' prodded Kleber.

The men nodded, serious, tense, ashamed of their lapse, aware once again of impending danger.

Not long afterwards they heard their *gnat* exploding at the end of its run. After *Vengeful*'s engines had stopped it had homed on *Mainwaring*'s propellers but its range was exhausted well short of the fleet destroyer and the torpedo's self-destruct mechanism took over.

'Level off at eighty metres, chief. Stand by to surface soon after that.'

'Surface?' There was surprise in Heuser's tone.

Kleber nodded. 'We have the up-wind position. We are close to the leading ships of the convoy. We shall make another surface attack.'

The set of the strong chin, the unwavering blue eyes, the steady voice, reassured the men in the control-room. Kleber did not tell them that his intention to surface so soon after sinking the destroyer was a calculated risk of a high order. Nor did they know of the apprehension he himself felt. It was outweighed only by his belief that he must do more to justify the faith the Flag Officer, U-Boats, Group North had reposed in his brain-child – Plan X. But the element of surprise had gone. Already escorts would be closing the area to hunt him. Now he pinned his faith in doing the unexpected, in tactical aggression. He would surface shortly and in the first confusion following the destroyer's sinking, U-0117, trimmed well down, would head for the approaching convoy at maximum speed. Once between its columns he'd make a swift attack and dive to the comparative safety of water disturbed by the wakes of many ships. It should not take long after that to find a temperature layer beneath which the U-boat could hide.

He looked at the second-hand sweeping the dial of the clock over the chart-table. In another twenty seconds he would give the order to surface.

The signal ordering *Mainwaring* to resume station inside the close-screen had concluded with the words *proceed with dispatch*.

Upon its receipt her captain, Lieutenant-Commander Bradshaw, turned his ship towards the convoy and increased speed to twenty-five knots. At 2008 he exchanged recognition signals with *Vengeful* coming up to take the billet on the outer screen which he had just vacated. As *Vengeful* passed up the fleet destroyer's side the latter altered course to starboard to pass astern of her. Lieutenant-Commander Bradshaw had no means of knowing that he had passed close to U-0117 a few minutes earlier, for *Mainwaring*'s asdic dome had been housed to avoid weather damage.

Thus, unwittingly, *Mainwaring*'s course had taken her between those of the U-boat and *Vengeful* which were approaching each other on roughly parallel courses. This was to have the most dramatic consequences.


## CHAPTER TWENTY-FIV

The first-lieutenant shut the door of the captain's sea-cabin and went through the wheelhouse up the port ladder to the bridge. He had just arrived there when three *S*s sounded in rapid succession on the asdic bridge-speaker.

'Hard-a-starboard, full ahead together,' he shouted, and leapt for the compass platform. Three *S*s was the emergency signal for 'Torpedo approaching on the starboard side'. O'Brien repeated the order by voice-pipe to the quartermaster in the wheelhouse below. The midshipman had already pressed the alarm buzzer for anti-submarine action stations. The signalman-of-the-watch was broadcasting the general alarm by TBS.

As the first-lieutenant reached the compass platform he was dazzled by a brilliant flash of light. The muffled roar of an underwater explosion seemed to come from under the bridge. Its force shook the ship, lifting it from the water and dropping it.

The first-lieutenant picked himself up. He was dazed but managed to yell, 'Stop both engines.' The midshipman repeated the order by voice-pipe. No reply came from the wheelhouse. Soon afterwards the siren, triggered by the explosion, drowned his voice. Above the siren's piercing wail little could be heard but the roar of escaping steam, the screams of trapped and wounded men, and the screeching of torn metal as the sea surged into a gaping hole on the starboard side and water pressure, built up by the ship's forward movement, broke away the plating.

The first-lieutenant grabbed the torch from the chart-table and shone it to starboard. The wing of the bridge had gone, jagged teeth of metal forced upwards by the blast showed where the break had occurred. The sprawling body of the starboard lookout lay across the debris. His anorak, caught on a broken rail, had stopped him going overboard.

A hand touched the first-lieutenant in the darkness. Someone shouted in his ear. 'The engines are stopped, sir.' It was Rogers the midshipman.

Redman heard the three Ss and ran into the wheelhouse. A blinding flash of light was followed by an explosion which hurled him against the port side. The ship lifted and shook as if in the grip of enormous forces. Lights went out and broken glass, splintered wood and metal crashed about him. The ship settled back in the water, listing over to starboard. He heard a muffled scream beside him, 'My chest! Christ, my chest!' The body which lay half across him jumped convulsively. It was the quartermaster. The roar of escaping steam, the shriek of the siren, the shouts and screams of the trapped and wounded, masked all other sounds.

He dragged himself to his feet and rang down *stop* on the engine-room telegraphs. Then he groped his way to the bridge. The ship continued to lay over to starboard, headed into wind and sea. He called at the top of his voice, 'Officer-of-the-watch.' The muffled reply was drowned by the noise of the siren. A figure loomed up alongside him in the darkness. 'It's me, sir.' It was the first-lieutenant. 'She's going fast. Hit beneath the bridge and in the boiler-room.' He shouted his report into Redman's ear. 'The ring main's had it, sir. O'Brien's gone down to see if anything can be done.'

'Did we get an A/S contact?'

'No, sir. O'Brien says we were getting wake effect from *Mainwaring*. Next thing heard was the torpedo approaching.'

The spray of a breaking sea swept over them, freezing where it fell. Snow began to fall. A thin patter, carried away by the wind shrilling in the rigging unheard against the siren's continuous wail.

The yeoman came from the after-end of the bridge with a battery-powered Aldis lamp. He directed the beam forward. Redman saw that the fo'c'sle was awash, seas surging over it, foaming up above the 'hedgehog' and the flash-shield to B gun. The first-lieutenant was right. She was going fast.

'Train that light aft, yeoman,' he shouted. The long beam swung aft and came to rest on a jagged hole in the iron deck. It ran from under the bridge to abreast the boiler-room. Sea poured in as steam gushed out in billowing clouds which were snatched away by the wind.

Redman took the Aldis lamp and shone it round the bridge. He saw the scared white faces of Rogers the midshipman and the signalman-of-the-watch; the torn metal of the bridge superstructure and the sprawling bodies of the bridge-messenger and a lookout. He took the first-lieutenant's arm. 'Clear away boats and rafts.' He yelled. 'Get everything that'll float over the side. Use the signalman and messenger to pass the word. Take charge yourself. Wounded men first. At the double now.'

The first-lieutenant disappeared into the darkness. Redman called, 'Yeoman!' From close at hand came an answering 'Sir?'

'Make by TBS – "*Vengeful* kippered starboard side" – Quick as you can.'

'Tried TBS already, sir. No main power so I switched to battery. No good, sir. Explosion must have damaged the TBS transmitter. Main W/T transmitter's also unserviceable.

178

But we've passed it by emergency W/T. *Mainwaring*'s been ordered to stand by us, sir.'

Redman patted the yeoman's shoulder in the darkness. *Mainwaring*, the nearest escort, a fleet destroyer, had passed *Vengeful* only a few minutes before.

Another sea broke over the bridge.

Someone bumped Redman in the darkness. 'Who's that?' he demanded.

'Chief ERA, sir,' was the shouted reply. 'We can't get the bridge on the phone or voice-pipe. I've come to report . . .' His voice trailed away. He took a deep breath and began again. 'To report, sir. Boiler-room's flooded. We're evacuating the engine-room. Some men trapped in the boiler-room and PO's mess.'

Redman said, 'Where's the engineer-officer?'

'Gone, sir. Doing his rounds in the boiler-room when it happened. After the watch changed. Trapped there with the others. Couldn't have known much about it, sir. All that steam and flooding . . .'

'Thank you, Robbins. Carry on now. But try to stop that bloody siren. See what else you can do . . .'

There was nothing else Robbins *could* do. Redman knew that. Nothing anybody could do. *Vengeful* had been torpedoed and was sinking fast in the fading stages of an Arctic gale. *Mainwaring* might be in time to pick up a few survivors. In those waters the difference between death and survival was a matter of minutes. She couldn't remain stopped for long anyway. Why hazard a second ship and her company? The rescue vessel was busy miles astern of the convoy trying to pick up survivors from the Liberty ship.

The list became more pronounced. The ship was lying across the seas now. They were breaking against the starboard side, their crests reaching up to the wheelhouse. *Vengeful*'s liveliness had gone. She was waterlogged, a hulk, lurching heavily as the waves struck her.

The siren's strident note grew suddenly weaker, hesitated, then cut off altogether. New sounds took over. The crash and roar of breaking seas, the shrill note of the wind in the rigging, the shouts and cries of men, the hiss of air venting from flooding compartments, the screech and groan of tearing metal, the bang and crash of loose gear in the compartments under the bridge.

Redman called out, 'Yeoman!'

'Sir,' came from somewhere near him.

'Pass the word to abandon ship. Make it sharp. There's little time. First check that radar, A/S and W/T offices are cleared. Use any men still there to help pass the word. After that every available man to get down to the waist and lend a hand with the wounded.' It was a forlorn injunction. What on earth could they do for themselves, let alone the wounded? But it had to be said.

'Aye, aye, sir.'

'And yeoman. Go over on the port side when you do. Away from the list. If the oil's thick try to swim under it. Long as you can.' Redman knew that was another pretty hopeless injunction.

The yeoman handed him the Aldis lamp. 'May come in handy, sir.'

Burrows went and Redman was alone. The list and the bridge slippery with frozen spray made it difficult to stand. He trained the beam of the lamp along the starboard side. The iron deck was awash but the gush of fuel oil had formed a slick which broke the crests of the seas. With difficulty he moved up the high side of the bridge, felt his way round the compass platform, past the asdic cabinet to the flag-lockers, and looked aft along the port side.

Carley floats, Denton rafts and float-nets rose and fell in the big swells, straining and jerking at the painters which secured them, their calcium flares reflecting ghost-like light on the scene of disaster. Knots of men were gathered in the waist, others on the oerlikon mountings abaft the funnel. The list had lifted the port side high out of the water but seas coming in from starboard surged across, swirling and sucking at the men, sheets of spray sweeping over them. An oil slick was spreading down-wind, smoothing the water in the lee of the ship.

The first-lieutenant had done predictably well, decided Redman. But it was hopeless. There was little chance of lowering wounded men into rafts under those conditions.

The ship's company just hadn't a chance. There was no electric power. Nothing worked. With the ship's broadcast out of action he was cut off from his crew. He switched off the Aldis lamp. It couldn't help.

Redman knew only too well that the first-lieutenant supported by those officers and petty officers who'd not been killed or wounded would be doing everything possible. They'd been trained for this. Every man knew his station and duty. But in the chaos of disaster pathetically little was possible.

The battery-powered loud-hailer? Why hadn't he thought of it? With sudden urgency he searched the slithery tilting bridge, using the Aldis lamp. At last he found it, wedged under the compass platform. Bracing himself against the steeply sloping side of the asdic office, he trained the loud-hailer aft and pressed the switch. It was dead. 'Oh, God,' he muttered, throwing it down in despair. 'Won't anything work.'

Somebody was coming up the bridge ladder, slowly, noisily. In the beam of the Aldis he saw Cupido staggering towards him.

'Get down into the waist,' Redman shouted. 'Chance of a raft there.'

The Maltese shook his head. There was a jagged, blood-stained tear in the side of his watch-coat. He said, 'The meal carrier's gone, sir.' He faltered, eyes blinking in the bright light. 'With the dinner . . . I was on the bridge-ladder . . . starboard side . . .' His face contorted with pain. '. . . everything exploded.'

'For Christ's sake, man. What does it matter? Inflate your life-belt and get moving.'

Cupido shook his head again. 'No good, sir. It's torn.'

The blood-stained tear in the watch-coat was on the steward's hip, below the Mae West. Redman saw the jagged indentation in the life-belt. The slither of metal that had wounded the Maltese had done that. 'You poor little bastard,' he said, taking off his duffel coat. He undid his own life-belt and tied it round the steward's waist. 'Where's your pick-up harness?' Cupido looked at him dumbly, frightened. He couldn't tell the captain he never wore it. It was too uncomfortable.

Redman said, 'You bloody little fool.' He took off his own, slipped it over the steward's shoulders and made it fast, plugging in the survivor's light and clipping it on to the harness. 'You're all right now, Cupido. Get down to the waist quickly. They'll help you there.'

The steward looked at him doubtfully. 'I'm sorry, sir . . .

about the dinner.'

Redman focused the beam of the Aldis on the port ladder. 'There's the ladder. Move, man. Don't waste time.'

When Cupido was half-way down, Redman switched off the lamp. While he'd been helping the Maltese the ship had settled deeper in the water. The broken tops of seas were reaching up to the starboard wing of the bridge.

Once again he looked down along the port side. Men were going over into the sea. Some were already on the floats and rafts. The wounded, thought Redman. Poor devils. Better to have been killed. A deck below he saw Cupido slumped in a heap at the foot of the ladder and went down to him, picked him up and half-carried, half-dragged him to the waist. In the darkness he found a group of men waiting to go over the side. Somebody shone a torch. 'Captain, sir?'

He recognised the voice of a leading-seaman. 'That you, Farrel?'

'Yes, sir.'

'Help Cupido,' he said. 'He's wounded. I must get back to the bridge.'

The leading-seaman said, 'Aye, aye, sir,' and took Cupido's arm.

Redman worked his way up to the bridge again. At its after-end, near the signal lockers, he found a halyard and lashed himself to the rail. The tops of seas were slopping over the bridge now, spilling in to where he sheltered in the lee of the asdic cabinet. His mind was confused but he knew he was about to die. There was a long and honourable tradition for what he was doing. Not that it made it any easier. Death was the ultimate terror. He was grateful that he was alone, his fear hidden from others. Now that he'd got rid of the Mae West and pick-up harness there couldn't be a repetition of the Yeoman Patterson incident. That was something to be grateful for.

A douche of spray spattered the bridge, freezing as it settled. It was bitterly cold. He bit into his lips to stop his teeth chattering. *Vengeful* shuddered as a big sea struck her and she settled deeper in the water. She's like a half-tide rock, he thought. He wondered about the depth-charges. Would the primers have been withdrawn or would the charges explode when she sank? No. That wouldn't happen.

Baggot, the gunner (T), would have seen to that long ago. Or, if Baggot had been killed, the torpedo coxswain, failing him a leading torpedoman. It would have been done. Long and thorough training ensured that.

Inevitably a question nagged at him: why had the asdic team failed to detect the U-boat before hearing the sound of its torpedoes? He was not to know that *Mainwaring*'s stern wake, laid between *Vengeful* and U-0117 just before the attack, had effectively masked his ship's transmissions in the brief but critical time which it had taken the U-boat to climb from the shelter of the temperature layer to periscope depth. Nor could he have known that even if *Vengeful*'s asdic watchkeepers had not been very tired men – which they were – it was doubtful if they would have had time to sort out the U-boat's echoes from those of the turbulent wake which masked them.

Redman heard the voices of men coming up the port ladder. They reached the bridge and the beam of a torch searched the darkness. He knew they were looking for him.

'Captain, sir?' It was Pownall's voice.

Redman said, 'Don't worry. I'm coming. Get down there and do what you can for the men.'

Two dark shapes loomed alongside him. 'Come on, sir,' said the yeoman. 'It's time now.'

Redman said, 'Go ahead, yeoman. I'll follow.'

They ignored his order, took his arms, one on either side, and pulled but couldn't budge him. Redman felt hands groping round his body. 'Christ,' said the yeoman. 'You've lashed yourself to the rail, sir.'

'It's no good, yeoman. I want to stay with her. You two carry on. That's an order.'

The yeoman was cutting the halyard. 'Sorry, sir,' he said. 'No future in being a bloody hero.'

Redman protested, ordered, begged them to go. But the lashing was cut and they were hauling him along to the ladder. He gave up the struggle. It could only increase their danger. 'All right,' he said. 'I'll come.'

'We'll look for a raft or a float, sir,' said Pownall hopefully. They reached the iron deck. *Vengeful* listed more steeply, the water rising in great spouts from the engine-room showering down upon them. The yeoman shone a torch aft. The upper deck was awash, apparently deserted but for the first-lieutenant. He was standing on the platform of X gun, lean-ing back against the gunshield which lay over to starboard at an oblique angle. The first-lieutenant saw the torch and yelled. 'You there! Get over the side. Shake it up. She's going.'

Redman called out, 'Captain here, Number One. Get moving.' Force of habit made him look at the luminous dial of his wristwatch. 2023. Seven minutes since the torpedo had struck. It seemed like seven hours. Where was *Mainwaring*? With fierce energy he pushed the yeoman and Pownall towards the guardrail. 'In you go, you two. I'll follow. Join you in the water.'

But they didn't trust him. Clawed at him, pulled him down the ship's side. 'For Christ's sake,' he cursed. 'Leave me alone.' He tried to break free. Then all three of them were in the water together, their anoraks protecting them from the first shock of immersion.

They swam away from *Vengeful*'s side, struggling through fuel oil, holding their breath, spitting out the choking slime between long gasps for air. Ahead of them calcium flares and a few red survivors' lights winked between the hills and valleys of the seas.

They swam towards them.


## CHAPTER TWENTY-SIX


At 2015, a few minutes after torpedoing *Vengeful*, Kleber brought U-0117 to periscope depth. Ausfeld had reported propeller noises ahead over an extensive front, the volume increasing. He estimated the distance of the nearest ships at three thousand metres. Because of the wide spread of these sound signals he could not satisfactorily answer the insistent question, 'Can you hear anything of the close escorts?' Kleber asked it even though he knew it was almost im-possible to distinguish the sound of the slow-turning screws of pistol-engined corvettes and frigates from those of mer-chant ships in the convoy, for the greater sounds enveloped the lesser.

And then, as so often happened in the war at sea, disaster

struck without warning. An unusual combination of awkward seas and a mistake by a tired apprehensive planesman caused Heuser to lose control of the U-boat's trim as Kleber began his periscope sweep.

'Hold her down, chief,' roared Kleber as the U-boat bounced to the surface. 'For Christ's sake! Hold her down!' There were notes of alarm and anger in his voice. They were approaching a heavily escorted convoy, already alerted by the sinking of the destroyer. It was sheer madness to surface before completing a thorough sweep with the periscope.

Before Kleber had finished the sentence, Heuser was shouting orders to the men on the flooding valves and hydroplanes and U-0117 took on a bows-down angle. A moment later Ausfeld – his calm and imperturbability for once abandoned – called excitedly, 'Propeller noises close ahead. Destroyer . . .'

He needn't have made the report. Every man in the control-room heard the roar of what sounded like a train entering a tunnel and, hearing it, crouched instinctively to shelter from the unseen terror. It had come upon them without warning, as if the attacker had been waiting for the U-boat with engines stopped and had somehow achieved this sudden frightening speed.

Kleber's urgent, 'Dive! Dive! Dive!' were the last words he was to utter. They coincided with a jarring crash, the sound of tearing metal, and U-0117 rolled over as the sea swirled in through a great rent in her hull. Though the men in the U-boat did not know it, the submarine had been sliced in two by the bows of the ramming vessel. The severed ends sank almost immediately but five men, a petty officer, three seamen and a mechanician, were blown to the surface by a blast of escaping air. One of the seamen was picked up by a corvette a few minutes later.

The U-boat's end was so sudden, so violent that neither Kleber nor his crew could have known what had happened. There was, however, an exception . . . Able-Seaman Gunter Holst, the sole survivor. After his interrogation by the corvette's first-lieutenant, Holst learnt that U-0117 had been rammed and cut in two by a destroyer.

He was not, of course, told that *Mainwaring* had travelled

a mile and a half past *Vengeful* towards the convoy when she heard the former's 'kippered' signal and turned to go to her assistance, Lieutenant-Commander Bradshaw informing the flagship of his intentions. These were approved, but he was ordered not to stop, simply to throw floats and rafts to the men in the water to assist their survival until such time as the rescue ship arrived. Thereafter, he was, with two corvettes, to hunt the attacking U-boat.

Since *Vengeful*'s bearing by radar was almost directly astern of *Mainwaring*, Bradshaw swung his ship through one hundred and eighty degrees. *Mainwaring* would, he then realised, be in danger of streaming back along her own wake. Aware of the problems this would create for his asdic team – and conscious that there was an enemy submarine nearby – he was about to alter to starboard when a U-boat bounced to the surface a hundred yards or so ahead. She was so close that she was sighted visually in spite of the darkness, and illuminated by searchlight. At the time, *Mainwaring*, having just completed her turn, was working up to twenty knots, and although Bradshaw was aware that ramming was frowned on by Their Lordships (it could cause severe damage to the attacking ship), he decided the chance was too good to miss. He also had in mind the need to reach *Vengeful* quickly and this seemed quite the best way of killing two birds with one stone. So he ordered 'Port fifteen – prepare to ram,' and the alarm signal sounded throughout the destroyer.

The U-boat attempted a crash-dive but was struck abaft the conning-tower, the destroyer's bows slicing the hull in two. As she passed over the submarine – or, more correctly, through it – *Mainwaring*'s rudder struck some wreckage and was damaged.

Bradshaw reported by TBS the destruction of the U-boat, his inability to manoeuvre, and requested the dispatch of another escort to assist *Vengeful*. Some fifteen minutes later *Mainwaring*, by then overtaken by the convoy, reported that the jammed rudder had been freed and, though damaged, was again serviceable. She was ordered to take station inside the convoy's close-screen.

Kleber died not knowing that Ausfeld's failure to pick up the destroyer's propeller noises in time was due not to any lapse in the sound-room but to the turbulence of *Mainwaring*'s stern wake which, combined with the heavy volume of sound from the propellers of the approaching convoy, had effectively masked the noise of her screws.

The movements of the three men in the black oil-fouled water grew slower, became spasmodic. The effort to breathe, to keep near-frozen limbs moving, to struggle against on-coming seas invisible in the darkness, led quickly to exhaustion.

Their eyes inflamed by fuel oil, the men in the water could no longer see the flickering lights towards which they'd been swimming. Now they floundered, gasping, splashing, spitting, while life ebbed away.

Redman, feeling himself slide into a dark abyss, clutched convulsively at the water before losing consciousness. Without a life-belt he was waterlogged, a deadweight which Pownall and the yeoman could no longer support. When he finally slipped from their grasp, they were too far gone to retrieve him.

Less than a minute later – it seemed to Pownall hours afterwards – the yeoman gasped something unintelligible, then fell silent. Pownall groped for the man in the darkness and found him, but the head was submerged, the body lifeless. The desperate knowledge that he was now alone hastened Pownall's end. Seconds later he too lapsed into unconsciousness.

The three men had gone quietly, the manner of their dying unnotable; little more, indeed, than gasps and gurgles and a mild splashing of the water marking their ends. Nor were they conscious of those last moments for the cold of Arctic winter froze their sensory perceptions, inducing a coma from which death effected the final rescue.

A dispassionate celestial observer might have noted that Redman died within a nautical mile or so of Kleber whom he had outlived by seven minutes. Not that these facts nor their irony were likely to have interested any observer, there being an abundant harvest of death at that time and place.

Next day in the Arctic twilight of forenoon, *Fidelix*, flying the flag of CS19, the Vice-Admiral commanding convoy JW137, followed the last of the merchant ships into the safe waters of the Kola Inlet.

Astern of the carrier, barely visible in the half light, came the cruiser *Nottingham.* She was followed by the Home Fleet destroyers, behind them the ships of the Eighty-Third Escort Group. The rearguard, the ships of the Fifty-Seventh Escort Group, were still at sea carrying out an anti-submarine sweep to seaward of the minefield which lay across the approaches to the Inlet.

As the Vice-Admiral watched the last merchantman move slowly down the Inlet towards Murmansk, he thought of the nine days which had elapsed since the convoy's departure from Loch Ewe. In his mind's eye he saw once again the great armada of weather-stained ships plunging on through the darkness of Arctic winter, buffeted by never-ending storms and blizzards, the targets of sudden attacks by an unseen enemy. The Vice-Admiral was no sentimentalist but it occurred to him that the convoy had about it a quiet dignity, a certain majesty; there was an implacable determination about its slow but steady progress towards its destination, undeterred by anything the weather or the enemy could throw against it.

The Vice-Admiral's pride in the men and ships under his command was tempered with humility. The price paid for the passage of JW137 in human lives and suffering, in the loss of ships, had been high.

Sobered by these thoughts he lowered his binoculars and turned to the Flag Captain. 'Well, Somers, it's taken nine days but it seems a lot longer.'

'It does, sir. Sorry we couldn't make more use of our aircraft.'

'Yes. Bad luck that. Your chaps must be very disappointed.'

Rory McLeod, the staff-officer-operations, arrived on the bridge. He saluted the Vice-Admiral. 'I've got the operation-room's latest tally here, sir.'

'Good. Let's have it.'

The SOO began reading from the list. 'Enemy losses – six U-boats sunk. Three reconnaisance aircraft shot down.'

'Remind me who got those U-boats, McLeod.'

'One sunk by *Vengeful* and *Violent* outside Loch Ewe on December the fourth, sir. Two near the Skolpen Bank yesterday afternoon. One by *Vectis,* the other by *Vallance.*'

'Splendid effort in those weather conditions,' said the Vice-Admiral.

188

The SOO nodded in gentle agreement before returning to his list. '*Iris* and *Peaflower* sank one during the second attack late in the afternoon. *Vengeful* sank U-0153 at 1836 yesterday.' He looked up. 'After that long stern chase, sir.'

'Yes. That was a damned good show, wasn't it?'

'And *Mainwaring* rammed and sank U-0117 shortly after it had torpedoed *Vengeful*.'

'Bradshaw had no right to ram,' said the Vice-Admiral with affected severity. He looked up and smiled. 'Damned glad he did, though.' He coughed as if to cover up an indiscretion. 'I call that a pretty successful brush with the enemy. Don't you, Somers?'

'I do indeed, sir. Extraordinary, though, that they tried the old wolf-pack tactic again.'

'Yes,' said the Vice-Admiral. 'I thought they'd learnt their lesson in 'forty-three. But it was a bold effort.'

'I'd say the weather made it possible, sir,' said the Flag Captain.

'Yes. They couldn't have concentrated if we'd been able to use our aircraft. And of course asdic and radar conditions were very difficult.' The Vice-Admiral paused, then added, 'And to be honest – let's concede it – the weather must have made things very difficult for their U-boats.'

'Can't see them trying another wolf-pack attack after those crippling losses. Can you, sir?'

'Unlikely, I'd have thought,' said the Vice-Admiral. 'But one never knows. It's the unpredictables that provide the problems.'

Politely the SOO cleared his throat. 'May I go on, sir. The recap of our losses?'

'Yes. Let's have them.'

'Two escorts, *Chaffinch* and *Vengeful*. The fleet oiler *Surfol*, and five merchant ships. Two of them ammunition ships. And, of course, two aircraft – a Wildcat and an Avenger.'

The Vice-Admiral was thoughtful. 'You haven't mentioned *Camden Castle* and the Liberty ship *John F. Adams*.'

'No, sir. We're excluding them for the time being. But I'm afraid their chances are pretty thin. Too many U-boats about.'

'Unless the weather's hidden them.' The Vice-Admiral looked at the dim outline of snow-covered mountains bordering the Inlet. He'd not enjoyed leaving the disabled Liberty ship in mid-ocean, nor making the decision to detach a corvette to look after her. But there were no acceptable alternatives. As always the safety of the convoy was the first priority. He abandoned his private thoughts and turned back to the others. 'Let's get the score in perspective, gentlemen. We've lost eight, possibly nine, of the sixty-four ships involved in JW 137. About thirteen per cent of our forces engaged. The enemy has lost six U-boats out of a total of . . . what was it, McLeod? Fifteen or sixteen?'

'Sixteen, sir. That's based on interrogation of German survivors.'

The Vice-Admiral was thoughtful. 'So there were sixteen U-boats engaged in the attack.'

'Yes, sir.'

'That means the enemy lost something like forty per cent of his forces engaged.'

'Plus the three aircraft we shot down,' said the Flag Captain, determined that *Fidelix*'s contribution should not be overlooked.

'Not bad. Not bad at all.' The Vice-Admiral fingered his chin. A meticulous man, he disliked the bristles which reminded him he'd not shaved for forty-eight hours. 'Very sad about *Vengeful*. Splendid effort of Redman's. Two U-boats on one convoy. That fine single-handed hunt. We'll have to see he gets something posthumously.' He turned to the SOO. 'Make a note of that for me, will you, McLeod?'

'I will, sir.'

'Incidentally. What *is* the latest news about *Vengeful*'s survivors?'

'Thirteen were picked up by *Grant Castle*, sir. Two of them were originally *Chaffinch* survivors rescued by *Vengeful* earlier in the day. I'm afraid four of the thirteen had died at the last count.'

'Any officers among those left?'

'One, I believe, sir. Groves, the sub-lieutenant.'

The Vice-Admiral shrugged his shoulders. His face was drawn with exhaustion as he moved across to the port side of the bridge. He looked down on the carrier's flight deck, took out a handkerchief and blew his nose. Admirals did not show emotion. It was bad for discipline and morale. When he'd recovered his composure he rejoined the others.

190

'Well, gentlemen. It will be pleasant to have a night of unbroken sleep. One gets confoundedly tired on these journeys.'

The Flag Captain said, 'I think the weather has a lot to do with it, sir.'

The Flag-Lieutenant came on to the bridge followed by the chief yeoman of signals.

'You look pleased, Flags,' said the Vice-Admiral. 'Thinking of that run ashore?'

The Flag-Lieutenant waved a signal and grinned. 'Just received, sir. From *Bluebird* by W/T. *Camden Castle* and *USS John F. Adams* have been sighted by the Fifty-Seventh Escort Group. They're bringing them in through the swept channel now.'

'Splendid.' The Vice-Admiral smiled warmly at the little group of men around him. 'Make a signal to *Camden Castle* and *John F. Adams*. "Welcome and well done."'

He moved to the far side of the bridge and stood alone, thinking of what lay ahead. The thirty-odd ships of the previous convoy had completed unloading in Murmansk and were awaiting the return journey. It was the Vice-Admiral's task to get those empty ships back to the Clyde. Today was Saturday. The south-bound convoy would sail on Wednesday. Until then his warships and men would rest briefly in the icy desolation of the Kola Inlet.

By now the German High Command would have ordered reinforcements to the Kola patrol line to replace their losses. In five days it would all begin again: the struggle with the weather and the enemy. It was difficult to say which was the worst.

The task is only half done, he reflected, and in that moment recalled Drake's message to Walsingham after Cadiz: *There must be a beginning to every great matter but the continuing unto the end until it be thoroughly finished yields the true glory.*